The Professor
A Novel

Elia Johnson

Copyright © 2023 Elia Johnson

Copy Editing by Carmen Riot Smith

Cover by Ever After Cover Design

All rights reserved. No part of this publication may be replicated, reproduced, or redistributed in any form without the prior written consent of the author.

This is a work of fiction. All of the characters, organizations, and events portrayed in this novel are either products of the author's imagination or are used fictitiously.

ISBN: 978-1-7370857-1-3

*For everyone who's had to learn to accept themselves a little later in life.
It's a hard journey but one that brings so many blessings.*

Contents

Chapter 1 1

Chapter 2 13

Chapter 3 24

Chapter 4 36

Chapter 5 50

Chapter 6 56

Chapter 7 56

Chapter 8 85

Chapter 9 89

Chapter 10 97

Chapter 11 106

Chapter 12 114

Chapter 13 129

Chapter 14 144

Chapter 15 153

Chapter 16 162

Chapter 17 177

Chapter 18 185

Chapter 19 193

Chapter 20 204

Chapter 21 213

Chapter 22 222

Chapter 23 235

Chapter 24 250

Chapter 25 257

Chapter 26 268

The Professor

Chapter 1 Confessions

"You know Professor Hutchinson and her wife are divorcing now?" Mya whispered to me right before class ended. My eyes immediately flew over to our professor, who seldom looked in my direction as she taught. I turned back to Mya.

"Really?" I asked and she nodded.

"Okay class, we're done for the day," Professor Hutchinson announced. "Remember that your essays will be due on Tuesday. Have a great weekend!"

Everyone began pouring out of the classroom, but I remained frozen on the edge of the damp cloth chair beneath me. My gaze was fixed on our professor. Mya also stayed in her seat, glued to her phone for the moment. My stupor was only broken when the professor glanced in my direction while speaking to another student. I quickly averted my eyes, then tapped on Mya's shoulder.

"What happened with the professor? How do you know she's getting a divorce?"

Mya's straightened black hair swung over her shoulder as she looked up from her phone. Her eyes were almost as dark as her deep brown skin. The set of thin gold chains around her neck matched her nose ring and made her look like royalty. "I went by her office today before class to ask about an assignment I forgot was due over fall break."

"The one about Freudian defense mechanisms?"

"Yeah, that one. Anyway, her door was cracked open, and I could hear her talking with someone. I'm pretty sure she was on the phone with her wife, but I'm not a hundred percent. She was yelling into the phone that she was done with 'the marriage.' She kept telling her wife—or whoever the hell it was on the phone—to leave her alone . . . and something about where to find her doesn't matter."

"Damn, Mya, you heard all that?"

"I couldn't help myself! And she was the one who was loud." Mya rolled her eyes. Nearly everyone had left the auditorium now and only a few students remained, talking with each other or with the professor. "Alright, you ready to go?" Mya asked, putting her phone and notebook away.

"No, I actually have to talk to Professor Hutchinson," I muttered distractedly as we both stood up.

She gasped. "About the divorce?"

"No. Of course not, Mya. About that upcoming assignment and the seminar she mentioned that's next week. I'm thinking of going."

"Oh yeah. That sounds boring as hell." She started walking down the stairs, and I followed.

"I think it could be a while though." My focus shifted again toward the professor at the front of the room. "I might just end up going to her office too. You should probably head to the library now."

"Are you coming when you're done?" she asked.

"Yeah, I'll be there." We reached the ground level of the auditorium, and the ding from Mya's phone shifted her attention.

"Okay, I'll see you later then." She spoke without looking up and walked out the door, along with the last student aside from me.

I scanned the room before nervously approaching the professor. She had begun packing away her books and laptop, her back turned to me.

"Miss Brentwood, how can I help you today?" she asked without looking up from her bag. I didn't at all appreciate her unusually stiff tone.

"Is it true?" I questioned her in a low voice as I stepped directly in front of her. "Are you and Teresa really getting a divorce now?"

Her body went rigid as she straightened up and faced me. "Who told you that?" Her russet brown eyes looked darker in the lighting of the room.

"Mya did," I blurted out uncomfortably. "But is it true, Alena?"

A pained expression washed over her face as she nodded.

My stomach dropped at the realization of what this meant, and a feeling of guilt engulfed me.

"How did she even know?" Alena questioned.

"She went to see you in your office this morning and heard you on the phone. She mentioned that you sounded really upset so she didn't go in. But she heard you talking about ending your marriage."

Alena bit her lip and looked away for a moment with creased brows. "I *was* upset this morning . . . and Teresa and I were arguing again." Her hand came to one of her temples and she closed her eyes and sighed. "But I should've kept my composure better than that and been quieter." She faced me again with a lingering sadness in her eyes.

"This is my fault isn't it," I suggested remorsefully. I searched her face for some form of animosity.

She only blinked at me. "Of course it's not your fault, Amelia. This isn't about you. This is about me and my wife. You know we haven't been doing well for a while now. My feelings for you are really only the tip of the iceberg."

I anxiously scanned the room, obviously concerned about being overheard, but it was empty.

Alena followed my eyes then looked back at me understandingly. "I'm sorry," she sighed. "Look, I never told you this, but I haven't been living with Teresa for the past month or so. I completely moved out when she gave me an ultimatum, but I have a friend who's teaching a graduate degree program in Georgia right now, and her apartment was vacant here. When she heard about the situation, she offered to let me stay there for a little while." Alena lowered her voice ever so slightly. "We should discuss what's been going on between us somewhere more private. If you're comfortable, you could come over to the apartment tonight."

I was stunned by the proposition, but I quickly recognized that she was right about discussing the matter elsewhere. I could only imagine who might hear us sorting through our emotions for one another in her office, especially if Mya had so easily overheard the news of her divorce. I was, however, fairly apprehensive about meeting up with Alena outside of campus. I had already gotten her number a couple of weeks ago, but we hardly even texted, and we definitely never saw each other anywhere outside of her office or the auditorium. It hadn't ever gotten to that point, although I secretly dreamed about the possibilities for some time now. I considered her suggestion for a moment before nodding in agreement.

She put a hand on my shoulder and gave me a reassuring smile.

To think that it all started with going to her office hours. Professor Hutchinson was so gentle and kind-hearted. I didn't understand how a college professor was able to command as much respect as she did without being either a pushover or a jerk. My professors usually fell somewhere between begging for their students' affections and being so strict and pushy that going to their class mirrored going to hell. But her class was nothing like the ones I had endured before.

I still don't exactly understand how Alena and I began falling into a romance of sorts, but it happened so naturally. I knew I had to visit her after my first day of classes because I was instantly enthralled by everything about her. By the second week, I'd started going to her office hours every single chance I had, and she never seemed to mind me doing so. During my first three years of university, I had of course talked with other professors and formed amicable bonds, but things were different with her.

It always just felt like *more*.

Alena was a poised woman with a serene and sophisticated sense of style. Her warm beige skin was flawless, her nose was broad, her lips were full, and her hair held long dark-brown curls with highlights. She always had a shining necklace adorning her chest, several rings lining her fingers, and a pair of dangling or studded earrings.

During our visits we often spoke about our interests in artistic measures. Mine were more visually representative while hers were more elusive. While I enjoyed art shows and museum exhibits, Alena preferred books and music—things you couldn't see but things that made you feel.

The first instance when I had expressly recognized my attraction to her occurred when I stopped in to see her around lunchtime one Wednesday. At this point, it was atypical of me to come to her office when it was not within the specified hours she offered. Truthfully, I had been wandering around the campus since both of my best friends were too busy for lunch that day. I only had one more class left before I could leave for good, but it was almost two hours away. I wasn't even sure if she would be in her office, but I knew that I wouldn't be as bored if she were and if I could speak with her.

I walked by her office and spotted her through the blinds of the small, square window on her door. She was removing a pan from a large plastic bag. She noticed me standing there, and her face lit up as she waved me in. When I opened the door, I was introduced to the spicy aroma of her food. She started to say she was on her lunch break, but once I explained that I had only come for a social visit, she invited me to join her and share her meal.

The Mexican food she'd bought was plentiful and I hadn't eaten yet, so I gladly agreed. A variety of carne asada tacos filled one foil container, another one held equal parts of rice and beans, and a large brown bag full of warm tortilla chips sat nearby. The queso and salsa containers were still in the plastic bag along with some brown napkins.

As we ate, Alena and I went from discussing road-tripping and crazy conspiracy theories to our views on the political climate. When she made a joke about how quickly the Obamas bolted from the White House once his term was over, neither of us could contain our laughter. That was when we both reached in at the same time to grab more chips. It wasn't a big deal in itself, but when her hand brushed mine, it amazed me to feel such exhilaration from the single, brief touch. It was like a light bulb switched on in my brain, and I suddenly realized just how attracted I was to her.

She looked up at me almost indifferently as she continued laughing, but I saw a flush of red in the cheeks of her light skin. I wondered if perhaps I'd had the same effect on her that she had just had on me, but I put the thought away almost as soon as it arrived.

But she *did* look at me as if she could see right through me, and it was mildly disconcerting.

My hand was awkwardly placed on the desk, and I gave her a nervous smile as our laughter dissipated. My demeanor shifted as I zoned out, gauging my now racing thoughts. Several moments passed before she moved her hand across the desk and placed it over mine. My breath hitched in my throat, and my heart began beating faster against my chest. I jumped back into reality.

"Are you okay, Amelia?" she asked kindly, a smile on her face.

"I'm fine," barely escaped my lips.

She removed her hand and graciously moved on to another subject as she finished the last taco.

"Why'd you choose this?" I asked abruptly toward the end of our conversation. She tilted her head and scrunched her brows together as she wiped at the corners of her mouth with a napkin. "Psychology," I clarified.

"Oh. Because I love learning about people. Studying human behavior is fascinating." She balled up the napkin and tossed it in the empty to-go bag. "Plus, I *love* teaching, so it's perfect. I can't get enough of interacting with so many people and students." She sighed. "What about you? You're getting your degree in sociology, right?"

I nodded, surprised that she remembered. I couldn't even recall when I had told her that—and she had many other students—so I was impressed.

"Why are you doing that by the way? And why are you taking Psych 200 your senior year? You don't need it, do you?"

"No, it's just a filler class that Mya and I could take together. I thought it would be interesting."

"So it's not interesting to you?"

"It *is* interesting!" I corrected myself with a nervous laugh. "What I meant was that we wanted to try it because of our interest. But back to my major . . . I think I like sociology for the same reasons you like psychology. Except the studies are on a much broader scale than just the individual, of course."

She nodded. "I see."

"I don't really care to do much with it honestly though." I moved my focus to her short pale green nails on the desk and slowly inhaled. "I want to study the arts, but not in college—in real life. I always wanted to be an art collector or curator or something. I think it'd be amazing to have a career like that." When I finally looked up, I met her eyes and saw that she was really engaged in what I was saying. It made me extremely nervous, and I felt the same electricity from when our hands had touched. "M-my best friend Gabe says it's something I could do. College may just not be the way."

"I thought Mya was your best friend?" she asked.

Damn. Does she remember everything? I nodded. "Yeah, she is too. They both are."

"So you have an eye and a passion for art, but you're almost four years deep in a major focused on people. How will that turn out?" She leaned back, and her chair squeaked. Her outfit wasn't one designed for cleavage, but I still couldn't help staring at her chest.

I shrugged, trying to focus on anything else but that. "Whatever works, I guess. I'm almost done, so I'll have my degree. I could get my masters and become a counselor or therapist at some point. It's at least something I can fall back on if my artistic dreams don't start up quickly enough."

Alena smiled. "I understand that. It's admirable. If it accounts for anything, I believe in you."

I paused for a moment. "Becoming a professor, funny enough, is one of my fallbacks too," I said. She laughed then, a shrill beautiful tone. "I'm serious! If I go get my masters, I could always have a teaching job with that."

"Now I see why you take such an interest in me," she murmured.

I swallowed hard, my heartbeat intensifying.

"Your grades in my class are fantastic, Miss Brentwood," she continued before I had another chance to speak. "You don't have to come to my office hours, but you do. And now it makes *that* much more sense."

I felt stuck in place. I was definitely taking an interest in her now, but not in the way she meant.

"I appreciate at least one student coming here," she exhaled.

"Oh, I'm sure plenty of them come." I wanted to squirm in my chair under her gaze and concentration. I wanted to flee the room right then. Did she always look this beautiful before?

"More like *twenty*," she chuckled. "And I have at least one hundred and fifty students across all of my courses. It's fine I suppose. Most do well . . . or average I should say. I get it though. I was once a college student too." She sounded disappointed, and wanting to cheer her up, I dramatically gasped and covered my mouth. "I know, I know. It's hard to believe." She grinned.

"Yeah, because it's surprising that you aren't still one. You could really be in class with me." I spoke without thinking but I was glad because she blushed at that, and it was a beautiful sight. I lowered my head to hide my pleased expression and swiftly strategized my escape. "Anyways, Professor, I have to go now." I wiped my mouth with a napkin then grabbed a plastic bag and began cleaning up my mess.

She held up her hand. "I can manage the clean-up, Miss Brentwood. Thank you."

"Thanks for lunch." I grinned shyly.

"You're most welcome." She stood and started gathering the trash I'd left alone at her request. "Feel free to see me again," she said. "Any time."

I felt dazed as I walked away, replaying the visit in my head. I had a new fear of being in there with her again. She was doing something strange to me. But I also felt a pull toward her for the same reason.

The following day, I had an undeniable urge to go see her again even though it was getting late. I'd missed my usual visiting time that day, but I was still on campus after attending several club meetings. I walked over to her office from my last meeting at six o'clock, hoping to catch her there despite the fact that her office hours would've just ended. As I stepped off the elevator, I noticed that most of the rooms were empty. This was typical at the end of the week, especially this late in the evening.

I rounded the corner and hurried to her office just in time to find her in the small room packing her work materials away with the door half open. "Hey, Professor Hutchinson," I announced with a smile.

She flinched as she looked up, clearly unsettled before she recognized me. "Oh, you scared me. Hello, Amelia," she greeted me warmly while motioning me in.

I sat before her, watching as she moved two spiral notebooks from her desk and zipped them up in her work bag. I placed my tattered laptop carrier beside my chair and viewed the familiar blue canvas painting behind her on the wall. I often admired it whenever I was in her office. The artwork was abstract and contained several hues of the dark blue color that dominated the piece. It provided a calming atmosphere and brought a much-needed brightness to the neutrality of the room. Without it, everything was boring. The stark white walls were bare and formless, and the carpet was an uncomfortable, prickly gray. A worn oak desk was placed almost in the center of the cramped office, but it was pushed closer to one side of the wall so that Alena was able to squeeze in from the opposite side. With the door closed, there was more space, but it was still a tight fit.

Absolutely nothing about the design of the offices in this building offered the impression of an education worth envying, but that was just the way it was in any of the liberal arts and science buildings on our campus. The engineering and technology students along with the student athletes had the best of everything. Everyone else was left with scraps.

Alena set her purse on the desk before sitting and leaning back comfortably in her chair. "What's the news with you today, Miss Brentwood?" she asked energetically, though her eyes looked tired.

"Oh. Nothing at all," I laughed. "I just had some meetings on campus and thought I'd come see you before your office hours were over."

"They actually are," she teased as she pointed to the paper on the door listing the times in bold. "But you know you're always welcome here. Nice of you to stop by to visit yet again. I do enjoy your company."

"I do too."

We stared at each other, and in the silence I felt strange. There was an urge to fill the empty spaces with some intelligent discussion or banter, yet I couldn't. A wave of uneasiness rushed through my body as I fully grasped how hard it had become from me to simply engage with my professor. I was ashamed because freezing up this much was highly unusual, but I just couldn't help that she made me so nervous now.

My eyes glanced over the place where a picture frame used to rest on the edge of her desk. I looked for the familiar picture but didn't see it. "Where's your wife?" I asked without much thought.

I remember how interesting it had been for me to find out that Alena was a lesbian. On the first day I visited her office, I saw the frame. It was silver, bordered with a design of mangled vines and roses. Inside was the picture of my smiling professor with her perfect white teeth. Another woman's arms were draped over her shoulders as they sat in a grassy field together. She told me the woman was her wife, Teresa. The woman had long curly red hair and a plethora of freckles covering her angular face. The two of them were truly a beautiful couple.

"Where's my wife?" Alena seemed to be both confused and amused by the question.

"The picture frame," I elaborated, tapping the part of the desk where it used to be.

She halfheartedly scrutinized me for a moment before the corner of her lips lifted. "I'm redecorating," she said, idly massaging the fingers on her left hand. Her lips twitched as if her smile threatened to fade into something morose.

I cursed internally after realizing that I had touched a nerve. "Umm, apparently school this week has drained me of my ability for good conversation," I disclosed as I awkwardly stood up.

She joined me, grabbing her purse off the desk and work bag off the ground. "That's totally understandable. You're a hard-working student." She winked at me. I took two steps toward the door before realizing I had left my laptop on the ground. I turned to retrieve it only to bump right into her, knocking her a little off balance before reflexively grabbing her wrist.

"Oh!" I clamored. "I'm sorry, Professor Hutchinson!" I was

mortified and couldn't make sense of why I was so flustered around her this week.

"It's okay," she laughed, apparently unfazed. "But do you plan on cutting off my circulation, Amelia?" she asked softly.

I looked at her confused before she glanced down to her wrist—which I was still holding—then back up at me. I released my grip, apologizing once again, but I did not make a move toward my bag. Her eyes stayed locked on mine. She stood several inches taller than me, especially because of the heels she had on. I kept looking up at her. She kept looking down at me.

"What has you so rattled this evening, Amelia?" she asked in a tone I had yet to hear before. It made responding to her even harder as the beating in my chest commenced.

"I—I don't know."

She gave me a wicked grin before turning around and picking up my bag from the ground. "Thank you," I said, taking it from her and holding it limply at my side. I swiftly turned around and walked out the room, quietly chastising myself as I launched down the hall.

"Have a good weekend, Miss Brentwood!" I heard her shout from behind me while she locked up the door.

I stopped and turned back for a moment. "You too, Professor!"

Chapter 2 Lucid

I don't recall how I ended up back in her office so soon, but it was a new week and here I was again, sitting in front of my professor and spacing out as she spoke to me. This wasn't at all my usual behavior in her office. I was normally fully engaged and conversed with ease, but now I just felt embarrassed and at a loss for words. *Why do I even come here anymore?*

She interrupted my spell when she cleared her throat. "Is everything okay, Amelia?" she asked, leaning forward with her hands clasped together. "You've been behaving odd lately."

"No, I'm fine," I lied. It had become increasingly difficult for me to be in the same vicinity as her when her presence was so unnerving.

"Are you sure there isn't something you need to tell me?" she asked once more.

"Like what?" My voice nearly cracked when I spoke.

"Like why you come to see me so late in the evening now? There's hardly anyone left in the building whenever you appear."

I internally froze. "Well . . ." I tried coming up with something sensible to say.

"Well, what?" she pushed, looking way too smug in her chair. "If I didn't know any better I'd think you have a crush on me," she continued tauntingly.

"I don't." My throat felt as dry as a desert, and I could hardly swallow.

"Then why are you always here, Amelia?" she challenged. "Explain that to me."

I was surprised how quickly I heard myself uncontrollably confess to how often she plagued my mind. Telling her just how frightening yet addicting her presence had become for me and how she was now interlaced into nearly every thought in my day. How I craved to take her into my arms and how badly I wished for her lips to crash into mine, even then. The words spilled out of me like water out of a faucet.

"Oh," was all she said as her pomposity altered into a state of wonder.

It only took a few seconds after returning her gaze for me to reclaim my senses. Shame then invaded my bloodstream so heavily that it was hard to face her. I sheepishly turned away, gathering myself before stammering out, "Professor! I apologize. That was inappropriate." I leapt up from the chair and would have sprinted through the door had I not felt a hand on my shoulder, stopping me. When I turned around, she didn't seem surprised or disturbed or whatever you might imagine her reaction to be in such a situation.

I could measure only one response on her face: *intrigue*. Not a single word escaped her lips as she walked around me and locked the door, tightened the blinds, then approached me.

"Miss Brentwood," she began, her tone admonishing, "you have to be very careful about what you say in this office." She stepped past me and leaned back on her desk. "Or what you do."

I was taken aback by her words and the look in her eyes. Uncertainty swirled inside me, and I doubted the obvious fact that she was inviting me in.

"Yes, I know," I said as composed as I possibly could. "I'm sorry." I walked over to her and timidly looked her in the eyes. "It won't happen again."

Her hand abruptly reached out and grabbed mine, pulling me toward her. "Who said I didn't want it to?"

I knew in that moment that I had two choices. I could either indulge in my burning desires or retreat from her and keep my feet firmly planted on moral grounds. I thought for sure I would've turned and walked away, but my sensual cravings took full control.

I leaned toward her, slowly, placing one hand on the desk and the other lightly against the side of her cheek. Her eyes moved down to my lips then up to my lustful gaze. That's when I impulsively pushed my lips against hers. I had simply wanted a taste, but it seemed I wasn't the only one. After one or two soft, sensual kisses I began pulling away from her, but she drew me back in. We made out right there in her office; it was a quiet, intimate exchange. I didn't want it to end, but it did when she gently pushed me away. She rose as she grazed her thumb lightly against the bottom of her lip, gazing into my eyes with a fiery passion.

♦ ♦

A loud beeping sound jolted me awake. Apparently, I had fallen asleep on the couch. As I looked down at my watch, I slowly comprehended that I had also overslept and was now late for psychology class. I threw on some jean shorts and a wine-colored halter top then rushed out the door.

I sped to campus as skillfully as possible while I replayed the scene in my head. It was hard for me to grasp that I had been dreaming about my professor, but it also felt like an epiphany. Ever since that day when we shared lunch and I had felt her smooth skin, my heart lurched nearly every time I saw her. I admonished myself for the feelings and tried to remember just how tacky it was for a student to have a crush on her professor. Aside from that, it was especially wrong because of the fact that she was a married woman. I'd mistakenly thought that my deterrent tactics had been working, but they hadn't, and my heart sank a little under the awareness of that.

Once parked, I power-walked to Province Hall, the main health and human sciences building. Alena was one of those instructors who didn't appreciate baseless excuses for tardiness, so I had to rush. I suppressed my heavy breathing as I stood outside the auditorium, peeking in through the side door where I normally entered. I quickly decided it was best for me to sneak in through the back instead. It happened to be my luck that day that I'd made it all the way to my seat next to Mya before the professor turned around from the screen behind her.

"Isn't it nice of you to join us today, Amelia?" she broadcasted to the entire class.

Shit, she saw me. Everyone turned in my direction. Perhaps I was not as lucky as I thought.

"Hopefully you have a good excuse for being late, but if not, this is your warning since you're usually on time. Come talk to me briefly after class, okay?"

I nodded as I dropped my backpack and got out my notebook. She resumed teaching.

"What happened to you? I called you like three times," Mya whispered.

"I fell asleep writing a paper for another class, and my alarm didn't wake me up in time. What'd I miss?"

"Umm, we have that online test tomorrow then we start our new section next class."

"Okay, okay." I sighed loudly and started copying Mya's notes. I contemplated telling her about the dream I'd had, and I nearly blurted it out to her several times throughout the class, but I couldn't manage to voice it. Not only was I deathly afraid of her reaction, I was also afraid of the truth of what I had been feeling and honestly suppressing for a while.

I studied my professor and her movements throughout the class. I thought about the way her smile lit up my atmosphere. The way I wished I could be stuck somewhere in the tangle of her curls. I so wanted to see those curls up close, her body bare before me. That and nothing else. Mya's hand was now waving in front of my face, breaking my trance. I tried my best after that to get a handle on the notes and lesson, but I couldn't remain focused for the rest of our time in class.

When Professor Hutchinson finally dismissed us, I packed up my things and let Mya know I'd meet her later. I walked to the front of the auditorium and sat in the first row, waiting for another student to finish speaking with the professor.

"Miss Brentwood!" Her attention finally turned to me.

"Professor." I stood up and approached her.

"Do you have a good excuse for your tardiness today?"

"No, I just, um . . . I slept in late."

"It must've been a pleasant sleep." She crossed her arms.

"Not necessarily. I had some weird dreams."

"Is that so? I'll tell you what, we can talk about it. Are you stopping by today?"

I hesitated. "I don't think I will."

"That's too bad. I ordered Thai food—far too much of it. I was hoping I could offer you some if you were coming by." As timing would have it, my stomach growled loud enough for her to hear, and she grinned. "It sounds like you could use some." She sucked in her bottom lip and seemed to hold in laughter.

"Oh alright," I conceded far too easily, my body growing warm all over. I had to avert my eyes from her lips in order to keep my bearings. "I have to do a couple things first, but I'll be right up afterwards."

"Very well. I'll see you then."

I waved at her before turning away and making my way through the side door. I spotted Mya standing in the hall, fidgeting on her phone. "What are you still doing here?" I asked, surprised.

"I was going to see if you might want to come over to my place until your next class. My Media Ethics class just got canceled, so I can leave campus now."

"Really?"

"Hodgins is sick, believe it or not."

"Hodgins the germaphobe? That's so weird."

"Isn't it?! That man's favorite words are 'get a Clorox wipe.' So, you can come with me, right? Just for a little while until your next class?"

"Umm . . . no actually. I can't go with you. I'm going to Professor Hutchinson's office hours today."

Mya groaned. "You're such an overachiever, Amelia. You literally have the best score in her class!"

"Yeah, and maybe going to her office hours helps me with that. I want to make sure I understand everything. Plus, I missed part of the lecture today."

"Whatever you say, Amelia." Mya sounded annoyed. "I won't lie though; you've been acting strange lately." Her tone switched to something more soothing and friendly. "Are you doing okay? You're not stressing yourself out too much again, are you? Or feeling anxious or depressed at all?" Her hand rubbed my shoulder.

Mya sometimes worried that I was bearing all the weight of my life issues on my shoulders as I had undoubtedly done on and off since the beginning of college. We didn't become best friends until sophomore year, but we met as freshmen. Adjusting to college in a different city and state was particularly challenging for me, and even though we'd just met, Mya helped me through. She was the one to include me in outings on the weekends and dorm movie nights. We discovered that we both loved watching this murder mystery show on Sundays at seven o'clock, and that's when the beginning of our unbreakable bond began. We texted and FaceTimed throughout that summer and decided on joining the same quad by the time the next semester rolled around. Even now, we often crashed at one another's place off campus, but I'd started isolating more as the semester grew increasingly difficult for me.

I thought again about telling her my dream and my recent thoughts about Professor Hutchinson, but for some reason I still couldn't. "No, Mya, I'm fine. It just eases my mind to make sure I stay in her good graces. But thanks for checking on me though."

"Hmm, okay." She sounded defeated.

The door to the auditorium opened then, and the unmistakable clack of heels sounded loudly on the hardened, vinyl floors. I turned from Mya and spotted Alena moving away from the room in her brown pumps. She smiled at both of us as she walked by.

I soon saw Mya off to her car where we hugged and gave our goodbyes. Afterward, I stopped by the director's office for some documents I had requested—which of course had gotten lost by an assistant somewhere down the line and needed to be reprocessed. I was irritable now, and my brain was tired by the time I stumbled into Alena's office. In spite of it, though, I did my best to appear normal.

"Perfect timing. My delivery just arrived a couple minutes ago." Alena smiled at me as she slid a Styrofoam cup of pho my way. She had already spread the food out on the mostly empty desk, but she didn't start eating until I sat down. I grabbed a spoon off the top of the container then lifted the lid. I blew on the steaming pho before sipping. While I ate, I observed how comfortable Alena seemed in her chair across from me. Something about the two of us sitting there eating lunch together felt very familiar, although this was only the second time we had done so.

I started to think about how Alena behaved a lot more formally with me in the classroom than when I was in her office. It was like two different versions of her, although I hadn't much noticed it up until now. I was overanalyzing everything because of the newly realized attraction I had for her.

"Are you going to tell me what's wrong?" she asked softly.

I looked up at her from my cup. "Nothing. I told you I just had a really strange dream."

"Is that why you were so distracted today too?" She straightened up and placed her half empty container on the desk, next opening another container full of shrimp and fried rice. "I just want to make sure everything's okay with you," she added.

I wondered why she would even notice my distraction in the first place. There were plenty of other students in the class to worry about. "Do you think dreams mean anything?" I casually inquired.

She scooped up the rice in her spoon. "It depends. I think they can. It could be something you consciously ignore but subconsciously cannot." The spoon hovered near her glossy, plump lips. "Why? What dreams are you concerned about? Maybe I can help you make sense of it." She finally slid the food into her mouth and chewed.

A lump caught in my throat. I knew what the dream meant, at least in theory, and how could I share that with her? It would inevitably change our dynamic, and by the time the semester was over, I'd only be a memory of a student she admired until that student admired *her* too much! I didn't want to be that memory.

"No, I can't tell you. You'll judge me," I nervously stammered.

She laughed quietly. "Now when have I ever done that?" That much was true. She was quite an open person and not judgmental at all. I hadn't shared anything too crazy with her as of yet, but I'd definitely made some questionable statements here and there which never seemed to offend. "It's completely up to you, Amelia. No pressure." She picked up her pho again and moved on to another topic, but I soon had us circle back to it.

"There's a professor here at GU that I dreamed of confessing feelings for," I blurted without fair warning in the middle of the conversation. "I confessed and then we kissed."

"Oh, *wow*." She put down the container in her hands and analyzed me with her eyebrows drawn together.

"I never even thought of it . . . of *her* like that before but now I can't let the idea go."

Alena's brow lifted at these words, and she blinked slowly several times over. "Her?" she repeated.

"Her," I confirmed. Despite my knowledge and obvious support of her sexuality, I had not expressly mentioned the fact that we shared the same love toward women.

She sat up stiffly in her chair and straightened her face. "Why do you think you dreamed about her?" she asked with a melodic lilt in her voice.

"I don't know. Maybe I'm attracted to her or something. I mean, I must be because when I woke up I felt the same way. I just never consciously considered it this much before." *Or maybe I just keep lying to myself about it.* I shifted uncomfortably in my chair.

She seemed to be pondering something deeply, and I wished I knew exactly what it was. "For how long? Did you know her when you were a freshman? Because that's not—"

"No," I interrupted her calmly. "It's nothing like that, I promise."

She let out a sigh of relief. "Okay. So, you had this dream about this professor. Is there a possibility that you want to carry out those actions?" she asked. "With her," she added astutely.

I exhaled as I lowered my head and pinched the bridge of my nose. "I should've told you before that I was gay."

"No, Amelia. It certainly wasn't my business."

"Professor Hutchinson, you're literally the only lesbian instructor on campus that I know of."

"Apart from the one you've been dreaming of I presume. Unless she falls somewhere else under the spectrum or isn't as open as me."

"It was only one dream! And she's—"

"Is she straight?" she interrupted with an unexpected critical tone. "Is it Professor Markham or Angela Foster—or perhaps it's Jody Singleton?" She began listing the names of other professors, some of which I did know from the department.

"No, it isn't any of them."

"Is she from another department then?" she probed.

"Professor, she's from this department, but that doesn't really matter. It'll never happen."

"How can you be so sure? It's rare, but sometimes it happens." She almost sounded distressed now, but I couldn't comprehend why.

"Yes, but I don't think your wife would apprecia—" *Oh shit.* I stopped myself too late. *What the fuck did I just do?* I stared at her like I'd been caught committing a crime, and her eyes were just as wide. It took quite some time for her to bring them under control. When she opened her mouth no words came out. "I didn't mean to say that," I murmured, breaking the silence, and I scooted my seat away from her desk.

"You . . . had a dream about me?" she asked reluctantly.

"I did." I nodded as I stood up. "I'm sorry. It's inappropriate, I know. I wasn't even going to tell you. I really didn't mean to," I fumbled out awkwardly. "It didn't mean anything, though! There are no worries, okay?" I blatantly lied. I began collecting my things even though I wasn't finished with my food. My ears and cheeks were burning, and my heart beat so hard in my chest that it hurt. I'd done something I felt instantly regretful about, but I also felt the relief of releasing the truth. I couldn't even fathom Mya's reaction to this admission, and now I had accidentally just told the source of my discomfort herself. Still, the feeling of liberation remained beneath the many layers of embarrassment.

"You don't need to be concerned about this, Amelia." Alena spoke calmly as she rose out of her chair. "We all have dreams and not all of them are ones to brag about. Don't feel like you have to go just because of that."

"I really think I should, though," I muttered, putting the lid on the pho.

"Okay." She seemed to force a smile. "Have a good day."

"You too." I rushed out of her office.

I was fully prepared to pretend that none of it ever happened. I could avoid all eye contact for the two days of the week I'd spend in her class and make sure not to incur any infractions that would make it necessary for us to converse outside of it. I spent the next day coming up with the perfect strategy to avoid her for the rest of the semester. My plans would've undoubtedly worked too, had they not been disrupted before I could even implement them. The first words Alena spoke when I sat down for class that next Thursday changed the entire trajectory of what I thought would be the end of our connection.

Chapter 3 On the Table

"Dreams. We all have them. We do. There are many who claim they don't, but they likely just don't remember them. Every night at some point we enter REM, and if you read the chapter for today you know exactly what that means. In this state of sleep, we dream.

"Some say dreams are a mirror to the inner self. Some dreams relay our deepest desires or our fears." Alena stopped pacing. "Sometimes we dream of things we want to carry out in reality." Her eyes fluttered to mine and stayed there long enough for me to notice. "Some dreams can be shared between two people." She turned and walked back to her podium in the middle of the auditorium. "There is so much about sleeping and dreaming that I can cover, but we'd be missing the entire point of our chapter. The idea that . . ." the rest of the words faded, and I remained distracted until the end of class.

I wondered if she was speaking directly to me or if I had somehow misinterpreted the lesson. But I couldn't have, because there was something calculated in the way her eyes had met mine when she spoke of sharing dreams. The *only* dream I told her about was the one when we were making out in her office. If her eye contact had, in fact, meant something, then there just may have been a possibility that the both of us shared a desire for one another. After running away from her office the other day, I believed I was destined for a semester of awkward Tuesdays and Thursdays. Now things seemed to be going in a different direction than originally expected.

I visited her office once again the next day, and we easily fell back into our normal routine—but only after we first addressed the elephant in the room. There was an obvious attraction between the two of us. We both acknowledged it, then immediately rebuked it. Alena was a married woman and, equal to that, it was against the university policy for relations to occur between an instructor and their student. We agreed to table our emotions for the time being while continuing our friendship of sorts and keeping our conduct purely professional.

It was an agreement that we made but never truly followed.

Our conversations swiftly grew more intimate, and our emotional bond intensified. Too often we were in her office chatting away—it didn't matter if the door was open, closed, or cracked. The eye contact between us now lingered, and if we were not careful, our chemistry was noticeable from miles away. We went from friendly lunches to flirtatious meetings. We'd sometimes even greet or depart with a lasting hug which left her delicious scent lingering on my clothes. She had soon told me that it was no longer necessary for me to refer to her as *Professor* and that I could call her Alena. Our growing closeness prompted a frequent outpouring of emotions that came with a sense of physical distance we both felt and both desired to close. But how could we?

I learned from our increasingly personal conversations that she and her wife had been separated for nearly a year now. She had long been ready to permanently end things, but Teresa would rather them stay separated while "allowing" Alena to date other women. This was obviously a poor alternative to being divorced and completely free, so dating had understandably been lackluster for her. Even so, Alena seldom felt anything for the women she interacted with because none of them had a connection that compared to the bond she once had with Teresa.

"You know, Amelia, you are the only person I've talked to that's made me feel again," Alena mentioned one evening, her eyes shut as she leaned back in her squeaky desk chair. The door was closed.

"Am I?" I responded, feeling properly flustered.

"Yes, you are." She opened her eyes and sat forward. "It's the way I know I should feel for someone. *Romantically*," she continued, sounding nervous.

The blank expression on my face was not indicative of the raging emotions beneath the surface. I didn't at all expect to hear the words she had just said to me. Sure, we still had obvious feelings for one another, but we had only verbalized them once.

"A couple of weeks ago you said you know it's wrong, but do you really think it has to be?" she asked earnestly.

"I never said it was wrong," I corrected.

"Yes, *inappropriate* was the word, I remember."

"Isn't it though? At least for now. And so are our lunches and our hugs and the way we look at each other. Maybe this is only temporary anyways, Alena. I may only be a thrill for you because things are risky with me, and when they no longer are, you'll date someone that's more aligned with you."

"I can't possibly imagine someone like that." She slowly shook her head.

"That's hard to believe," I bitterly disagreed. I denied her confession so vehemently because there was absolutely no way reciprocity could be true. How could anyone dream up perfection like this?

"I want more than a fling with you, Amelia. You're not a silly thrill for me." She stood up and walked to the front of her desk, sitting on the edge of it with her arms crossed. She took in a deep breath, leaned closer, and placed her hand gently under my chin. "*You* make me feel, Amelia," she repeated with a certain conviction. She remained there, her minty breath inches from my face as her fingertips moved from my chin and lightly brushed across my cheek.

It felt like my dream again, but the terror of its merging reality was sickening. I was scared to go beyond what could easily be left behind. Flirting and inside jokes, even an emotional connection could be abandoned without the same guilt as a touch, a kiss . . . or more.

I was rationalizing in my head when I found my hands gripping her thighs. I saw it in her eyes and felt it in mine, the longing, and I wanted to take that plunge. Everything in my being wanted to; everything except my brain, which held my values and better judgment. Still, I stood, and my face edged closer. My lips lingered only an inch or two from hers, but she did not close the gap. She waited for me to do so, but I couldn't. I removed my hands from her thighs then her hand from my cheek.

"I'm sorry," I whispered. I collected my things as she straightened her lilac-colored suit and readjusted her curls into a bun.

"Don't be," she said.

When I finally fled the room, I could barely think straight. My thoughts tumbled through my head, relentless and insistent: *What does this mean? What the hell was that? What about her wife? What about her job? Could this become something?*

As I approached the parking lot, I thought about how awful it was to be any part of the reason why someone would break up with their significant other. I never wanted to be anyone's secret, especially when they were already in a relationship—and Alena was married. I couldn't fathom that my chemistry with her would have gone as deep as it had, growing deeper with every passing day. I also couldn't justify our connection despite the agreement she had with her wife.

That's all that happened that day, so I continued visiting her. We grew more and more attached throughout the next weeks, and Alena eventually told me how her increasing feelings for me were only driving the nail in the coffin regarding her separation with Teresa. I told her that I should stop visiting if that were the case, and I avoided her for about a week.

Alena proved to be talented at hiding her emotions. There was no obvious tell that I had hurt her feelings, but in the one or two times our eyes met after she'd dismissed the class it was clear that I had. I needed time to think this through for myself and to honestly see if I'd be able to disregard my feelings for her altogether. I found that it was extremely difficult to do so, and I quickly discovered that my attempt would be futile if I knew that she equally desired my presence.

She never said anything to me about it that week—but the next Tuesday on our way out, she handed us our most recently graded tests, individually. When it was my turn to collect the test, she mentioned how my grades were excellent and how I was succeeding in the course. She politely smiled and called the next student, and as I walked away, I noticed a sticky note tightly fastened to the top of the paper.

I miss your visits, Amelia. But if there is no need to see me in any other way, I can do nothing but respect your decision and try to understand it.

There was no signature and no indication of who had written the note. I refrained from turning back in her direction as I walked out of the room, a gut-wrenching feeling rising in my stomach. I tucked the note into my bag.

It had torn me to shreds that day, but I couldn't think of a better way to handle our situation. The distance wasn't helping me extinguish my feelings toward her, but it *was* minimizing a consistent rate of growth between us.

I still felt weak from the note when I arrived at class today, seeing how beautiful she was for yet another Thursday. Then Mya told me the news of her divorce. And now here I was, finding myself waiting for our first off-campus meeting. Tonight.

I shivered as I walked out of Province Hall and quickly threw on my jacket. The weather in North Carolina could never decide what it wanted to be around this time of year. After three years of attending Greenwood University of Technology & Arts I thought I'd be used to it, but I wasn't. Regardless, I otherwise enjoyed my life at this school. It was one of the best in the state for the value, and I had been able to snag several scholarships that made it easier to pay for my out-of-state tuition. Not only were the academic points of the university good, but so was the social aspect of it. It wasn't a party town, but there were always plenty of things to do.

I walked with my hands in my pockets as I made my way toward the library. My soft, yellow sweater complemented my blue jeans and brown boots. Alena had been dressed in black slacks with a black and gray tribal-designed cardigan. Her wild, brown curls enveloped her face as per usual, and the wardrobe amplified her flawless skin. She was beautiful; too beautiful and too warm and too caring and too *married* for me.

I couldn't help but wonder why she wanted to leave her wife in the first place. What issues could there possibly be that would drive such a wedge in between them? It was frightening to think about how unpredictable something as established as marriage could be. It didn't matter if two people went into it with love if there were big enough problems to extinguish it.

Alena hadn't yet conveyed too many details about her relationship with Teresa, but I could tell solely by the way she spoke of her just how in love she once was. I could also see how hurt she was by the forced absence with her old lover. It made me further question why she refused to stay and fight for it. Maybe Teresa just needed more help than the average person and in time things could be salvaged. Perhaps the circumstances between Alena and I also made for some difficulty. I started to have an inkling that my presence in her life was a block for their potential healing, and I didn't want that for her even if she was convinced that she wanted to be set free.

Yet, simultaneously, I wanted her.

I wanted to learn her deeply and spend copious amounts of time with her. I wanted to take her out for nights that turned into mornings together. I wanted so very much to feel the softness of her skin and taste the sweetness of her lips. Her aroma was like a drug shooting into my veins on impact, and I wanted to be surrounded by that in her bedsheets.

But she was still married, still my professor, and I was still her student. And this was only a budding romance. It could very well be that the feelings for me that Alena spoke of were only fleeting. If this were true, the fact remained that the risks of sneaking around with a student were not worth the thrill. Being expelled from one's primary form of work while enduring a messy divorce would be the last thing anyone might desire.

I inwardly debated everything as I walked across the cool, windy campus. I hardly even registered the crinkled leaves beneath my feet when I passed underneath the bright orange and yellow trees. The seasons were changing around me nearly as much as my emotions deep inside. It was fall, and I was *falling*. The leaves were turning brown and becoming fragile remnants of life that could only drift to the ground. They mirrored my dwindling hope for discovering love.

The connection between Alena and I was effortless and incredibly strong. Our attraction to one another was electrifying. We both saw each other so clearly, and it was as if we were soulmates—but only at the wrong time. She was the one person that consumed me and ignited a roaring flame, but there were still so many obstacles standing in the way of *us*.

At last I stood in front of the library. Its brick exterior looked old, but it had been completely remodeled and modernized within. That was how most of the buildings were on GU's campus, but it wasn't the university's external appeal that brought me here as much as its ratings and distinguished academic programs.

I made my way inside and found Mya tucked away near the back of the third floor. She sat studiously at a wooden table with her books spread out and her left-hand scribbling vigorously on a piece of paper. As I approached her, I thought of what I might say about the lecture I had apparently discussed with Alena. I hated lying to my friends, but I didn't know exactly how to tell them of my seemingly mutual crush on my professor. This was, of course, worse since she was also Mya's professor.

Psych 200 was one of the few elective courses we discovered we could take together during our final two semesters of college. It wasn't supposed to be very challenging, though it wouldn't have made much of a difference for either of us because we were both quite astute, academically and otherwise. Mya was easy to talk to and was excellent at networking. She was also extremely well-spoken, so it was no surprise that she pursued a degree in journalism. Her goals were vast and expansive, but she had them planned in neat, organized steps. For now, she just appreciated being able to work in television at all, even if she was only behind the cameras.

"Gabe's on his way," Mya muttered, looking up from the table as I took a seat across from her.

"Can you ask him to pick me up a soda from the machine down in the lounge?"

"Why can't you ask?" she tossed back.

"Never mind," I huffed.

She set down her pencil. "Did you get everything straightened out with the professor?" she asked with a raised brow.

"Yeah, I think so." I shifted uncomfortably in my seat.

"How is she though? With the divorce and all." Mya leaned in as if we were gossiping in a high school cafeteria.

"Why the hell would I know about that?" I answered defensively, my throat dry and my chest fluttering. Alena and I would be discussing exactly that tonight, so I was more annoyed by the question than I should've been. Mya absolutely could *not* think that our professor ever spoke about personal matters with me.

"Whoa! Chill, okay," she laughed. "I'm just joking. Anyways, I'm really just irritated that you made me walk by myself. I ran into Taj again, ugh." I listened to her complain about her encounter with her ex-boyfriend and his new girl. Mya spent all of sophomore year dating Taj and much of junior year being cheated on by him. He had promised her he'd changed his ways, but with some newly gained self-respect and the help of me and Gabe's rightful slander of him, she finally decided not to take him back.

At last, a tall, deeply tanned figure emerged from behind some bookshelves carrying a Fanta Orange, Skittles, potato chips, and a Twix bar. His dark eyes stared in our direction as he approached. The single braid of hair he kept at the back of his neck swayed behind him while the rest of his brownish-black hair lay in a shaggy, unkempt pile of waves on top of his head. He shook away the hair that fell over his brows as he reached the table.

"Hello, beautiful ladies," his low, crackling voice heralded us as he passed out our treats. A thin layer of hair stretched across his upper lip and his smile was presently obstructed by the silver brackets pelted across his teeth.

"You know us so well!" I said, reaching for the soda. Of course, we were not supposed to eat in the library, but we were tucked far enough away from the librarian stations to not chance getting caught.

"Thanks, Gabes," Mya cooed out her nickname for him.

"You two are going to take all my money eventually," Gabe grumbled, and we laughed as he shook his head. "So, what's going on? Anything new today?" he asked, sitting down beside me. An earthy and woody smell permeated the air around us. The two small diamond studs on each of his ears briefly glinted from the overhead lights.

"Yeah, Amelia here might have some details for us." Mya pointed in my direction, and I stared at her blankly, not understanding what she meant. "*Professor H*," she hinted.

"Oh my God, Mya, why can't you leave that alone?" I turned to

Gabe. "Mya here has been eavesdropping today and found out that our professor may be getting a divorce." I didn't want to talk about it, but I knew Mya would mention it first if I didn't.

"Ooh, that's juicy, Mya," he said.

"Gabe, don't encourage her," I admonished, obviously joking. I wanted to keep our discussions regarding Professor Hutchinson as lighthearted as possible, but I felt a rush of guilt for even engaging in the conversation at all. I changed the topic as quickly as I could, and we began discussing the next movies we should see and what art exhibits we might travel to in the spring.

Though Gabe had his fair share of male friends in school, he often preferred to keep close company with Mya and me. He'd met the both of us at the beginning of sophomore year when our other two quad mates hosted a kickback in our shared living room. At first it had been odd to have these random gangly boys in our space, but they all turned out to be really sweet. They were our lone neighbors at the end of one of the halls on the second floor, which was probably the reason we were able to turn into a trio so quickly. Whenever Gabe was tired of being around the guys, he would request to come hang out or study with us. This meant that he often accompanied us to and from the library, which he was more than happy to do, especially when it began to get darker earlier in the evenings. I attributed Gabe's good manners and his respect for women to his family and the fact that he had four sisters. Two of them were older, two were younger, and he also had twin brothers.

Gabe enjoyed watching our crime show too but preferred our movie nights, especially when it came to the low budget films. He was fascinated by what could be done with a little money and a lot of creativity. We were all imaginative people and often bonded over our prevailing love for anything artistic. Mya's voice could carry just about any tune, and she knew how to play a variety of instruments. Gabe liked music as well, but he preferred creating abstract paintings, woodworking, and organizing historical maps. I enjoyed viewing and critiquing paintings and statues, so we frequented museums as a group. I wanted to travel the world someday and witness the best art. This dream admittedly had almost nothing to do with my major, but it was a common theme for most college students anyway—to end up not using our majors post college.

The semester after we all became friends, Gabe and Mya ended up sharing a math class where they grew especially close. Gabe was an engineer, which basically meant he was a mathematical genius in our eyes. He helped Mya pass her math centric classes for two semesters, and he also helped console her with me through many nights after she discovered Taj's lack of loyalty. I'd never seen Gabe angrier than when he'd heard of how reckless Taj had been with his loving friend's heart.

"Oginalii, where are you?" Gabe waved his hand in front of my face.

I looked up from the table. I'd been staring, thinking about Alena again. "I'm here, I'm here. Sorry."

"She's been acting weird, Gabe. I don't know why. She won't tell me." Mya spoke as if I weren't sitting right there.

He turned to her, his brows furrowed. "What do you think is bothering her?"

"I have no clue," Mya muttered.

I cleared my throat. "I'm right here."

Gabe turned back to me. "My apologies," he said with a sheepish smile. "Let me ask *you* then. What's up with you, Amelia? Are you working too hard?"

"No, I just have a lot on my mind."

"Which is exactly why we need to have a weekend out!" Mya interjected. "Dinner and movies on Friday then the club on Saturday!" she exclaimed.

"Mya, I don't know if I'll be up to it," I said.

"I think it'll be fun," Gabe concluded.

"It will! Amelia, there's no reason for you to keep adding pressure to yourself. You need to blow off some steam, maybe even get a little steamy . . . find you a girl," Mya said.

"Woman," I corrected.

"You know what I meant." She rolled her eyes.

"Mya's right," Gabe tried again. "This is our senior year, and we can't be so stuck on our studies that we don't have any fun. When's the last time we went out anyways? Maybe the first week of school?"

"Okay, duly noted," I said. "But we had fun the first three years of college. Don't you think it's time we get used to being more serious?"

"Hell no!" Mya shouted in disapproval, and I motioned for her to quiet down.

"Mya," I said, hushing my voice and hoping she would too. "We're almost in the real world now."

"Yeah, exactly—you're proving my point, Amelia." Her eyes narrowed. "Life is too short not to have *any* fun."

Gabe silently nodded with his lips pursed and a hidden laughter in his eyes.

I groaned dramatically. "FINE! What is it you want to do again?"

Chapter 4 *Is This Okay?*

I collapsed into my vehicle and let out a loud sigh. I had just completed my final class of the day, along with the journey from the opposite side of campus, and I was beginning to surrender to fatigue. Everything in my life was growing so complex. Not only was I actually having some sort of romantic affair with my married professor, but I was also blatantly lying to my two closest friends about it. Mya did not for one second believe that I was okay. She had genuinely grown concerned about me, and Gabe felt the same way. It was quite upsetting how much my secret feelings for Alena had become lethal to the usual honesty I shared with them.

The sky looked harsh and gray as I sped away from campus, and the engorged clouds threatened to release a freezing rain. It wasn't long before I faced the familiar black door of my apartment and quickly unlocked it. I walked straight past my living room and kitchen and into my bedroom where I recklessly threw myself onto the bed.

My arms sprawled out beside me, and I became aware of a throbbing pain in my head. *Of course I have a headache with all of this shit going on!* I lay still in the quiet room until the chirping phone in my pocket revived me. I supposed that it would be Alena since she hadn't yet given me directions to the apartment. My heart was beating erratically as I checked the newest message which confirmed my guess. She had sent me the address and suggested I come over around seven o'clock to see her. I sent back an *okay* and spent the next hour mentally preparing myself for every possible outcome of this visit.

Would Alena tell me that she thought things over and wanted to cool down our communication and focus on rearranging her life? I personally couldn't imagine balancing even a standard breakup, let alone a divorce, in the midst of a new love affair. But could this even be called a love affair? Perhaps it could if given the right opportunity, but that would depend on Alena's desire to involve herself even further with me. There was at least a morsel of a chance that it would happen, and if it did, I would have to seriously consider what it might be like to secretly date my professor. The coinciding fear and thrill surrounding this idea was tantalizing in the best and worst ways, and it made me shudder.

As the thoughts accumulated inside of my head, our planned meeting time neared closer and closer. I ended up having to rush my shower before a failed attempt at making a sandwich. I tripped and dropped my masterpiece almost immediately after completing it then silently cursed to myself as I cleaned up the mess.

With mere minutes to spare, I pulled a thick jacket around my arms before tossing my bonnet aside and putting on my shoes. It was now six thirty-two and I was dressed expressly for comfort. I spread perfume that smelled of vanilla and honey crisp apples across the pulse points on my body. Though Alena would not encounter my usual fashion sense during this visit, she would unquestionably know that I always smelled good.

Before I left, I gave myself a once over in the full-length mirror that hung on the back of my bedroom door. I admired my rich brown skin as I stared into my tired eyes and pulled at the dark, shrunken coils growing out of my head. I then flashed a mostly straightened smile.

I was ready for my meeting with the professor.

A baseball stadium sat seventeen miles away from where I lived and across from it was the Brookfield Apartments. I found solace in the fact that the high-end development was everything but affordable for the average college student. This made it highly unlikely for me to run into anyone familiar from school while I was there.

The sky was already darkening when my little ash gray Camry slipped into a convenient spot near the front of the 500 building. The shortening nights and frosty touch of the air further signified fall's incursion of summer.

I remained motionless in my car for several minutes. I wasn't entirely certain if it was because I needed to gather up the courage to go inside or because I knew that the icy air awaited me. After reconfirming the address, I exited my vehicle and hastily made my way up the three flights of stairs.

I blew warm breaths onto my fists as I approached the door with the brass numbers Alena had texted me earlier. I started to imagine just how nice it would be to be all alone with her at her place, and it made my heart flutter. I surprised myself by being more excited than nervous, and I even reprimanded myself for the thoughts. But I was still happy that there would be no barriers between us, nor any distractions or worries, if only for a short time.

I sucked in a deep breath and knocked three times. Within moments, Alena was at the door welcoming me in with a genuine smile. The warm air from inside of the apartment wrapped itself around me as I entered. I examined the room with its shining, cherry-wood floors and its coffee-brown walls. There was a sizeable living room to my left with a black velvet sofa set, and to my right was the kitchen, furnished with black wood grain cabinets, black-and-white marble countertops, and stainless-steel appliances. A circular glass table sat between the kitchen area and a bookshelf. It was surrounded by four chairs with legs that matched the cabinets. Everything looked brand new.

"Wow," I gasped.

"It's beautiful, isn't it?" Alena spoke with what sounded like hidden excitement. "Here, let me take your jacket." She was slipping it off me before I could even assist.

"Thanks. Yeah, Alena it's . . ." I paused, catching a glimpse of her captivating brown eyes, "it's beautiful." Her gaze was fixed on me. She must have been analyzing my every move from the moment I entered the apartment. Noticing this made me feel embarrassed in a way, especially because I could tell she knew that I knew.

"Come over here, Amelia, let's talk," she insisted warmly as she walked over and hopped onto the left side of the L-shaped sofa. She was wearing a tight, long-sleeved knit top with gray sweatpants bottoms. The pants had a faded emblem on them and seemed ages old, so I assumed they held a sort of sentimental comfort for her.

I thought about sitting at the end of the couch that was farthest away from her in hopes that it might ease the tension I was now feeling. She just sat there so freely. She had thrown herself onto the couch with the youth of a teenager and now waited for me with one leg on the floor and the other tucked beneath her. I also couldn't help but notice how her thin yet muscular arms were so defined beneath the sleeves of her shirt. I had to work hard to control my breathing as I watched her chest slowly rise and fall. I longingly imagined what lay beneath the fabric as my eyes indiscriminately skimmed the area where her nipples poked through. I was grateful that my dark exterior couldn't expose my transfixed thoughts on her figure.

"Did you have any trouble finding the building?" she asked attentively.

"No, not at all," I said as I hesitantly slid down next to her on the sofa. "I'm just not used to the cold yet, so I stayed in my car too long. I'm sorry about being late. I know you don't like that."

"It's fine." She leaned back and inhaled a deep breath. "Mmm, you smell good."

"Thank you." I felt my cheeks heat up as I crossed my legs. "So, is your friend loaning you this place for free?" I asked awkwardly.

"I wish," she snickered. "Her name is Jess by the way."

"Right. Jess." I nodded.

"I'm currently paying her a discount for the rent," she said.

"Couldn't you just take over the lease completely?"

"I could, but she isn't ready to give it up just yet. She may come back next year which is why I'm hoping to be out of here by then."

"And you don't want to move back home?" I nervously questioned.

"No. Teresa can have the house, I don't want it," she firmly rejected the notion.

"I guess you can just get your own apartment here or somewhere nearby then." I inwardly cringed at my words. I felt like my conversational skills were rendered absolutely useless once again tonight.

"I don't know, I may want to move further away from the campus." Her gaze shifted ahead of her toward a stream of steam rising from the stove. I hadn't even noticed the pot there when I first walked in and inspected the room. She stood up, sauntered over to the kitchen, and switched off the stove. I couldn't pry my eyes away from the curve of her ass as she moved.

"Would you like any tea, Amelia?" She briefly turned around.

I cleared my throat and shifted my gaze. "Sure."

I watched her open a cabinet and effortlessly pull two blue ceramic mugs off the top shelf. She poured the tea into them, mixed in some sugar, and slowly walked back toward me.

"Thank you." I blew on the surface before taking in a steaming sip. When I looked up from the mug, I met Alena's penetrating gaze. We both silently exchanged looks for a moment as a warmth spread throughout my body. I wasn't sure if it came from the tea or from her observation of me.

"Amelia," she breathed out with a quiet frustration. "You are infuriating for me. Do you know that?" She sipped the tea, eyes still locked on mine.

"No—well, what do you... what do you mean by that?" She had caught me off guard which caused me to stumble on my words as I responded.

"I mean that you make it hard for me to keep things professional. I know that's what you said you wanted." She sounded dissatisfied as she placed the mug on a golden rose-shaped coaster on her coffee table.

"That's not what I really want." I lightly shook my head. "I just think that it's best, given the overall situation."

"I understand that... or at least I'm trying to, but it's hard." She errantly examined my body on the couch. "I'm extremely attracted to you," she added, a helplessness staining her voice. "You have a certain charm about you, Amelia. I even felt it the very first time we met. Your entire aura thickens the atmosphere wherever you go. Any place is a little bit lighter once you've entered and left. I'm sure each person you meet is a little bit happier too."

"I don't know if I'd say all that," I shyly denied, placing my tea down on a different coaster. I was stunned by the complexity of her compliments and the boldness of her flirtations. What the hell was I supposed to make of her praising me like this? Her expressions regarding me were far more intricate than I could have ever imagined them to be.

"It's true. I apologize if that makes you uncomfortable," she offered, but it didn't seem sincere as the corner of her lips turned up before she grabbed her mug and took another sip.

"I still just find it hard to believe that my feelings for you are even mutual," I explained.

"Why? We have good chemistry, shared interests, a similar moral compass. Our conversations are exhilarating and the way we laugh together is addicting. What more do you need for a mutual attraction?"

"Okay, so maybe we do have all those things going for us. But what about Teresa? I don't understand why you're choosing to split with her now. The timing just bothers me." My leg bounced uncontrollably as I looked at her. It was clear that I was troubled, and I wasn't trying to hide it. "It makes me feel guilty or responsible somehow." I frowned.

"You have no reason to feel that way, Amelia. Teresa and I have long held our differences. The reason our marriage has been on the rocks is no fault of yours." Her mug hit the coaster with a small clank, and she repositioned herself on the couch. "I know you have these thoughts that whatever has started up between us in some way contributes to my desire to leave her, but I can promise you that it doesn't."

"Then why did you mention that I was an additional source for the wedge between you two?" I huffed.

She released a long breath and rubbed at her brows. "When I said that my feelings for you are the tip of the iceberg, I meant just that. The rest of the issues that Teresa and I have are the reason for the sinking of our marriage. Not you." She pushed back her curls. "I do view you in a very positive light though, especially at this point in my life. You are easily someone beautiful and . . ." She tapped a finger to her bottom lip now—the one I wished I could bite. "How can I put this?

"I've never taken an interest in one of my students before. I mean how could I have anyway since I'm married. But my marriage is over now, and you are . . . different." She licked her lips. "Amelia, I honestly started feeling something for you after the third week you came into my office." She blushed. "You tripped on your way in, and it was adorable. I'm sure you didn't think I noticed, but unfortunately for you, I notice everything."

She stood up and collected the two mugs. She carefully rinsed each of them in the sink then turned around and leaned on the counter while vainly tucking her curls behind her ears. I thought of the moment she mentioned, which I unfortunately remembered as well. I definitely almost ate the carpet of her office that day, but I thought for sure I had saved myself from the embarrassment. Yet somehow the calm in her eyes eased the rising anxiety resulting from her remarks about it.

She stepped a few paces back in my direction then stood blinking at me. "It wasn't long after that week that I began paying more attention to you—a little in class, but mostly whenever you came to my office. I couldn't get you out of my head. It was like every time you were there, I noticed something new and fascinating about you. You were also funny and kind and pure." She paused. "All the feelings that started floating around inside of me were hard to admit to myself at first. They were more than I've felt for anyone in years..." Her voice trailed off and for a split second she even looked guilty.

"When you told me about your dream, I was shocked. I used to sway myself from indulging in any thoughts of more between us by telling myself that you were as straight as an arrow. I convinced myself that you would never have the same feelings for me that I was developing for you, but then you did." She returned next to me on the sofa. "So you see, Amelia, you're not the only one in disbelief here." There was a hint of sass in her tone, although her face remained kind.

I hadn't before considered her perception of things due to my unfortunate habit of externalizing my personal experiences with others. This made it difficult for me to comprehend their point of view. "I never really thought of that," I admitted. "But I think this would be much easier for me if you weren't—"

"Married," she exhaled the word out indignantly. "I told you about the 'agreement' I have with Teresa—though it doesn't make a difference anymore. I don't believe in cheating, Amelia."

"Does she already know about me?" I never dared ask the question before.

"She does. She knows that you're my student and that the two of us have a romantic connection as well. It isn't really her business, but I did tell her."

A wave of fear permeated my insides now, and I felt a little sick. Panic also rose from somewhere inside of me resulting from her articulation of our mutual affections. "Has she mentioned anything about it?"

"No. But she's very upset by it. I can tell." Her brows drew together, and she frowned. I had never heard the version of sadness that currently stained her voice. "I hate it," Alena continued. "She blames me but not herself when *she* was the one neglecting our relationship in the first place." The pangs of anger could now be picked up in her speech. "I told her before that I wanted a divorce, but she refused to discuss it. The separation was her way of keeping me for longer, hopeful I might change my mind. But I just need to be free." Alena's voice trembled as her façade wavered, and the anger that faded revealed a thick layer of sadness.

"I tried, Amelia, I really did. And for so long. She was neglecting my needs for her work. I understand being passionate about her career because I definitely enjoy what I do, but I would never abandon someone I loved for it." She shook her head as a tear trickled down her cheek. Without a second thought, I embraced her. I was not expecting the flood of tears that came as she wept in my arms. I hated to see her break down like this. It was the first time I had seen her strength falter and observed her as a weakened shell of herself. It was gut-wrenching and painful to watch yet somehow intimate to experience.

I struggled to keep in my own tears as I comforted her. "I'm so sorry, Alena," I murmured as her cries got quieter. Her fragility was clear in the way she clung to me, and there was absolutely no way that I was going to let her go until she was ready.

Minutes later, she finally pulled away. She excused herself, standing up and walking through an open door behind the wall of the TV. I heard water running and concluded that she was cleaning herself up in a bathroom. I looked down at my shirt, which was now saturated with her tears, but I didn't care about it at all. I was glad to be here for her, and I felt fortunate that she would share so much with me. Despite our current dynamic and age difference, she had always treated me as her equal and nothing less.

When she returned to the living room, I could see just how red and puffy her eyes had become from all of the crying. "Ugh, Amelia, I ruined your shirt. I'm sorry," she uttered apologetically after noticing my tear-stained tee.

"It's fine." I waved my hand in the air.

"No, let me loan you another shirt. It looks like you got hit by a hurricane." She laughed softly, though a defeated tone still plagued her voice. She then disappeared into the room across from the bathroom door and moments later called to me to get changed.

I strolled over to her room and peeked in, promptly scoping it out. The bedroom decorations flaunted a beautiful purple and teal color scheme. The dark wooden bed frame and matching dresser and wardrobe took up most of the space. The walls were a pearl-gray color which pleasantly accentuated the colorful bedspread. I stepped in right as Alena closed a drawer across the room.

"I love the design in here," I noted as I approached her.

"Isn't it cute? I actually helped Jess decorate the entire apartment when she first rented it," she explained as she handed me the shirt. "I would've gone more for green and beige myself."

I rubbed the linen between my fingers as I studied her. The red in her eyes had lightened into pink, and she looked more drained than when I first arrived.

"If you have any more time, we can finish our conversation so you can be on your way," she suggested.

"Yeah, I think that's a good idea," I hesitantly agreed. I did want to finish talking, but I didn't want to leave. The vulnerability we had already achieved in this setting was very satisfying for me. Our emotions ran free in this apartment in a way they never could on campus.

"Okay, I'll be in the other room waiting for you." She walked out and closed the door behind her.

Upon her exit, I threw my shirt over my head, replacing it with the thick, fitted burgundy top she'd loaned me. The shirt was far too lengthy for my arms and my bare nipples peeked through the fabric, but I shrugged it off. I cuffed the sleeves several times and bunched the bottom of the shirt into my sweatpants. I then grabbed my top off the ground, opened the door, and walked back into the living room.

Alena sat there waiting for me on the couch as I entered the room. I held up my tear-soaked shirt, and she handed me a plastic bag to temporarily dispose of it. She had thrown back her hair since she'd left the room, and her curls were now falling into a tousled veil around her head. I felt stimulated as I silently bagged my shirt and set it next to the apartment door before returning next to her on the sofa, sitting closer to her this time around.

"I hope I didn't put too much on you, Amelia. I feel so comfortable around you, but I'd hate to overwhelm you with everything going on in my life," she said anxiously.

"Alena, you can tell me *anything*." I spoke softly. "I'm always going to listen to you because I care about you. We have a bond—a friendship above all—so just know that I'm here for you no matter what."

She nodded with a slight grin. "Thank you."

"I know this may feel like a lot, and it is." I leaned forward. "But from what I can see and from what I know about you . . . you are more than capable of overcoming it all. I really believe that." I instinctively placed my hand on hers. It was merely an automatic response—a friendly gesture—but the emotions between us, especially at this point, were far from friendly.

The patter of my heart sounded like a drum in my ears as she left her hand under mine, searching my eyes in our closeness. Time crept to a halt as the distance between our lips diminished. She was almost close enough to taste by the time she stopped edging toward me. That's when her hand slid from underneath mine.

Damn, I thought disappointedly, but I was pleasantly surprised when the same hand that had just pulled away now rested on my face. My heart palpitated violently as her long, cool fingers moved slowly across my cheeks.

"Is this okay?" she whispered, her warm breath tickling my nose. I nodded my head, not taking my eyes off her. When she started nearer to me once more, I hastily bridged the gap between us. Finally, her soft lips were pressed on mine.

There was a release I wasn't quite prepared for once our lips touched, and the relief of it was indescribable. Right in the living room of Alena's apartment, an unspoken rule I'd made for myself was now being broken. Crazy signals shot through the length of my body as warmth filled my entire being. The gravitational pull from within me to be nearer to her moved me forward, and I found myself pressed as close to her as physically possible.

Alena's hand dropped from my face then and latched onto the sides of my hips. There was a rising heat from her touch there. She pulled me inward, causing her own body to compress onto the couch. Her hands slid lower, and she kissed my neck gently while squeezing my ass. A knot of guilt went straight to my stomach when I felt a familiar tingling in the lower half of my body. I knew that I craved her terribly, but now wasn't the right time. It couldn't be.

I abruptly pulled back from the kiss and looked down at her below me. I was stunned. Her beauty and warmth and the lust in her eyes taunted me, but the knowledge that fought its way back from below extinguished the heated feelings. I shut my eyes for a moment, struggling to recapture a firm grasp on reality. When I finally did, guilt weighed on me like a ton of bricks.

Alena's hand seized my face which was undoubtedly filled with anguish as I opened my eyes. I turned from her immediately and tried my best to suppress the tears that were threatening to fall.

"Amelia, what's wrong? Is everything okay?" she asked worriedly, sitting upright. Did I—" she froze.

I supposed that she feared my reaction to the kiss, but I loved it—more than any kiss I'd ever received in fact. It was equally as intense as it was sweet and tender, but I still somehow managed to feel terrible about the experience. I thought about Teresa who had longed for the same lips and missed the touch I was now receiving. It gave me such a dreadful feeling that I couldn't speak or even look in her direction.

"Amelia, say something," she impatiently urged.

"We shouldn't have done that," I whispered as I met her entrancing brown eyes and immediately lost myself in them. "I told myself not to."

"So, you're not uncomfortable? You didn't feel any pressure to kiss me?" Alena sounded frightened. She seemed so worried about breaching my boundaries, which was admirable, but not the point.

"No, I wasn't. It isn't that I didn't want to kiss you." I fidgeted with my hands. "It's just that some things you can hope for but still know that you probably shouldn't do."

Alena was quiet for a long moment. "You're right." Her eyebrows pressed together. "But you're also wrong. If we both wanted to, I can't see the problem with the fact that we did."

I couldn't think of something I wanted more than to taste her lips again. Actually, I could—but my mouth would still be the main character collaborating with her body. Yet the dilemma remained. "What if you and Teresa get back together?" I asked warily.

"We won't. How can I convince you of that, Amelia? I started the process already, months ago, but she won't even sign the initial papers. I'm not holding on to her, she's holding on to me." Somehow her tone remained soothing despite the obvious traces of distress in it.

I knew that Alena and I were running in circles, but I was having a hard time outrunning my conscience. "I hate this," I admitted with watery eyes. I wanted nothing more than to freely take a chance on Alena, but things were just so complicated. My frustrations would have bled out through my tears had I not stifled them.

Alena was still clearly able to see how upset I was, and she pulled me into her arms and held me tightly. I felt completely protected with her and didn't ever want to leave her embrace. She kissed my forehead for the first time, which put me at ease all the more. The tension was soon broken when my stomach erupted in a loud, gurgling sound. I looked at Alena, my mouth hanging open, and she laughed which sent my heart fluttering a little faster.

She released me from her grip. "Did you eat anything this evening?" she asked skeptically.

"I tried," I guiltily admitted. "I made a sandwich before I came, but then I dropped it on the ground."

It was obvious that she held back her laughter. "You're a clumsy one, aren't you?" She seemed to weigh the next words in her mind carefully. "I wanted to make tacos for dinner before our meeting tonight, but I didn't get the chance. You're welcome to stay while I cook and eat dinner with me afterward if you'd like."

Is she nervous? I grinned. I was extremely pleased with the offer to stay with her longer. "I do love tacos."

Chapter 5 Hate to Love

Mya was exhilarated now that I was willingly going along with her plans for the weekend. Ever since I'd left Alena's apartment the other night with an invitation to return this Sunday, excitement became my personality. I couldn't help but eagerly plan coordinated outfits with Mya for the club on Saturday or assist in the vote on what movie we would see tonight. Gabe had been allowed to choose the restaurant without objection since we had conspired against him on both the film and the location of the club we were visiting. He would much rather have seen *Venom,* but Mya and I were set on watching *The Hate U Give.*

Gabe decided on taking us to a Japanese steakhouse near the theater for dinner. He had only been to it twice before, but he continuously raved over it, and for good reason. We sat around the grill with strangers and watched the chef spin his knives and spatulas in between cooking the food and agitating the fire just for fun. We devoured our teriyaki chicken, shrimp, and steak with the rice and vegetables that came with it. Mya and I also drank our fair share of sake since Gabe was the designated driver.

Almost as soon as we entered the theater—Gabe, with his bottomless pit of a stomach, made a beeline to the concessions stand while Mya and I slipped away to the women's restroom. By the time I had finished and washed my hands, Mya was playing around with her hair in the mirror, so I decided to wait for her in the hall. She came out giggling to herself and walked over to me.

"Guess who I just ran into in the bathroom?" she asked.

"Who?"

"My old Biology professor from sophomore year." She grabbed me and pulled me further away from the entrance. "Ugh, it's just so weird seeing your professor in public, let alone the bathroom! Thank God I just finished making my weird faces when I was putting on my lip gloss."

I couldn't help myself as I chuckled at her. She shoved me forward right before Gabe stepped into the hallway and waved us over. He had gotten us snacks which we gladly accepted before we all made our way to Theater 7. We settled into our seats just as the commercials came to an end.

Not even half an hour into the movie did I have to use the restroom once again. I squeezed past Gabe who was sitting next to me, then past two couples and a group of teenagers. Once I safely made it through the dark room, I breezed to the bathroom and promptly took care of business.

While washing my hands I heard the door open. I didn't think anything of it until I heard my name being called. I whipped my head around to find Alena standing there in jeans and a sage green sweater with a surprised yet satisfied expression on her face. My heart leapt into my throat as I stepped over to the hand dryer. It blew fiercely as she advanced toward me without releasing her focus.

"I promise I didn't know you were here." She smiled. "I thought you were going to the club this weekend," she said as she opened her arms for a hug. I gave my hands a little shake before eagerly embracing her, my eyes staying locked on the door's entrance while I did.

"It's funny, Mya just ran into one of her professors. I guess it was my turn next." I grinned.

"I'm glad I have the pleasure of being the one. What movie are you two watching?"

"It's three of us actually. And we're watching *The Hate U Give*."

"Me too! How did I miss you?"

"Maybe it's the dark room, Alena . . . I don't know," I said sarcastically.

She playfully nudged my shoulder. "Don't be like that."

The door suddenly swung open, and some lady rushed in with her toddler in tow. My immediate unease quickly traveled to my face, and Alena gave me a knowing look. She placed a hand on my shoulder before starting toward a stall.

"Nice seeing you, Amelia." She held up a hand in goodbye.

"You too, Dr. Hutchinson."

I pushed the restroom doors open and stood outside contemplating. I should've headed left, toward the theater and my friends, but an uncontrollable urge held me back. I somewhat enjoyed that brief moment of uncertainty when Alena and I were interacting in a public setting. It wasn't to the point where I would suggest purposely going out with her just yet, but it was enough to motivate me to sneak around a little.

Instead of walking into the theater, I stepped behind a pillar that sat tucked away in a long hall of doors. I waited patiently for her to emerge, and when she did, I whistled to her and waved her over.

"What? What is it?" She giggled as I jerked her further out of view.

"We weren't finished talking," I reproached jokingly.

"Oh. Was there something else you needed to tell me right at this moment?" she countered in the same manner.

"I just wanted to see if you were on a date," I teased. The sake was clearly running its course through my system.

Alena tilted her head and stepped forward, towering over me in the corner. "I think you know better than that if I'm not here with *you*."

A sudden jolt of electricity ran through me. Even being in public wasn't enough to keep me from being aroused by the way she looked at me. A fight or flight response started then, and I wanted to run. "Okay." I grinned nervously, heat flooding my cheeks. "I need to get back before my friends come find me. I'll go first."

"See you Sunday then?" she asked.

I nodded as I slowly wandered away from the pillar, but before I could get far, she snatched me into a tight hug. The aroma of berries and pomegranates flowed from her hair and caused me to float away in my mind for a split second. I forgot about everything—all that was going on and even that we were in public. Reality held me captive again only once she released me. I was blushing, though it wasn't apparent, and I began to stumble away. I looked back one last time, still flustered. "Goodbye."

As I emerged from behind the pillar, I caught a glimpse of Gabe's backside as he disappeared into the men's room. *Damn, I wonder if he saw us.* I was slightly concerned, but I was mostly still in disarray from the unanticipated crushing of Alena's body into mine. She was still behind the pillar waiting for the distance to grow between us as I walked on. *Why the fuck does she smell so good?* My thoughts threatened to turn erotic as I entered the theater. Before I knew it I was seated a chair away from Mya again, and she was glaring at me.

"Took you long enough," she huffed before facing the screen again.

Gabe soon reappeared beside me and smiled as he whispered, "What'd you do? Fall in the toilet or get a new date?"

I froze in my seat. "What do you mean?" I whispered back as casually as I could manage.

"You took forever. I almost went to look for you, but then I saw that *gorgeous* woman you were talking to. Did you get her number?"

"No." I sank into my seat. I was on edge, yet pride still swelled in me at the mention of Alena's beauty.

"Good! You're supposed to wait until tomorrow for that."

I didn't understand what Gabe meant.

Nearly the entire drive home, I had to endure Mya's unending questions. She grilled me about missing the "best part" of the movie, and she kept asking me why I had taken so long. Gabe eyed me through the rearview mirror as she complained, but he made no mention about seeing me with a woman outside the theater. I thought it smart to subdue any curiosities Gabe might develop if I didn't mention Alena, so I admitted to seeing "Professor Hutchinson" in the hall and speaking to her for a moment.

"What?!" Mya fumed. "You were disturbing our *professor* with class shit while we were out one of two nights of *ever* this freakin' month, Amelia?!"

I bit my lip to calm the laughter that wanted to escape due to her theatrics.

"Promise me you won't do that tomorrow," she whined.

"You act like I'm planning to see another teacher or something, Mya."

"Dammit, Amelia, just promise me!"

I finally broke and laughed hysterically.

"Keep it down you two, you're going to make me crash the car," Gabe petitioned as he drove with one hand and picked at his braces with the other. He had a hard time giving up on his favorite snacks despite it being bad for his teeth.

"*I'll* make sure of that if Amelia doesn't promise me," she threatened.

"Oh God," Gabe groaned nervously.

"Okay, I promise, Mya!"

"Thank you." She smiled angelically before turning back around. I noticed how she often sat in the passenger seat nowadays whenever the three of us carpooled. I didn't comment on it, but it did make me wonder since we used to fight to the death for that spot she now assumed was hers.

Gabe approached my apartment first since he and Mya lived at the same complex. I squinted my eyes at both of them as I exited his car, then I boldly presented a middle finger in their direction once I was safely in my doorway.

At some point during the trip home, I'd learned what Gabe meant at the theater with his comment about getting someone's number. He and Mya had revealed their secret plan for us to go to a lesbian club tomorrow instead of the one *I thought* Mya and I had chosen together without him. I was annoyed because I had been excited about going to LUXX, our favorite club. A club was a club in the end, but I knew I would be uninterested in any of the women there. It was hard as hell to see anyone besides Alena.

When I was finally out of my clothes and laying on my semi-comfortable bed in the dark room, my thoughts roamed. As I began to drift off to sleep, memories of the embrace at the theater consumed me once again. I yearned for Alena's body to be on mine, and the anticipation of seeing her again on Sunday kept me from sleeping. When I finally dozed off, I was with her again. I was in Alena's office—my hands on her thighs, our lips locked together, enjoying the exhilaration of a forbidden pleasure.

Chapter 6 Nightly Bliss

I was radiating with excitement by the time I pulled up to the Brookfield Apartments. It was a quarter to seven on Sunday evening, and Alena had suggested that I arrive hungry since she was cooking. It was easy to submit to her request, especially because I was still a little hung over from the night out on Saturday.

Visiting her apartment the second time around was far more intriguing. I wasn't as nervous about it, so I was able to notice things I hadn't before. The bookshelf near the front door held many small green plants. Near the television was a photograph of a family of four. Another picture included a second family of equal size but with only one familiar face from the previous picture. There was also a portrait of what I assumed to be Alena's graduation from grad school. The last frame was a picture of the most adorable Teacup Yorkie.

I sat at the kitchen table while she worked fervently in preparing our meal. The candle that burned on the glass table reminded me of a handful of summer nights long ago. I nostalgically described to her how I'd gone on several camping trips when I was a small child. I gushed about how much I used to love scorching marshmallows so that I could create a black crust around the ooey gooey goodness of its insides. I talked about the fishing ventures where we seldom caught any fish but still enjoyed the process. The entire time I spoke, Alena appeared fascinated by my ramblings. After I was done reminiscing on the past, I gave her a brief overview of the mundane clubbing night I'd had with my friends. Alena was familiar with Beck's, the club we went to, but she confessed how she hadn't been to a club in town in over a year. She wasn't too keen on running into her students when she wanted to have a good time.

"Are these your plants?" I asked, now standing at the bookshelf.

"Yes, the entire shelf is mine." She named the two or three plants that rested on it as well as the ones on the floor—my preferred one was the Monstera.

"Which book is your favorite?" I asked as she began to set the table.

"The book of poetry there, by Maya Angelou." She pointed to the right of the shelf. "I absolutely adore her."

I grazed my finger along the spine of the tattered book before she came beside me and picked it up, turning the pages deliberately.

"I hope you've heard this one." She began to read aloud about the caged bird. I knew this poem well, and hearing her recite it so passionately made me wonder if she felt like her life mirrored that of the bird.

"That was beautiful," I murmured once she finished the poem. I was admittedly smitten by her reading to me so unexpectedly. "Maya Angelou is a treasure for sure and definitely a staple in our community."

"I'm glad you know her." She tapped the book lightly on my head before replacing it on the shelf. "It may have been a good reason for me to kick you out before dinner if you didn't," she teased.

I shook my head and turned back toward the books. "No wonder you're so poetic when you speak. Most of these are poetry books," I said, sliding my finger along each spine of the remaining books before turning around.

"It's definitely my favorite genre to read. I also write a little poetry as well," she declared while grabbing wine glasses and paper towels for the table. "Maybe one day I'll show you some of my poems. I think I left them in a box back at my house." She stepped closer to me. "Anyway, shall we eat now?"

A cocktail of orange juice and amaretto sat on the table next to our plates. A spread of organic hard scrambled eggs with spinach and vegan cheese, pancakes and berries, and turkey bacon went along with our drinks.

"Who are all the people in the pictures over there?" I asked as I slid a slice of bacon between my teeth.

Alena looked across the room, and pointed with her fork as she spoke. "The left picture is of me with my father, mother, and my brother, Langston. The other one is of his family: his wife Naomi and his two girls, Emma and Nicole." She picked at a bare pancake.

"Those little girls are adorable." I swallowed my bacon and started on my eggs.

"They really are." She drizzled syrup on the fluffy rounds. "I wish I got to see them more often but they're in Colorado now, and I'm here. We all used to be in California with my parents."

"I remember. That's where you were born too, right?"

"Mm-hmm, good ole Palo Alto." She took a swig of her cocktail.

"What about the dog?" I asked.

"That's my baby, Pompeii." She frowned. "I miss him so much, but he's staying with Teresa." She cleared her throat and looked away for a moment before returning her eyes to me. "When do I get to hear more about *your* family, Amelia? You have two brothers and one sister, right?"

"Right. I'm the second oldest. My brother Jordan came first, and I was born three years after that. My little brother, A.J., came next and he's sixteen now. Julia is the youngest and my favorite. She's fourteen."

Alena chuckled and took another sip of the cocktail. "It sounds like a full house."

"In a way, but I always liked the company." I shrugged.

"I bet that was nice." She sighed. "It got kind of lonely with just Langston and me. We were pretty much polar opposites too. He was always quiet and reserved, and I was a lot more rambunctious than him." The corners of her lips lifted. "But he always stood up for me and stood by me, especially when I came out. My parents were in disarray for a little while after that."

I nodded as I held a berry between my fingers. There was a warmth emanating from my cheeks as the liquor slowly spread through my system. I could tell that it wasn't a lot, but it was still enough to loosen me up.

"Do you like cats or dogs?" Alena suddenly asked, reclaiming my attention.

"I don't *love* cats, but sometimes they're okay. I love dogs though! My family has a Beagle-Husky mix named Pinky."

"Aww, how adorable."

"She's *so* cute! She's our princess. I'll have to show you pictures of her—her blue eyes are gorgeous! Let me get my phone." I jumped up to grab it from a charging dock on the edge of the counter.

"You seem a lot calmer tonight, Amelia. I like that," Alena said, dabbing her face with a napkin. Her plate was nearly empty.

"I'm not gonna lie, I was nervous as hell the first time I came here to see you."

She lowered the napkin. "I'm sorry you felt that way. I hate to think that I made you uncomfortable."

"*You* didn't make me uncomfortable, Alena, the situation did. I just didn't know exactly what to expect, that's all."

"Oh." There was a tenderness in her face.

"I was also excited," I added casually as I moved beside her and scrolled through my phone. I showed her pictures—first of my dog, then of my siblings and parents.

"You have a beautiful family." She grinned. "And uh, I was excited too when you first came, by the way." She looked up at me and I could see that her cheeks were a light pink. "Just like I was when I spotted you on Friday."

I bit my lip shyly as I set my phone down.

She ran her hands through her hair before lifting herself from the table and grabbing our dirty plates. I quickly joined her, snagging the empty cups and the saucers she had set out for the fresh fruit and butter. I helped her clean the rest of the table as well as the stove and wash the dishes.

Her movements around the kitchen were so light and nimble that it sparked something in me. I had the urge to dance with her. I wanted to hold her close in my arms and move harmoniously around the room together. I also wanted to smell the fruity aroma of her hair and get a nice view of her lips. To feel the warmth from her body in the room as we touched. I yearned for this but shied away from the suggestion. I had gotten more comfortable than I was the last time for sure, but I was still getting used to all the newness with her. Instead of dancing, I settled for nestling beside her on the sofa once the kitchen was finally spotless. The only remaining lights in the room were the burning candle and table lamp, which magnified the highlights on Alena's curls. It also made her warm brown eyes look especially inviting.

"Is there anything in particular you'd like to do tonight? My cocktail wasn't too strong, but I still don't want you to drive for at least another half hour or so."

"I want to hear some of your poetry. Do you have anything you can remember off the top of your head?" I asked eagerly.

"That's not exactly what I had in mind." She blinked demurely. "But yes, I do know some of my poems by heart. Most of them aren't appropriate though. My *normal* poems are in that box I told you about."

A surge of intrigue swept over me. "I'm a big girl, Alena, I think I can handle it."

She laughed. "I believe you, but I'd rather uphold my wholesome exterior for as long as I can manage."

This comment sent my imagination spiraling into the deepest reaches of sensuality. Overly erotic imagery consumed my mind, and I struggled to keep it all controlled. "Fair enough," I conceded.

"I usually watch this crime show on Sundays, but since you were coming over I recorded it so I could look at it later. We could just watch it together right now if you're interested?" she hesitantly asked.

"Is it the *Murder in Camp Maroon* series?!" I shrieked.

"You know that show?" She seemed pleasantly surprised.

"Do I?! That's how Mya and I became friends. We watched it almost every Sunday even before we lived together on campus. We still watch another series that's similar, but she missed too many episodes of *Camp Maroon* and gave up on it a couple months ago. I've been watching it alone."

"That's too bad for her." Alena was already flipping through her recordings. "But at least neither of us have to watch it alone anymore."

We both focused our attention on the fictitious recounts of a crime concerning two wayward lovers that had met at their workplace. The younger man had killed his older female lover who was cheating on him with someone closer to her in age. It was a crime of jealousy and passion, but I couldn't help but empathize with the felonious character. The show brought back some insecurities I'd recognized earlier in my connection with Alena. Differences in age—even small ones—could be problematic in a romantic situation.

"That was horrible," Alena muttered as she muted the television while the credits were rolling. "What'd you think of this episode?" She turned to me with a frown.

"I think it was tragic. I can't believe he did that. But what she did was pretty awful too."

Alena nodded, her brows and mouth still turned down. "Yes, but not enough for her to be killed because of it."

"Definitely not," I agreed. "But . . . do you think she had a point about him?" I asked carefully.

"What do you mean?"

"How she related more to the man that was her age, so she chose to be with him. Don't you think she was right to find somebody that was better for her?"

"She could've broken it off if that's what she wanted to do, Amelia."

"Yeah, I know." I looked away from her intense gaze. "But it makes sense, right? I mean the age thing in general. Like with us . . ." I turned back to her, focusing on her forehead instead of her eyes.

She cocked her head to the side. "With *us*? You're twenty-one, aren't you?"

"Yes, and you're nearly in your thirties."

She scoffed. "Damn, Amelia. You act like I'm ancient or something." She backed away and crossed her legs. "I just turned twenty-eight, and by the end of the year you'll be twenty-two. That's six years apart. It's just a number." There were traces of agitation in her voice.

I sighed and shook my head. "I didn't mean to offend you."

"You didn't." She took a deep breath and spoke in a softer tone. "You should know that your age doesn't matter to me, though. At all. If it did, we wouldn't even be here right now. We're both in our twenties and you're about to graduate, so I think we're just fine on that front."

"Yeah, I mean that makes sense." I tugged at my shirt.

She raised a brow. "But?"

I exhaled. "I'm no killer, Alena, but I do understand the uncertainty I saw in that man on the show. She shouldn't have cheated, but it makes perfect sense that she would want someone who had *more*. More than he did . . . more than I do."

"More than *you* do? Why are you even saying that?" Alena looked perplexed.

"Because it wouldn't be the most outrageous thing for you to come across someone that has more than I can offer right now. I mean, I've dealt with that before." I lowered my head, feeling the sting of embarrassment from my unsuccessful romances of the past.

I had always been a passionate lover—even when I was closeted throughout high school—but nothing ever stuck. No one ever stayed with me. The last time was the hardest with Reyna. She had promised me the distance wouldn't change things when she transferred the second semester of our freshman year. It was admittedly a short time for us to be together, but it felt like we were soulmates. In the end, she couldn't handle the distance, so she found somebody else.

Alena didn't so much as breathe while I spoke my piece. She had listened intently to my words and compassion spread across her face. "Amelia, if we were together, I would never hurt you like that. And I don't want to be with someone because of their age or their career or their finances. I want to be with someone because of their character and their heart."

"*Are* we planning on being together?" I asked her anxiously as an unwelcome wave of frustration swept over me. "Where is this leading us to anyways? What exactly do you expect from me here?"

She clicked off the TV and stared into my eyes. "I truly enjoy every moment I spend with you, Amelia," she said. "I adore seeing you, talking to you, and being around you." She grabbed my hands. "I want our connection to grow into something serious in time. I know it'd be complicated, but I think we could make it work."

"*Could we?*" I asked, my voice riddled with uncertainty. "It's not only about your age or marital status. There are also rules at the university forbidding everything we're doing. What we're *feeling*."

"Then discretion can be our friend. But only if you're in for that, Amelia. I'm in no position to be implementing my will above yours."

She let go of my hands and rocked back on the sofa again. "For me it's simple. We are two consenting adults who should be able to have a romantic connection with one another if that's what we choose." She paused. "Maybe it's wrong, maybe it's not. I don't care about the standards of society or even the university for that matter. I fully understand that I'm in a position of authority over you as your professor, but I would never intentionally place any pressure on you because of that. There's also no way I'd *ever* offer you an unfair advantage." She shook her head. "It's against everything in my nature as a serious academic."

Anxiety filled my lungs as I digested her words. It was true that as adults we had the right to choose who we interacted with, but it was also true that it was inappropriate for us to engage in any way other than professional right now. I'm sure there were plenty of cases where people in this situation had undoubtedly favored the person they were interested in when it came to their grades. I'm also sure there were instances where the opposite occurred after one of the parties broke off the connection. I couldn't imagine Alena being angry at me for denying her, especially to the point where she would try to cause any harm. I also didn't think there would be anything I could do in order to make her give me a grade that I didn't rightfully earn.

"I want nothing more than to be sure of this like you," I murmured. "You'll just need to give me the time to adjust." I placed my arms around her, and her hand grazed my back as my head rested on her shoulder.

I couldn't recall a better sensation than to be in her arms. Despite my reservations, I felt so much for her—more than I even cared to admit. I was hoping I would be able to control my feelings because I knew just how fast I could fall in love. Maybe it would be a "young" thing for me to do, since I hadn't had my heart broken enough times before. But truthfully, I rarely opened myself up to many people in the first place, so every time I did I was taking a huge risk.

"Do you want me to go?" I asked when we both pulled away. I briefly glanced toward my coat and shoes by the door.

"It is getting late, isn't it?" Alena swung her arm over the sofa and checked her phone on the side table. "It's ten fifty-two. Are you ready to go?" she questioned.

Hesitation colored my voice as I spoke. "Not necessarily, but if you want me to, I can." I didn't want to be too clingy, but I also wanted to express my interest in spending more time with her tonight.

"Don't you have classes tomorrow? I know I do."

"Yes, but that never stopped me from being a night owl before." I grinned.

She sighed lightly. "I don't really want you to leave yet. But what kind of person would I be for allowing you to indulge me in such a way . . . by letting you stay?"

"Is that some of your poetry coming through? Give me more lines, Alena! Don't keep it from me!" I chanted while snapping my fingers. She burst into a laughter that I soon joined in, and as we calmed down, I found it hard for my heart to do the same. It was far too difficult when I was staring at this portrait of beauty—the lightly-melanated woman sitting next to me on the sofa. I began to feel tingly sensations emanating throughout every area of my body. Her almond eyes remained on mine—as breathtaking as ever—and her full lips were set so beautifully on her face.

Why had I not kissed them once again? I'd been here even longer than the first time, yet I still did not seek out what I craved. We had the privacy along with the desire, so why not indulge?

Can I kiss you again? is what I meant to say, but "Can I stay a little longer?" came out instead.

"Sure." She smiled, and I felt a sense of relief.

"Will you read me more poetry from the shelf?" I asked.

Alena obliged, leaving me on the sofa while she grabbed a book. "This one is new, but there's this poem in it that reminds me of you."

She sat back beside me, propped up on her left leg.

Her soft trills carefully reviewed the page. She occasionally glanced down at me, and I peeked up at her several times before our eyes finally met without straying. She stopped reading then and closed the book before advancing in my direction.

It happened so quickly—one moment we were gazing at one another and the next, her mouth was crashing into mine. I tasted a faint hint of cherry and almonds on her lips as they fought mine for control. A familiar warmth flooded my cheeks as the flavor of her mouth consumed me and there was an arousal of heat from deep within. The softness of her lips and the intensity of her kisses were enough to drive me crazy.

I didn't even have sufficient time to notice her pinning me down on the sofa and pressing the length of her body against mine. She felt even more muscular than she looked. Her arms and hands were strong, but her breasts were soft, and so was her ass. My hands molded the soft flesh as she remained flattened on top of me.

I was utterly failing at maintaining control of my carnal desires despite my best efforts. The pounding of my heart and rushing of blood eventually created a familiar wetness that reminded me of where an interaction like this might be headed.

And for that, I was not yet ready.

There had never been a more memorable or infuriating pain than when I realized I needed to stop. I grasped her hips and gently pushed her away. Disappointment plagued me as she stopped blessing my lips with her own. The way she now appeared mirrored exactly the way I was feeling. Dazed and euphoric. She looked as if she'd had two glasses of wine in one gulp, and I couldn't help but smile at her. She returned the gesture as she sat up on her knees and inspected my form below. I wanted to beg her to kiss me again, but even the thought of her edging closer to me once more sent a rippling inside me that I knew I would be unable to control.

"Too much?" she asked, running her fingers through her beautiful curls.

Not enough. "It was, umm . . ." I didn't have the vocabulary for the way she made me feel or the things I now wanted to do to her and with her. "Maybe I should go?"

"That bad, Amelia?" she asked with clear amusement.

I shyly looked away as I sat up and straightened my clothing.

"Oh, I'm just playing." She placed a hand on my shoulder as she sat down beside me. "Anyway, you should stop giving me that look so much. It drives me nuts."

"What look?" I asked defensively.

"The one you give me when you want me to kiss you."

My chest tightened. I had no clue of this so-called look that I gave her, but it was embarrassing to hear about.

"You gave me that look the other night too," she continued. "I've really been trying to behave myself," her grip tightened on my shoulder, "but I seem to have this urge to give you what you want."

And there it was. An exact replica of the seductive slur in her voice that she'd once used with me the evening in her office when I had nearly knocked her to the ground. The sultry tone was brand new then, but the shock of being faced with it once again weighed just as heavily the second time around. I had an inkling that she enjoyed riling me up this way, and I was nearly wheezing when I stood up and told her that I had to use the bathroom before heading back to my apartment.

After I'd finished, I noticed a lamp shining from her room and wandered toward it. She was sitting in the bed with a serious face, scribbling onto a notepad. "What are you doing?" I asked as I entered the room.

"Writing down this idea that just came to me."

"For what?" I sat on the edge of the bed.

"A poem." She looked up now, locking her eyes with mine.

Her features were soft and her expression was relaxed.

"A wholesome poem?" I asked with a grin.

She smirked and shook her head as she looked back down to the pad. "I'm almost finished, give me a moment."

I scooted closer to her with my lips pouted. "Can't you read it to me?" I asked as sweetly as possible.

"Amelia, I don't—" She peered up at me. "Fuck," she whispered lowly, putting down the pen and scowling at me. "I never should've told you my weakness."

"I would've figured it out on my own," I countered with a smile.

"I'll read it to you, Amelia," she relented, and I beamed as she waved me closer to her. I lay beside her on the bed in my baby blue joggers. As she lounged next to me, she placed a kiss on my forehead that left my skin tingling behind it. "I don't like reading a poem that I haven't let marinate, but here goes nothing."

She began to describe her perception of a woman that she had dreamed of encountering but had yet to meet. This woman was dignified and varied, zealous and wise, and beautiful in every way. She had thought it impossible to actually cross paths with such a person until she noticed that this very woman was materializing in her real life.

She detailed the passion always bubbling up in the woman's deep brown eyes, the arch of her brows, and the imperfect curve of her smile. She talked of how the woman's neck was missing sweet kisses and an expert tongue. How her entire body, in fact, deserved the same. How her breasts were ample and lips supple. The longing to see what lay beneath any nuisance of clothing she wore. How she imagined the woman's scent coated with the sweetness of an erotic sweat. How she would make the woman sing a tune created only for her.

The poem that she'd scrawled in a matter of minutes seemed to go on without end and my heart drummed at the words. I could only assume that I had at least partially inspired it. There were no words to describe my excitement for the moment or for the entire night.

Unfortunately though, my fatigue overtook me before I could give Alena proper warning that I was slipping away. It might've been the lull of her soft, melodic voice reading to me or the fact that she was doing so as I leaned my head against her shoulder in that very comfortable bed. Whatever it was, I was surprised to soon open my eyes to a dark, unfamiliar room. I was clinging to the sleeping woman I currently admired, which explained where I was and why. I promised myself to wake her in two minutes' time so I could return home, but I lost consciousness again, and that never came about.

Knock, knock, knock. I heard a persistent noise at the front door and thought I was dreaming, but I could feel myself slowly returning to consciousness. I tried to fall back asleep, but the noise persisted. *Knock, knock, knock, knock.* I was now fully awake from the knocking, and I lay facing the bathroom door in Alena's room. All I saw was darkness as I opened my eyes—meanwhile the sound grew louder.

I felt a movement in the bed and eventually heard Alena jump out of it. The sound of her footsteps trailed halfway to the side of the bed where I lay, so I shut my eyes and remained unmoving. She then paced farther away and left the room, closing the door behind her.

After a few quiet moments, I caught the unsettling utterances of a woman who was obviously upset. I could barely make out the angry voice that was shouting at Alena for reasons I didn't know. The voice was unfamiliar, but I could only think of one person who would have that much familiarity with Alena for her to even entertain the idea of opening the door at this hour: her spouse. *Shit, it's Teresa.*

The last thing I wanted was to be caught in bed with Alena even though nothing was happening other than actual sleep. I started to regret not forcing myself up as soon as I'd realized that we had both nodded off. I wanted to be back in the safety of my apartment or to be anywhere but here. I feared that the woman at the door might barrel past Alena somehow and find me lying here in her bed. That fear made it impossible for me to move.

Alena raised her voice for the first time, and whatever she had said stopped the dispute almost immediately. The other woman quietly uttered a few more words before the door was firmly shut and locked. I finally exhaled and regained the use of my limbs as a stillness settled over the apartment.

Alena returned to the room with a dreadful look on her face, and she let out a deep breath as she shut the door behind her. I glanced at the alarm clock on her bedside table and saw that it was just past six in the morning.

"Was that Teresa?" I questioned her as I sat up.

She sat down at the foot of the bed, half facing me. "Yes, that was her." She rubbed at her eyes. "I'm sorry she woke you. She was headed to work and decided to stop by for some reason. Apparently, last night she found out that I was staying here." Alena looked at me with an anxious expression.

"What? But it's so early. Who told her you were here?" I sleepily rubbed my eyes as well.

"Jess. She knew we were separated and that I wanted a divorce, but not that I already had another person in mind that I . . ." she paused and bit her lip as she glanced at me. "Jess isn't too judgmental in general. But Teresa told her we are divorcing *because* I was cheating on her with you."

"What?! Doesn't she know you've been dating other people already?"

"She does." Alena was now wrapping a blanket around her body. I only then noticed that she had changed into shorts and a tank top. "Teresa has a way of sounding very convincing with her half-truths and fabrications." There was a trace of venom in Alena's voice.

"What made her decide to leave?" I imagined that something must have been worse than what she had told me so far since she was obviously petrified.

"She freaked out when she saw your coat and shoes, but I told her that it didn't matter—that there was no fixing this. That I meant what I said about getting a divorce and that I needed her to stop trying to win me back." She paused, her breath going uneven. "She told me that it isn't right for me to be with one of my students and . . ."

"Shit. Alena, what is it? What else did she say?" I persisted, although what Teresa had said so far was already bad enough.

"That she should report me to the university."

My mouth swung open. Surely the sweet looking, redheaded woman from the picture wasn't that cruel. She had to know just how detrimental it would be for her to release such information. Even threatening to do so was an insane move, especially if Alena had ever meant anything to her. I now understood why Alena's face was twisted the way that it was. Her career could be at stake, and for nothing. The school code was clear on student-professor relations. It was prohibited as long as there was any possibility that the participants could be in a classroom setting together: "*So as to ensure fairness and equality for all students in the university.*" If caught in such a situation, the instructor was always reprimanded the harshest.

This is insane! "I can't do this," I muttered as I flung off a blanket that had been placed over me. I looked around on the floor, not knowing if I'd hurled my phone there by accident, before I remembered that I'd left it in the other room.

"What are you doing?"

"I have to go, Alena." I walked past her into the living room where I grabbed my phone off the coffee table and looked at the time along with a string of messages on the front screen. I then picked up my white sneakers, slipped them on, and sat on the sofa tying them while Alena silently watched me. Her arms were crossed over her chest and there were goosebumps scattered along her exposed skin. She looked grumpy and tired and adorable.

Get it together, Amelia. "Alena, this isn't worth it." I tried to sound stern, but I think it came out more distressed than anything. "I can't let you play Russian roulette with your job! Sure, Teresa is being unfair, but we can just stop this now so it won't negatively impact you. I won't even go to your office hours anymore. We can talk again next semester or something." I felt defeated, and my shoulders slumped as I spoke. I was distraught by the mere idea of seeing her without being able to engage. I was also weak from the thought of having to hide all my emotions and feelings and longings for this incredible woman. It didn't matter that she was my professor or even that she hadn't yet gotten a divorce. I hated the notion of any portion of my life that would hold her absence. But I would try my hardest to stay away if that was what was best for *her*.

She calmly walked over to me and placed a hand on my shoulder. "*No*. That's not what I want, Amelia. You don't have to do any of that for me. I know the risks here, and I'm willing to take them." Her eyes were tired, but she spoke with precision and certainty.

"Alena, you love your job," I reiterated. "I can't allow you to do this. I'm not worth it, I promise."

She dropped her hand from my shoulder then and rubbed her palms together. Before speaking again, she took a step back and drank in a deep breath. "Amelia, your worth is *not* a variable here. I appreciate your concern for me, but I am getting really tired of people thinking they have the authority to allow or disallow me to make a decision for myself." She spoke sternly. "If you want to walk away from this for *you*, I can't stop you, but you won't choose anything for me." She peered into my eyes, a fire raging behind hers.

"I didn't mean to—"

"I know," she stopped me. "Last night you mentioned that you needed time to adjust, so I'm going to give that to you. Take however long you need, Amelia." She sounded frighteningly morose.

My resolve faltered, and I was speechless as a new fear threatened to control me now. Did she actually want me to take time or was she getting over this entire situation? I wanted to do what was best for her, but not if it meant that she would hate me for it. We both stood there in silence for several moments as I searched for something to say.

"Does this... does this mean that you don't even want to try anymore?"

"No. Of course not." She lightly shook her head. "I just want to respect your needs the same way I expect you to respect mine."

I nodded in agreement. "I apologize for what I said before, Alena. I just don't want you getting into a dangerous position because of me."

"You're forgiven." Her hand consolingly rubbed at my shoulder. "I think you should head back to your apartment now."

"Yeah," I agreed. "I tried getting up earlier once I realized that we fell asleep—I don't even know what time it was—but then I nodded off again."

"It's not all your fault," she admitted, averting her eyes from me. "You fell asleep before I even finished my poem, and I couldn't bring myself to wake you. You just looked so peaceful and beautiful."

My heart leapt at her words. I fumbled as I attempted to grab my keys off the glass table next to the sofa. "I guess I'll go now." She pulled me into a tight hug before stepping back and placing her sweet lips on mine. Adrenaline rushed through me, and my head was light afterward.

"I think you should weigh all your options, Amelia. I definitely did." Her eyes shifted away. "*Really* think about everything and... let me know if this isn't what you want to do anymore. I support whatever you decide, and I don't want you to rush for my sake either. I already have so much going on."

Had her tone not been so glum, I might've thought she was trying to sway me with the kiss before she'd said these words. But I could tell that she was being sincere.

"Okay. I'll probably only need a few days just to process it alone."

"Of course." She smiled flatly, and I could see a layer of pain concealed behind it as she opened the door. "Be safe, Amelia. I'll see you in class tomorrow." She watched me as I walked toward my car, and her door didn't close until I was inside of my vehicle. The amalgam of emotions that now raced through me were almost as dizzying as her unexpected kiss. I could definitely get used to her affections but hopefully not the uncomfortable feelings that inevitably came with them.

My main concern had now become the possibility of us getting caught because of Teresa. I thought that if I could somehow speak to her and convince her that she'd only be hurting Alena it might solve things. But I didn't know Teresa at all, so there was no chance for that.

The idea that Alena might put her reputation in danger for the mere possibility of us did not sit well with me at all. I didn't want anyone questioning her professionality simply because of our attraction to one another. If we were ever interrogated about our connection and decided to be honest, there would one hundred percent be consequences. If we were to lie instead, but they found proof that we were doing something improper, then Alena would surely come to ruin.

Deciding to continue our conduct with one another wasn't a good idea. By nearly every standard, our feelings for each other were wrong, yet somehow everything we shared was undeniably right.

Chapter 7 Caution to the Wind

The next two days of psychology class were hard for me to endure. I knew I would have to avoid Alena in order to better clear my head. It was already a challenging task to begin with, but when I finally stepped into the auditorium on Tuesday afternoon, the difficulty increased.

Alena wore a plain blouse along with a black blazer, and she had on a medium-length skirt to match. She didn't typically wear skirts, but whenever she did—I was allowed a delicious view of her lean calves. I couldn't help but bore my eyes into the crevice where the V-line came together on her top. I was mesmerized by her as she flawlessly presented the lesson for the day.

An outsider looking in might assume Alena to be a person with a life free of any drama or troubles. The gritty truth hid beneath her unblemished presentation. She always carried herself well, and in a way I hated it. Not many people knew how much she endured and, more than that, how magnificently she handled it all.

By the time class ended, I was weak and longing for a reconnection with her. I was in my head about it the whole walk to the library, and when Mya and I arrived, I remained trapped there. Both Mya and Gabe mentioned my distance and worriedly asked if I was okay, and I again lied. They eventually moved on to our usual topics of art shows, galleries, movies, and such—but it was obvious that neither of them believed me.

Regardless, spending time with them was so helpful for me. The familiarity we shared allowed me to easily fall into a comfort and forgetfulness that I didn't often attain with others. I felt the same with my younger siblings and some old friends from high school, but none of them were here to keep me from drowning in my sorrows. Alena too permitted me to slip into a more blissful version of the real world around me. But she was also the one that currently shook my foundations.

After the remainder of my classes, I drove to the Greenwood City Ministry to volunteer as I often did whenever I was available between Mondays and Wednesdays. The building was fairly large and had an office for counselors, a food bank and storage, and a safe shelter for women and children in need. I worked in the food pantry where we packaged up meals for the families around the area.

I walked through the long hallway and greeted everyone as I came into the stockroom teeming with tall metal crates of empty boxes, bags of supplies, and food. There were six carts lined up and ready to go for the orders. Two girls made produce bags, while an older man packaged meat. A young guy with freeform twists was the cart runner for now. Rodney, a big burly man with long dreadlocks, was there as well and gave me a wave when I came in. I rushed into another room to log my arrival and when I got back to the stockroom, I saw Tasha arrive.

Tasha was my favorite volunteer advisor. She was the same age as me, yet she had snagged a job working here with an agency as opposed to being a volunteer. I smiled at her as we extended pleasantries, but in the back of my mind all I could think about was Alena. It physically pained me to remember the buried sadness in her expression when I saw her the morning before. She didn't glance in my direction once during the class period, and it made me sad.

"What's wrong, girl?" Tasha's voice snapped me back into reality. She had just finished weighing some food and was about to roll it to the back.

"*Food for two*" the intercom sounded, and I decided to make my escape.

"Nothing, I'm good," I responded quickly, rushing away to get the ticket order.

I was relieved to have a suitable distraction for a few hours since a lot of families came in to get food. I tried my best to suppress my melancholic emotions while I was there, but they had apparently slipped through the cracks.

"Are you sure you're okay?" Tasha whispered to me later when business had slowed down. "You've been moping around here since yesterday, so I've heard." She glanced around the room, her eyes staying on Rodney. Tasha had Mondays off—so, theoretically, she shouldn't have known how I was doing.

I exhaled loudly. "I guess my bad moods are popular talk, huh?" She stifled a laugh as she nodded. "I'm just dealing with some complications in this romantic situation of mine," I admitted quietly.

"Aww, I'm sorry." She softly patted her hand on my back. "So, what'd he do?"

I laughed. "I'm glad I didn't get the automatic blame here."

She chuckled. "I know how guys can be. What happened?"

"It isn't really anything they did. It's just that they aren't completely separated from someone they were with for a long time."

"How long you talkin?" She folded her arms.

"About three years."

"GIRL! That's marriage."

If only you knew. "Yeah, but we're not even doing anything as far as a relationship yet. We're just really good friends starting something, but the other woman doesn't want to break it off. She's trying to get other people involved too." That much was true.

"That honestly sounds messy. I wouldn't try too hard with it; you might get yourself hurt," Tasha advised. "If he really wants to be with you, he'll work it out."

She was really good at listening, and I wanted to tell her more about it, but I didn't want her to look at me differently because I had developed feelings for someone who was still married. Although her advice was sound, I wasn't much worried that Teresa was a romantic threat to me anymore. Alena did well in convincing me that the situation was truly over between them.

The intercom sounded once again, and I started pacing away. "She's actually the one who's trying to work it out. I'm the one on the fence about it." I ran away and picked up the new order cards.

It didn't occur to me that I'd outed myself until I returned to find Tasha with her arms crossed and a big grin on her face. When she asked if I thought that she was homophobic, I realized what I had done. We then both had a good laugh about it as we worked on more orders and took them out to the clients. The rest of our conversations during my shift were converted into inquiries solely about me. Tasha wondered what other secrets I might've held from her. *If only you knew.*

I was practically famished by the time Thursday hit. My craving for Alena had become so unruly. She had even slipped into my dreams for two consecutive nights, but they were no longer comprised of erotic office scenes. I was now in her bed, and she spoke to me with that lovely trill of her voice. We shared kisses, but her intoxicating eyes stood out to me more than anything during those dreams. It felt like someone had injected a dose of some dangerous drug into my veins when I finally encountered those eyes in class.

Getting through the hour and a half period was just as hard as it had been on Tuesday. I yearned for Alena in a way that made me feel pathetic. It hadn't even been a week, and I was already pining for her so profoundly. Today her eyes flitted toward me a couple of times and each instance sent chills through my body. This solidified my decision to visit her office after class, even if it was just to see how she had been since Monday morning. Unfortunately, my plans were demolished when class ended and she announced the cancelation of her office hours for the day. I wanted to ask her why she had decided to do so, but it seemed dangerously unnecessary to inquire about that in the auditorium. I chose to continue my day with the unanswered questions.

By the time I finally arrived back in my apartment around seven, I was ready to call Alena and meet up. I was in no way whatsoever done with her or the situation between us, and I had gained whatever clarity I was seeking concerning the complications. I sat in my kitchen after a shower, drinking my second glass of cheap Chardonnay and rehearsing what I would say during the call. I was almost ready to make my move when my phone buzzed unexpectedly.

"Damn, Amelia, what's up with you?" Mya immediately shrieked into the phone.

"Hello to you too," I scoffed.

"Are you still coming over?" she wailed agitatedly.

"Oh shit! Mya, I completely forgot!"

She groaned into the phone.

"I'll be there in—" I looked at the quarter drunken bottle of wine. "Damn it."

"What now, Amelia?"

"I was drinking my wine already because I thought I was in for the night."

"God, Amelia, I can't with you!" I heard a commotion in the background.

"Mya? I can get a Lyft ride over; it just might take a little longer."

"NO!" she exclaimed. "I'll be there in nine minutes."

I smiled to myself. "Okay, Mya, don't speed."

"I never do," she shot out aggressively then hung up.

I set my phone down and judged how ready my living room was for guests. Luckily, one of the side effects of me having to make a tough decision was becoming anal about everything else. My apartment was spotless.

I placed the wine bottle next to the sink and brought my glass with me to the coffee table where Mya and I would be working together. Alena had assigned us a project outline for the final that was due in December because she wasn't a fan of last-minute planning. Mya and I had of course partnered up, but the draft was assigned Tuesday and due Friday night. She refused to wait until then because she wanted to return to the club Friday. She swore up and down that there was a completely different vibe then compared to on Saturdays, and she still wanted me to find a woman that would sweep me off my feet.

Little did she know that I was already swept.

It didn't take us long to finish the outline since we had already begun drafting it in the library. We perfected it before copying it over to a document and posting it on the class's website portal.

"Done!" Mya gleamed excitedly, giving me a high five. She then slammed her laptop down hard.

"Dammit, Mya! Why are you always so keyed up?"

She laughed. She loved to push at my buttons when it came to her carelessness with technology . . . or car doors or refrigerator doors or chairs or any damned thing that would eventually break from her use of it.

"You're such a prude," she mumbled.

I rolled my eyes. "That isn't even how you use that word, Mya. I know you know that."

"I do." She smiled. "It's just fun annoying you." She stood up and skipped over to my bottle of wine. "I think I deserve a drink for all that hard work."

"I'm sure you'll help yourself," I said.

"Indeed!" She was already pouring herself a glass. After her first sip she groaned. "Why'd you get this garbage, Amelia?" She clearly hadn't read the label; it was the cheapest of the cheap wines I could find in the grocery store.

"Because it gets the job done faster than the good stuff." I shrugged.

She stuck out her tongue in disgust as she plopped back down beside me. "God, that's disgusting!" Her complaints didn't stop her from drinking the wine though. "Why do you 'need the job done' so much anyways, Amelia? I know there's something you're not telling me."

My chest tightened as I glanced over at her. I so did not want to have to lie to Mya tonight.

"Don't you dare say it's nothing either." She rotated her glass around carefully before taking another sip that ended in a grimace. "It's definitely something."

"Mya," I started hesitantly. The urge to tell her was almost as persistent as the beating of my heart. I had to remind myself that discretion was still my end game for now, even with my friends. "What if I told you that whatever is going on is something I can't talk about yet."

"Honestly? I'd say it's horse shit. I'm your best friend, and you should be able to tell me anything." I didn't expect a different answer from the bull-spirited Mya. "But as your friend, I also respect your choices and your privacy so, as long as you tell me soon, I'll be okay." She smiled before standing and putting her glass in the sink.

"Thanks." I stood too.

"Are you down for an episode of our show while I'm here?" she asked.

"Sure, it's not that late yet."

"YESSSS." She shook her fist happily and ran to open a cabinet.

A bag of popcorn popped violently in the microwave while I

flipped to our current weekly show, *Rendezvous Priory*.

"Are you ever going to finish *Murder in Camp Maroon*, Mya? It's still so good."

"Aww, I bet it is." She sounded disappointed. "But I'd hate to skip forward, and I know it'll take forever for me to catch up now."

"Yeah, it would," I agreed with a chuckle.

"Hopefully tomorrow night we can find you a new gal to watch it with." She winked at me.

Guilt tugged at the edges of my conscience because I couldn't tell her I already had somebody to watch it with. "All this damn matchmaking for me while you're single. It doesn't make sense, Mya," I casually remarked despite my misgivings. For the first time of the night, she was quiet. I looked over to her. "You *are* still single. Aren't you?"

Mya's eyes shied away from me as she responded. "I *am*. I just don't care to look for anyone right now."

"I thought you wanted someone by the end of the year?"

"I still do, and I am pretty sure I will have a man by then. It's just . . . who am I to rush fate?"

"Sure, Mya," I responded skeptically. I was taking it all with a grain of salt. If she wanted to confess to whatever it was that she was hiding, she would do so when she was ready. Who would I be to judge her anyway when I undeniably held the biggest of secrets between us.

We enjoyed the rest of the night together without any more mention of it. Mya even decided to sleep over once we started taking shots during the show. We then put on *Murder in Camp Maroon* so she could slowly get caught up.

At the end of the night, I lay opposite her in my bed, thinking of sleeping with Alena instead. I imagined her holding me tightly against her and the sweet smell of her hair flowing through my nostrils. I missed her and was more than ready to make my return.

"Hey, Amelia, I'm sorry. I was already on the phone when you called earlier."

"It's okay. How are you?" I eagerly awaited the sound of Alena's voice again, but she didn't speak for several moments. I had finally decided to call her after I finished all my school activities for Friday. Mya was back at her apartment, grabbing her dress and a couple changes of clothes so she could spend another night with me after the club. She and I had been together most of the day besides our classes.

"I've been better," Alena finally sighed out.

"What's going on? I'm ready for us to talk, but if you need to—"

"Hold on." She began speaking to someone on the other end. "Ugh, I'm sorry, Amelia, my mother's here—and I'm helping her switch to another hotel room."

"Oh." My breathing stilled.

"Don't go anywhere, I'll slip into the hallway." A few more moments passed with a string of voices and commotion in the background, then a door closing. "Hello?"

"Your mom is in town?" I asked surprised. She hadn't spoken too much about her mother, which made me assume their relationship might not be so harmonious.

"Yes, she told me last minute about her trip here. It's a short one though. She'll be gone Sunday morning. She just wanted to check on me with everything going on with Teresa." Alena didn't sound too confident about the motivations of her mother. "Did you say you wanted to talk with me?" she asked, remembering my words. "Do you mean in person?"

"Well, yeah. I had enough time digesting everything. I want to try to—"

"Alena!" *I heard a muffled voice yell on the other end.* "What are you still doing out there? I need help with my outfit for dinner." I assumed it was her mother.

"Just another minute," Alena called back to her. "I'm sorry,

Amelia. What were you saying?"

"I think we can find a way to navigate this . . . situation between us," I muttered out. "However difficult it may be," I added. "I just can't see us *not* moving in a forward direction together."

"I feel the same way, Amelia. Truly," she said before she exhaled. "This is great." I could hear the smile in her voice. "Maybe you can come over on Sunday, then? We can speak more in depth about everything."

I couldn't help the grin on my own mouth nor the throbbing of my heart. "Okay," I breathed into the phone.

"How does *Murder in Camp Maroon* and *AA* sound?"

I burst into laughter. "AA? Alena, I know we both drink a lot sometimes, but—"

"I didn't mean it like that," she chuckled. "Both of our names start with an 'A.' I just thought it was clever."

"Oh. Well then maybe it was just a little bit clever," I admitted. "So, I'll see you Sunday. Six-thirty?"

"Sounds like a date."

My chest thumped excitedly. "Don't eat too close to the time. *I'll* be bringing the food and libations too."

"Libations?" she repeated. "My poeticism is rubbing off on you."

"I've got some tricks up my sleeves," I teased.

"Okay," she chuckled. "I have to go now before my mother throws another fit."

"Gotcha. See you soon."

Chapter 8 Beck's

The drive to Beck's was terrifying since Mya decided to take on the role of designated driver. This would have been perfectly fine if only she could drive like a sane person. She maneuvered her vehicle so harshly that I was surprised one of the tires didn't pop off and swerve in front of us on the road. "Land!" I shouted dramatically as I escaped the car immediately upon our arrival.

Beck's was something between an upscale club and a bar. It was one of those fun, familiar establishments where everyone felt at home. The bright flashing sign that hung on the gray brick exterior looked like one you might see for a drive-in movie theater. We paid the parking fee then clacked across the road in our heels to the club's entrance.

The sparkling black dress I was wearing clung to my ass for dear life in the same way Mya's green backless dress did. I could've sworn Gabe was even drooling at her a few times. He too came dapper down in silky black slacks and a red blazer—and combined, the two of them looked like Christmas.

Beck's was relatively spacious on the inside, and the atmosphere of the club was lively and sophisticated. There were dark leather booths to the left of the entrance and a throng of high tables bordering the dance floor. On the opposite end was a lengthy, burgundy-colored bar where two bartenders in striped formal vests served alcohol. Mya purchased our drinks from the auburn-haired bartender right away and forced us to take one shot each before we did anything else. Once we'd taken our shots, we all went to the dance floor and got busy.

The music here was the perfect blend of hip-hop, rap, old school, and pop—though I would've danced to just about anything with my inebriation. I usually became a flirt once any amount of liquor invaded me, but tonight was different. Alena stayed front and center in my mind for the duration of my time at the club. I either danced alone or with my friends but with no one else. Several women still came up to me and tried to join while others tried to offer me drinks. A brave two or three even went straight for the phone number, but they all got declined.

At some point, I realized that I had lost my two friends in the sea of women, and when I found them I couldn't believe my eyes. There was a corner near the bathrooms that had blue, cubed seats. Gabe sat on one while Mya stood in front of him, their eyes locked on one another's as they spoke. I didn't have to guess what I might be witnessing next if I didn't walk away. I was too tipsy to feel the betrayal that would come later if I'd accidentally just discovered that my two best friends were fooling around behind my back. Even then it would no doubt be softened by my own shortcomings of a comparable variety.

I stumbled over to the bar to order a lemon drop when a robust, bronze-skinned woman approached me. Her dark locs hung midway down her back over the purple jersey she had worn with bleached gray jeans and a purple pair of Jordans. A faded scar sat high on the inside of her left cheek as she smiled at me and offered to buy my drink along with hers.

She introduced herself as Sarin, and though my brain wasn't working at full capacity, I could've sworn that I had seen her before. I soon discovered why she was so familiar as we talked and drank with one another. We had shared a class sophomore year and even co-presented a group project. The group had been large enough that I wasn't a completely awful person for not immediately remembering her. She was also one of the guards on our women's basketball teams, so I'd seen her on the posters displayed throughout our campus. Admittedly, Sarin was quite attractive and smooth talking. She also had many hidden talents that piqued my interest, but I still didn't have the inclination to flirt with her. Nevertheless, her number was the first one I accepted tonight along with a loose plan to meet again before the semester ended.

When Sarin returned to her friends after our drink, I spotted another vaguely familiar woman laughing and drinking with three others at a table next to the bar. The woman had on a dark gray pantsuit with a relatively risqué lace corset top. There was no way I could have missed the fiery red hair especially under the flashing lights. The loosely flowing curls stretched down just past her shoulders, and when she smiled, I realized for the first time that the pictures didn't do her justice. It was *Teresa*.

I didn't know what to think, and I certainly didn't know what to do with myself, so I pretended to look for someone in the direction of the dance floor. I eventually started scoping out Mya and Gabe, and I soon spotted them two tables behind where Teresa sat with her friends. I drank down the extra cocktail that Sarin had bought for me, hoping it would be enough to suppress my fear of having to pass Teresa to get to them.

It was hard not to look the woman's way as I started toward them and even harder to ignore her brilliance. How had Alena so elegantly worded my aura when she was literally married to someone whose mere presence could disintegrate me into nothing. And when she stepped in front of me before I could even make it halfway to my friends, I nearly vanished.

"Hi!" she shouted above the music, an inviting slur in her voice. Her piercing green eyes looked me up and down. I wondered if she knew who I was, and that fear kept me struggling to swallow the dry lump that was stuck in my throat. "This ensemble is simply beautiful." Her hand moved in a downward motion, emphasizing my dress. Her eyes sparkled. "You look stunning tonight."

Does she know who I am? I couldn't stop thinking it, but something from inside me finally came up with a word to say: "Thanks." Never did I think I would meet Alena's wife at the club and then be complimented by her. Even in my looming drunkenness it finally occurred to me there was no reason at all for her to know who I was. Alena and I didn't take pictures yet or go out in public, and I'm sure whenever she mentioned me that it wouldn't have been by name. So the wife of the woman I was secretly seeing was genuinely either drunk out of her mind, or tipsy and attracted to me.

"Would you like to dance?" she asked smoothly.

"I can't, sorry."

"You can't dance or just not with me?" Her eyebrow was raised but the cheery expression on her face never faltered. "I'm kidding." She placed a hand on my arm. "I can take a hint."

Teresa kept talking to me for several minutes after my rejection and, unsurprisingly, she was a fantastic conversationalist. She was whimsical, exciting, and *happy*. Why was she so happy? Shouldn't she be angry or upset? She was losing the woman she supposedly loved to divorce. Her wife had moved out and was talking with other people—one of her students even. Of course there was no need to be sad about anything 24/7, but she still looked *too* happy.

Before she let me go, she slipped a card into my hand and suggested that we continue our conversation another night if I so desired. It was the second and last number that I accepted.

Chapter 9 Unfaithful

"Amelia! You're finally here!" Alena was beaming as she swung open the door. "*Ugh*, why didn't you call me to come help you?" She snatched the two large brown takeout bags from me that I had stubbornly carried from my car to her doorstep. This allowed me to carefully move the bottle of wine tucked underneath one of my armpits into my hands.

"Thanks." I trailed behind her and shut the door. I placed the bottle next to the bags on the counter, and she sniffed loudly as she started unpacking the food.

"This smells amazing," she murmured as I slipped off my shoes. I tugged my hoodie over my head just in time for her to turn around and yank me into her arms. The thin blue woolen sweater that she wore scratched my neck as she released me.

"What's with the scratchy sweater?" I rubbed at my neck.

"My mother," was all she could manage through gritted teeth as she shook her head and reverted her attention to the food. A satisfied groan escaped her mouth. "This pasta is so good! I still remember it, and I've only been to Bertolli's once."

"I used to go all the time my sophomore year. Here, let me help." I stepped forward, but she shooed me away. I narrowed my eyes at her then reached for the bottle of wine. *I'm helping with something,* I chuckled to myself as I placed the bottle on the table and snagged the glasses that were already next to the sink.

I'd arrived around six-thirty so that we would have enough time to sit at the table and eat before *Murder in Camp Maroon* came on. It only took us a few minutes to set everything up on the glass table, and soon after, we were happily eating the small spread of bread and pasta. We finished right before it was time for us to move to the sofa and watch a new crime unfold.

I'd had about two glasses of wine since arriving at Alena's apartment which was beaten by her three and a half glasses. "Your mother's visit must've been fun," I muttered sarcastically as she swallowed the remainder of her half empty glass. The credits now rolled on the screen.

"Don't remind me about that," she huffed. "Hopefully I can forget it."

I placed my hand on her back and she tensed up momentarily before relaxing into my touch. "Do you want to talk about it?" I asked as I began rubbing her.

"I haven't told you much about my mother yet, and trust me there's a lot to tell." She took a deep breath. "But long story short, she came here to try to get me to rekindle my relationship with Teresa."

"What?" My hand dropped from her back.

"My mother has a very self-centered way of thinking. I told her about my definite decision on divorcing Teresa, but she somehow still believes that she can swoop in and save the day for us. It's almost been a year now since that was even possible. On top of that, this just shows that she really doesn't care about my pain. I've spoken to her on several occasions about our issues and about how Teresa kept hurting me." A quiet anger was apparent in Alena's voice.

"That's awful," I muttered quietly.

"Yeah," she exhaled sharply before standing and slowly walking to the kitchen with the empty glass. "I'm starting to feel this now." Her eyes closed as she rolled her shoulders back and took a deep breath. "I'd better stop. I have to be up early in the morning." She turned around to me and seemed only then to fully recognize my presence. "We still have to talk about *us* don't we?"

I nodded as I stood and walked toward her, my face showing concern. "Yes, but you have more to say about your mother too." I was more worried about her predominating agitation than 'talking about us.'

She swatted her hand to the side. "That can wait until afterward or even another time." She seized my hand and hauled me back toward the sofa, damn near pulling me onto her lap in the process. "What's bothering you the most about us, Amelia, and how can I help with that?" she questioned, looking attentively at me.

I remembered a certain encounter from two nights prior and I visibly shuddered. "Teresa," I admitted with a frown. "Have you spoken to her since she came here that morning?" I asked nervously.

Alena's face mirrored mine. "Yes, actually. *She* was the one who told me my mother would be coming into town." Her brows drew together. "My mother really is insufferable sometimes. It's insane that she would tell her before me and even use her to get the message across." Alena's hands were now clenched into fists. "Teresa called me right before class on Thursday which is why I had to cancel my office hours."

"Damn. I was wondering about that." I slid down, more onto the couch than on Alena's legs. "It was last minute, and that's not you."

"At all," she groaned. Her mouth set to say something more, but I beat her to it.

"I was going to stop by your office that day." My heart thudded as if I had released a kind of secret.

"Really?" Her surprise seemed genuine.

"Yeah, it was getting hard for me."

"I thought it was just me." She patted my hand.

I shook my head. "Definitely not."

She slid a hair tie far up her wrist and began to run her hands through her curls. "It would've been nice to see you—one on one," she said as she tied her hair into a messy oversized knot. "Especially since I had to pick up my mother. The next night I even had to survive dinner with her and Teresa."

"*What?*"

"It was later, after I talked to you on the phone that day. I wasn't aware of the extra company until Teresa showed up. They had planned *that* behind my back too, apparently."

"Why would they do that?" My heart set to a rapid pacing as both anger and nervousness consumed me. Why was Teresa so adamant about getting to Alena now? From what I'd been told, she had been content to lose her for nearly a year at this point. Why jump through hoops at the end of it all?

"Your guess is as good as mine. And Teresa was all too eager to hint at my being with a student of mine the entire dinner. Can you believe that shit?" She spoke fiercely now. "That's something *I* want to tell her whenever I'm ready. Thankfully my mother didn't take her seriously, but she did allude to it being normal that Teresa and I had been having such big problems. 'Every marriage goes through its ups and downs, you know,' she said. Just like everyone suggesting that you settle in love likes to say."

Alena had hardly taken a single breath as she spoke, and she was now pacing in front of me. It was as bad a time as ever to mention my seeing Teresa, but I knew I shouldn't withhold it from her. "That sounds terrible, Alena. Do you know what Teresa did after dinner?" I questioned timidly.

"No, of course I don't. Nor do I care." She folded her arms.

"I saw her," I blurted out despite my dread of revealing it.

"She was at Beck's that night."

The corners of Alena's mouth twisted into a frown. "You went there again? I thought you were going to LUXX this time?"

"We were originally, but Mya was determined to go back to Beck's. She's trying to play matchmaker—very unsuccessfully I might add." My fingers dug into the sofa.

Her eyes widened. "Well you didn't talk to her did you? To Teresa?"

"No—well, yes."

Alena sat down again. "You did?" She looked afraid of something rather than angry at me.

"It was an accident, I think. Well, she spoke to me . . . she complimented my outfit and—" I stopped myself. "She seemed pretty intoxicated, but she was with a group."

"It was probably Marina, Adrian, and Solana." She nodded assuredly to herself, her eyes glancing over at the bottle of wine. "They always used to go out together, even before we were married." Her jaw went taut before she spoke again. "She flirted with you, didn't she? That's what you were about to say before, right?"

"Yes," I hesitantly let out. The last thing I wanted was for her feelings to be hurt even more by anything concerning Teresa.

"She does that when she gets drunk. Some things don't change." Alena shrugged and her attention again shifted to the bottle of wine on the counter. "It was always more fun for her to woo strangers than her own wife," she finished as she walked away and placed the bottle into the fridge. She grabbed two cold waters and passed one to me as she sat back down. Apparently, there was a lot to unpack this evening.

I thanked her for the water and took some gulps while she stretched herself more comfortably on the couch. I was appalled that Teresa's behavior seemed so ordinary to Alena. "Was Teresa ever unfaithful?" My voice was grim when I asked her, but truthfully I was seething with an anger deep within me—an anger I had not often known. How could anyone behave so insolently to the goddess of a woman that was Alena?

"Maybe," she answered lazily. "I honestly don't know." She began twirling a curl around her pointer finger and staring at the knots it made. I didn't want to pry, but I did want to know more about Teresa. Was her glittering, enigmatic aura not so golden after all?

"What happened to you two, Alena?" It was a question I'd seemingly asked over and over, and every time the answer was more revealing than the last.

"We were only in love for two years." Alena exhaled while carefully examining me. "Do you really want to hear about all this stuff?" she questioned hesitantly.

"If you're comfortable sharing it, then yes, I'd like to know." I scooched closer to her and turned my body so that I didn't have to crane my neck to see her.

"I've known Teresa since undergrad, but we didn't start dating until a couple years after that." She spoke carefully. "The first year that we dated and the one we married were our best years. In hindsight, it really didn't take long for our relationship to unravel, but at the time it seemed to happen slowly." Alena's entire body had gone rigid, but she continued. "For months at a time, we argued about small things that grew into bigger things. We pushed at each other's buttons, and she always poked at my insecurities. Eventually, she started hiding things and grew more distant. By then it was just over a year and a half that we had been married. Now of course, in between all the mess—there were sweet moments, pleas for forgiveness, and resolutions. But none of it ever lasted." There was now a frustration in her voice as she spoke.

"It's like she grew accustomed to shutting me out and enjoyed her life better that way. I wanted to retreat earlier on, but she apparently still wanted me around at her convenience. There were several nights of no check-ins with me while she was on work trips, followed by anger at my obvious discontentment. By then it had already gotten to the point where I needed the physical distance to match the emotional because she was affecting my energy so badly. The argument that she'd used to excuse her lack of communication was that she was an adult and that I wasn't her mother. But that has nothing to do with being respectful to one's spouse or partner, does it?" she asked rhetorically.

"Teresa puts on an act—and that's all it really is, Amelia. She will virtually convince the entire world that she is doing better than she is." Alena's voice weakened. "Dinner went horribly the other night, and she still wanted me to see her afterward and 'talk things through,' like my mother had suggested. But I denied her. It's just like her to go and party it off and pretend it doesn't hurt."

"I hate that you're going through all of this," I sighed, placing my hand on hers. I didn't know if bringing up Beck's turned out to be such a good idea after all. Would I have wanted to know about my ex clubbing after a night of practically begging me to take her back? Probably not.

"I'm numb to it, Amelia. It's a good thing to be because it used to hurt me so badly. I cried more than enough tears for Teresa. I'd be lying to say I won't shed any more, but it won't be from anything new with her."

At this, Alena finally withdrew. Like lungs with no air. Like an ocean with no water. Like the sky with no wind. She was still and quiet. I felt like an intruder sitting there, yet I remained.

It was clear that the mood of the evening had soured. Alena's disposition never recovered from the discussions of her mother and Teresa. She didn't seem to have enough energy to hold up a front any longer. I watched her nod off on the couch after we finished talking, and I soon suggested she go to sleep. She saw me off into the night only after giving me a kiss I was sure to remember in my dreams.

It wasn't long before I was lying in my own bed considering the rest of our discussion, however brief it was. Alena hated the idea of it, but she knew she should try to make sure Teresa would keep quiet about our relationship. She also enlightened me on the fact that she never mentioned me to Teresa by name, which was another weight off my shoulders. This meant that Teresa would've had to stalk me to know my identity for any other reason. If that were the case, she would be damn near crazy to fake like she didn't know me when she'd seen me at Beck's.

On another note, I thought again about the two numbers I had acquired Friday night at the club. I examined the card Teresa gave me with the aid of my bedside lamp. She was a media management director and music curator as well. No wonder she was so well spoken and intriguing. She was actually living a life I might've wanted for myself, at least in terms of the curation.

Sarin had texted me at some point when I was with Alena, and her text had included an invitation to a pickup basketball game the last Wednesday of the month. She was going to support a friend for a special Halloween event and wanted to take me to a nearby café afterward that had some murals and other artistic representations nearby. I didn't want to decline a friendly invite, but I also knew how anything could be more than just friendly given the right conditions. I was utterly stuck on Alena, although I didn't mind the idea of new platonic connections. I decided to give it a chance.

I agreed to join Sarin for the event and she quickly texted back, confirming the plan. I hoped Alena wouldn't want to see me that night or day, but if she did there wasn't much we could do inside. Even then, I would happily spend weeks and months doing nothing in her quiet apartment if it meant that we could be together.

Chapter 10 I Want Moore

"Is everything alright?" Alena asked, peering up from where she sat at the kitchen table. A pair of reading glasses that she almost never wore sat atop her nose while she leisurely flipped through a novel from her bookshelf.

I had been in the middle of staring into space and allowing my thoughts to drift slowly through the atmosphere when she interrupted me with her question. I was also ruminating on our changes in conduct during the continual office hour visits. Our conversations there now remained strictly cordial while any romantic talk or banter was reserved for the time we spent in her apartment. On this particular night, she had invited me over for a "study hall" since we both craved one another's company and simultaneously needed to complete our work. It didn't take her long at all to finish grading papers and revamping her upcoming lesson plans. Meanwhile, I had only touched the surface of my work. All I had finished so far was one full assignment from my internship class and half of an assignment from African American Studies. I was currently stuck between completing the other half of it and starting on my psychology paper. It wasn't due until the middle of November, but I didn't mind finishing it earlier.

"Yes, I'm fine," I finally answered as I rubbed my eyes and readjusted myself on the couch. But I truly wasn't. I was highly agitated by the limitations we had regarding what we could and couldn't do together. It didn't matter how much I loved being here with her in her apartment because even with all of its style, wonderful smells, and good vibes—the place was starting to feel like a prison. I longed for date nights at a rooftop bar or a restaurant or bowling alley. A picnic in the park on an abnormally warm day in Fall. Holding hands in a museum. None of these desires seemed possible.

"You know . . ." She lowered the glasses in a way that was disturbing to the rhythms of my heart. "It's a lot easier to get work done at the table," she offered. "It might benefit you to sit up straight and leave your phone over there too so you have less distractions."

"I think sitting in front of you would be the biggest distraction," I retorted.

"Oh, would it now?" She raised a brow.

"Absolutely." I stared at her, unblinking.

Alena shrugged and removed the glasses from her face completely, setting them carefully on the table along with the book. Her arms extended into the air as she stood up and exhaled loudly. She moved toward a pot on the stove that was now simmering with a purpose and switched it off. Without even asking, she made me a cup of tea to go along with hers, adding sugar cubes and a sprinkle of cinnamon to both.

I already felt extremely spoiled tonight because as soon as I stepped into the apartment I was greeted by the wonderful smell of chicken, vegetables, and a broth of some kind, permeating my nose. Alena had the meal spread out on the table for me because less than three days ago I idly mentioned that I missed my grandmother's home cooking. Alena claimed that she cooked the meal so she could present her skills as worthy to me while also alleviating my ache until the holiday season when I would see my grandmother again.

She was now beside me, her warmth and perfume overriding my heartbeat's previous calm. "Thanks for the tea," I said.

"You're welcome." She nuzzled her head into my shoulder while holding her steaming cup a safe distance away. "What are you working on?" she asked, briefly examining my laptop.

"Your paper," I answered, not having made the decision to actually work on it until then.

She gasped and set down her tea. "This early? You know the way to my heart." She fawned over me.

"You're the only professor I'd do it for." I indulged her.

Her hand gripped my arm, and with a light squeeze she whispered into my ear, "Good girl."

There was no way she could have cared about my focus at this point because it was currently being depleted due to her behavior. She began to kiss on the back of my neck as if she'd read my thoughts and taken them for a challenge. I could feel her breasts press against my arm as her hands held fast to my hips. It was not an overly erotic gesture in and of itself, yet it still had me eager to lose a few items of clothing.

"I—I need help with a question for your paper!" I stammered out, trying to get her to retreat.

She stopped kissing me. "Could it be sent in an email that I would respond to on time?" Her lips were on my ear as she spoke, which didn't at all help my cause.

"Yes!" I gasped.

"Okay." She moved far enough away from me, to where I could breathe a less seductive air again. "Ask away." She smiled innocently, and it made me want to melt. She was no doubt playing an evasive game with me and my reactions must have been amusing for her. She promptly answered my questions in between sips of her tea, but I had yet to touch my own cup since I had immediately set it down out of fear that I would tremble and spill it.

"Thank you," I said once she finished helping me. After I notated everything that needed to be included in the paper, I started typing out the introduction. By then she had finished her tea and remained beside me, but she was no longer taunting me.

"You're very welcome," she said.

"I won't do that anymore though, just so you know." I stopped typing and looked in her direction.

"Do what?" she questioned.

"Turn you back into 'Professor Hutchinson' while we're together outside of class."

She laughed. "Don't worry about that. Even if you weren't in my class I would've tried to help you with anything confusing." She began to play with the soft coils in my hair.

"That's sweet of you," I cooed, "but I still don't want it to be in our dynamic when it doesn't have to be."

"I appreciate that, Amelia." She grinned. "And speaking of my title. Once the semester is over, no one will be able to call me Professor Hutchinson anymore. You can even get started early and call me Professor Moore."

"Why is that?" I scoffed, thinking it was a joke of some kind.

"Moore is my maiden name. I want to start getting used to it again." She sounded a little glum but optimistic.

"Okay, then I love it! Alena Moore is fantastic!" I overstated.

"Are you making fun of me?" She poked me in the stomach.

"No, of course not! I just want to be excited with you about this."

She flashed me a smile that sent a chill down my spine. "You're the sweetest, Amelia." She leaned toward me, her lips gently making their way onto mine. Tenderness encompassed every action she made regarding me tonight in a way that fatigued me. Her body was speaking a language of desire, one that I knew full well but had not yet fully partaken in before.

Her lips moved to my neck again—this time at the front—and

they drew a slow line down to my red and black button-up blouse. I could hardly breathe. She brought her fingers to the collar of my shirt and pulled her lips away from my neck. She gazed into my eyes as her fingers settled on the top buttons. I could tell from her expression that she would've preferred to rip the buttons off without so much as another breath, but she still politely asked, "May I?"

I desperately wanted to tell her yes, and I wanted to beg her to take everything else off me while she was at it. I wished to equally undress her so that we could both be naked, and when we were, she could make good use of her tongue across my entire body. I didn't at all want her to stop, but I also didn't want her to keep going before I had a chance to reveal a certain truth.

I placed my hands over hers. "You shouldn't yet."

She bit her bottom lip, removed her fingers from the buttons, and retreated.

I grabbed her hands. "Alena, before we go any further," I nervously stammered, "I just want to make sure that you know . . . well, I don't think that I'm ready for too much right now." I ineffectively tried to explain myself.

"It's fine, Amelia. I don't want to do anything that you'd be uncomfortable with," she assured me.

I tugged on her hand. "I promise you it's not that I don't want to do more, Alena. I just never have before so I'd like to move a bit slower. I mean, what we were doing is fine. I just want to make sure we don't get out of hand if some of our clothes come off." I shyly looked away from her, but I could feel her eyes still trained on me as she tapped my shoulder. When I glanced up, I saw an unperturbed expression painted on her face.

"You haven't? Had sex, you mean?"

"No." My lips pursed miserably as embarrassment nipped at my ego.

Her hand cradled my face, and she looked deep into my eyes.

"There's nothing wrong with that." The words came out so effortlessly that it settled my apprehension almost immediately. "Just continue to let me know what you're comfortable with, okay?"

I nodded, thinking again of the buttons. This time I took initiative by nearly launching myself into her arms. She took a firm hold of my hips, stroking her thumb along the bare skin where the hem of my shirt lifted. Her kisses were intense yet preserving in a way, and I could tell she wasn't even using half of her strength. Her fingertips brushed along the bones of my chest, close to the buttons. She was avoiding them it seemed, so I put my hands over hers to guide her there.

One by one, each button on my shirt parted ways with the small slits in the fabric. My ears pounded from the anticipation as if a bomb had been set for each one. The look that Alena gave me while halting to examine my now shirtless form was enough to send me into cardiac arrest. Every touch from her was slow, tantalizing, and torturing. She took her time, even though what we were doing did not even touch the surface of what I hoped would come.

I didn't have any more air to provide my lungs so I could simply imagine what she looked like underneath the loose tee that hugged her—but in one fell swoop, I lost air all the more. She had so quickly hooked her shirt around her hands and lifted it over her head that I now had the inclination to release tears of joy. Only after she was solely dressed in a tight bra in front of me did she decide it was the perfect time to put her hair into her familiar bun.

I ogled her as she positioned herself above me on the couch. While she straddled me, my eyes moved from hers, down to a small gold link chain necklace swinging from her neck, then even further down to the soft flesh that spilled out of her bra. My hands instinctively caressed her stomach, and I noticed a small, shimmering jewel on her navel. I then grabbed a hold of her hips and pulled her into me. Her warm skin was now pressed so close to me that I could feel the palpitations of her heart.

The concept of breathing was growing more and more foreign, and I nearly had to gasp for air when I felt her teeth ever so slightly graze my neck. She flicked her tongue across it next, alternating with her lips, and I couldn't help but release a silent moan. So much was left to the imagination as she licked and sucked on my neck. *How would this feel somewhere else,* I wondered. A coinciding drip from below answered the question. It would feel how she always felt to me.

Alena's head lay on my chest as I stroked her beautiful curls. The lamp beside her bed was lit well enough for the highlights from her hair to shine. I found it hard to breathe evenly because of how breathtakingly beautiful the woman laying on me was. All things considered, I was finished with my schoolwork for the night. Before I had even come over, I figured it would be too hard to focus with Alena in the same vicinity as me, but she had assured me she was a great work partner. She was definitely the opposite of that tonight—at least in an academic sense.

"You're so beautiful . . ." she mumbled tiredly with her eyes still closed. She was tracing a random pattern on my exposed thigh. ". . . and soft and warm. I love your fucking body, Amelia."

I was certain that she could hear the orchestra of my beating heart because a smile slowly crept onto her face. I continued to run my hand through her curls and lightly stroked her exposed back. She had released her hair from the bun at my request once we'd moved to the bed in order to cool down and cuddle more comfortably.

"I think I'm going to have flashbacks during class from the things we do," I murmured lightly.

Her eyes shot open. "Why would you say that?!" She gripped me as she shook with laughter. "You are something else," she whispered after she finally calmed down. A single finger of hers drew a line from my cheek to my chin while she lay there staring up at me. "I hope you know that that wasn't even a morsel of the things I have planned for you, Amelia."

Her tone was too soft and too easy for the words she released, so much so that it frightened me. I swallowed hard.

"And speaking of plans." She sat up and faced me. "I want to take you on a proper date." She crossed her long legs, and her eyes were set ablaze.

"A date? Like in public? How can we do that?" I questioned.

"I don't know. It's something I've been mulling over, though. I don't only want to keep you locked up here in my personal dungeon." She paused. "Well, I sort of do . . . but not for the dates."

I wondered about the things that went through her head. "Okay, say we did. What did you have in mind?"

"I'd take you to an art museum, of course. They have plenty around the state. We can go wine tasting before that, and afterward, a nice dinner at a Mediterranean restaurant." She leaned forward. "Have you had Mediterranean food before?"

I nodded. "Once or twice."

"Great! So we can do all of that, and to end the night we can watch the stars together from the sunroof of my car." She gestured with excitement as she passionately discussed the plans she had intricately worked out in her mind. "It's kind of chilly to be outside, but even then I might bring a blanket so we can do that instead. I'll bring my favorite books and read them to you too."

"It sounds lovely," I hummed.

"So let's make it happen!" she declared. "If we go somewhere out of town, we have less to worry about. We can stay a night or two in a hotel," she paused and furrowed her brows, "if you're comfortable with that."

"Yeah!" I assured her. "Let's have a real date somewhere." Her excitement was rubbing off on me. "Far enough so we can sneak a kiss in the park and hold hands."

She nodded eagerly.

"But when?" I questioned. "It's the end of October and once November hits, everything accelerates."

"Sometime soon," she promised, turning from me and nestling on my chest once again with closed eyelids. "Will you stay with me tonight?" she asked.

I didn't expect the question. Clearly, I hadn't prepared for an overnight stay, and it was especially worrisome due to the interruption of the first accidental one. I figured Teresa hadn't been back since then because Alena hadn't mentioned it. Instead of asking and potentially souring her good mood, I used that logic as a sign that we were in the clear. I also admittedly desired to sleep in her arms every single night at this point. I had no issue being patient with the timing of that, but I definitely wouldn't mind if we started doing it now.

Alena's eyes remained closed as she pointed out where I could find a pair of pajamas. I changed in the bathroom then, unlatching my bra and putting on the dress of a shirt with similarly lengthy pants. By the time I returned to the room, I could see Alena's discarded clothing laying on the edge of the bed. I'd thrown her another pair of pajamas before I escaped to the bathroom, but she didn't appear to have left the bed in order to change into them. She was already snoring lightly when I turned off the lights and lay beside her. My back was turned to her, my butt only slightly brushing up against her thighs as I stared into the darkness. I shut my eyes after a few moments, and she soon pressed herself up against me and draped an arm over my side.

"Goodnight, Amelia," she whispered drowsily.

I relaxed into her embrace. "Goodnight."

As I drifted off, I happily thought about our growing bond with one another—the emotional, spiritual, and physical. Though we had not gone far at all tonight, every new moment shared between us was special.

Chapter 11 My Type

My arrival back on campus on Halloween night was timely. I lowered my radio as my Camry casually crept around to the front of the gym. I had proposed that Sarin carpool with me to the pickup game and let me drive her home afterward. I thought it was better than her original suggestion to hitch a ride with her friends.

It was a relief for me that Alena both knew about and encouraged my plans with Sarin for the night. She wanted me to enjoy myself and send her any good pictures I took of the art near the café we were going to afterward. She would be at a friend's costume-dinner party in Raleigh for the evening, and I was pleased that we were both going to have a fun time.

As I waited for Sarin, I happily replayed the moments I had shared with Alena the previous night. It had been extremely sweet of her to reassure me when I was wary about getting intimate. I admittedly lacked in sexual experiences, but not because I hadn't had the opportunity. I'd just always held the idea that I wanted my first time to be meaningful. I hated the thought of sharing myself with someone I didn't already care deeply for, and I didn't want to regret anything.

A few minutes before six o'clock, a tall figure emerged from the gym wearing light wash moto-stitch jeans, a black pair of Nikes, and a nice brown leather coat. The scar on her cheek was raised as she smiled and waved at me while strolling toward my car. A sweet scent flooded the vehicle when she entered, and she shed a large plaid bookbag from her back and placed it on the floor in front of her.

"Amelia, this is a nice ride," Sarin remarked in her soft, raspy voice.

I chuckled. "This old thing gets me from point A to B, and that's all."

"Nah, you're definitely not giving her enough credit. She's a beaut." Sarin's dark eyes glowed softly as she stretched her arms toward me. We hugged awkwardly in the small space between the seats.

"Now let's go, woman!" she playfully urged. "I don't wanna be late."

I had never been to Terrabridge Park, a new development with a nice community center, for which Sarin gave me precise directions to. It was only twenty minutes from campus, and it sat beside a large grass field and coliseum. The night was chilly, as expected—but my fleece-layered hoodie, along with our laughter and banter, kept me warm. The Halloween game had a fun setup with team names like the "Skullduggery Crew" and the "Petrified Pumpkins." Most of the players wore face paint and some even had on costumes. The atmosphere was more representative of an organized carnival than a pickup game—especially with all the music, snacks, and raffles.

I was thoroughly enjoying my time with Sarin as we discovered so many new things about each other. I learned of her love for the arts, which wasn't like mine, my friends', or Alena's. She was interested in theater but didn't have much time on her hands in between basketball, ROTC, and being a full-time student. She'd starred in several plays throughout high school, but her scholarship prevented her from being able to juggle acting while keeping pristine grades. Sarin also had an accent that came from Philly, the city she grew up in. She said a lot of "jawns," "shorty's," "drawlins," and "ards," as a result.

When we arrived at the coffee shop, we were met with an open stage where someone stood singing into a mic. Sarin told me it was *The Word* open mic night, but as a Halloween special. There were whimsically themed pastry items, coffees, and juices. The atmosphere was diverse and blended, and people of all ages and backgrounds were in attendance. We were forced to find a spot in the back of the bar area because it was packed.

I was surprised when the host announced Sarin as the next person to showcase their talent. I turned around, my face a portrait of disbelief, as she cracked a smile and handed me her coat. She confidently stepped up to the stage and closed her eyes. When they opened, it was hard to ignore the raging fire inside them.

She spoke eloquently of growing pains and of the falsehoods of past people in her life. She tactfully expressed that she didn't deserve to go through what she did but that she also wouldn't be the same without those painful experiences. She discussed the shortcomings of her father and her mother but the saving grace of her aunts, brothers, and grandmother. She thanked God for the blessings in her life and the will to continue to live when she so many times wanted to give up. As she quietly ended the spoken piece, her eyes watered, and she bowed her head.

It was breathtaking. The room erupted in loud applause, shouts, and whistles. This was definitely not a regular poetry night. A couple of people dapped her up on her way back to me and several complimented her too.

"Where did that come from?!" I exclaimed.

"I speak a little word every now and again," she replied far too modestly.

"A little?!" I responded with shock. "You were fantastic, Sarin. I really teared up there. It was beautiful."

"Thank you. Now let's order something to eat."

The two of us combed through the crowd to the front register. I decided to order a caramel pumpkin latte along with a raspberry bloody bagel. I also ended up trying some of Sarin's skeleton-shaped lemon pastry, and she had some of mine while the rest of the performers blessed us with their talents.

As the evening came to an end, Sarin suggested that we should look at the art another time. She asked if I wanted to meet up with her again when we were both available, and I agreed. I had clearly discovered a new friend who was perfect for me, and it was thrilling. It did not at all occur to me that the stir she incited could even compare to the way Alena made me feel.

"You should come to one of my games sometime," she proposed as I pulled up to her apartment complex. "The season starts next week, and I can already tell that we're going to be good this year. I even have some scouts coming to see me."

"Wow, Sarin, that's exciting!"

"Yeah, it is. If you come to any, bring your friends too. I don't know who you hang with, but if they're anything like you, I know they're cool peoples."

I bit back my smile. "Okay, Sarin. I'll check the game schedule and make sure we make it to a few."

"Do you promise?" She held up her pinky finger.

"Yes." I briefly locked mine with hers.

"Okay." She looked pleased as she grabbed her bookbag before getting out. She walked around to my side of the car and motioned for me to open the door. "I need a proper hug goodbye. The one at the beginning of the night was mediocre."

"Yeah, it was awkward as hell," I agreed with a chuckle.

"Now you ain't have to say all that, Amelia." She joined in my laughter and then brought me into her arms. "Better," she said with a sure nod of her head. "You be safe, and text me when you make it back," she instructed before backing away.

"Okay, I will." I got into the car and rolled the window down. "Thanks for the good time! I enjoyed it."

"Me too." She grinned. "Goodnight, shorty."

I waved and rolled the window closed.

"Hey, Amelia!" Mya called to me as I walked toward her on the second floor of the Student Center.

"Hey, girl." I smiled as we hugged. I sat down next to her on the burgundy banquette seats. Her computer sat on her other side while she chewed on some waffle fries.

"Where the hell have you been the past couple of days?" I questioned her.

"*Busy.*" She rolled her eyes and chuckled. "Do you want some?" She offered the food.

"Don't mind if I do." I snatched three fries from the paper bag.

"How was your Halloween date?" she asked casually.

"Mya, it wasn't a date," I sternly objected.

"Okay. Whatever the hell it was—how was it? You never gave me any details." She leaned toward me.

"It went really well actually. I think Sarin and I will be pretty good friends." I smiled.

"Umm, you have *me*. . . . You don't need any more friends," she chided.

"Whatever, Mya." I wiped my hands free of the salt from the fries. "So! Do you wanna go to a basketball game with me next week?"

"Since when do you like basketball?" Her face scrunched up.

"Just answer the question." I furrowed my brows.

"How about you show me what *Sarin* looks like first?" she challenged.

"If you go to the game with me on Tuesday you can see her for yourself."

"Oh!" Mya gasped. "Your new girl plays basketball? That's so cute! She probably towers over you." She laughed.

"Mya, she is just a friend," I reminded her through clenched teeth.

"Yeah, if you say so." She rolled her eyes again. "I'll go with you. I'd say we should invite Gabe too, but I'm not sure if he'll be able to come. Apparently, he's doing some 'guy stuff' sometime next week."

"Eww," I said, my nose wrinkled.

"I know right?! It's gross," she agreed, then sighed. "I guess we finally became too much for him."

"Ahh, it's understandable." I waved my hand. "The three of us have been attached at the hip since sophomore year. If he hangs out with two women all the time, how is he going to find a girlfriend anyways?" I shrugged, and Mya tensed.

"You don't think that's what 'guy stuff' means, do you? Do you know if he's talking to someone?" she asked worriedly.

"No, but would it matter if he was?"

She looked away from me, embarrassed. "No, I guess not."

"Mya?" I tapped her shoulder "Would it?" I asked again. "Do you like him or something?" *I know you do.*

"What?! No!" she exclaimed, unconvincingly.

"Oh my God, *you do*!" I bellowed out excitedly. "I knew it!"

"Amelia, no! No, no, no! You can't tell him! Our friend group will be *ruined*!"

"You're so dramatic," I chuckled.

"I'm serious. I only like him because he's the one nice guy I know right now. All those other guys are so fake—but I know it's just temporary, okay, so please don't make a big deal out of this."

I stayed quiet for a moment and eyed her suspiciously.

"What?" she questioned.

"I saw you two at the club a few weeks ago. By the bathrooms." I let my words marinate for a moment as her eyes grew wide. "Doing God knows what."

"We were just talking." She looked down and fidgeted with her hands.

"You don't look like that when you talk to *me*," I teased.

"Keep messing with me, and you'll be in the bleachers alone," she threatened. "Drop it, okay?"

"As you wish," I held up my hands.

"Now back to Sarin." She leaned forward again. "I think I deserve a little word of thanks for my help."

"For your help with *what*?"

"Umm, you met her at the club on Friday! I said that you would meet someone if we went on Friday!"

"Technically, I met her sophomore year," I taunted.

"Really, Amelia?" she growled, then she looked down at her phone. "Shit! I gotta go." She began packing her bags in a hurry. "Did you want to work on that essay later on tonight?"

"I'm already finished with it for the most part."

"Damn, really? Okay, I'm still coming over though. But right now I have to get to class."

"Shorty!" I heard a raspy voice from behind us. I turned in time to see Sarin approaching with two other women of similar height following her.

"Is that her?" Mya whispered with a smirk; her bag was now around her shoulders.

"Yes, but please don't be weird." I replied in a rush.

Sarin swooped me into a hug. "Amelia! How you been? What's goin on today?"

"Not much, just taking a break. I've been good. Uh, this is my best friend Mya. Mya, this is Sarin."

Sarin hugged Mya and they exchanged pleasantries. "These are my teammates, Liz and Brady." She introduced me to a lanky blonde woman and a heavier set, dark skinned woman with glasses and short thick dreads. They both waved, but the blonde woman sported a cheeky smile.

"So, you're the one who stole our friend on Halloween night," the woman with glasses said.

"I guess so," I answered nervously. Sarin's face flattened as she looked down at me.

"Don't make it a habit," the blonde woman teased.

"Ard, Liz," Sarin snapped. "We're gonna roll." She tipped her head back. "See ya shorty. Nice to meet you, Mya." She waved, and they walked away in longer strides than my short legs could ever provide.

Mya was giggling uncontrollably as soon as they left our view.

"Friend or no friend, she is definitely your type."

"Don't you have somewhere to be?" I asked unkindly. "And I don't have a type."

"You *don't?*" She took a step back. "Okay, how does this sound to you?" She put down her computer bag and listed her next set of words separately on each finger. "A brown skinned woman that is tall. She is feminine looking in the face with a masculine presence—and you know exactly what I mean by that. Someone who is sweet and quirky yet strong and passionate about *something*—for Sarin that's basketball. But really, it's the artistic side which is the only thing you mentioned to me about her before today. What does that give you, Amelia?" She lifted her chin and gave me a smug look.

"My type," I sputtered out with a new realization.

"Ding, Ding, Ding! We have a winner!"

Chapter 12 Caught Up

"Are you certain you brought enough clothes, Amelia?" Alena questioned me sarcastically as I shoved my oversized suitcase into the backseat of her black Cadillac.

"Why pack light when you can pack right?" I winked at her, and she chuckled. "Okay. Let's go up now, I'm freezing." I threw a small duffle over my shoulder and followed Alena up to her apartment.

Once we entered the front room, she shed her shoes and hung her black leather coat on the rack. I tossed my duffle at the entrance of her bedroom then walked over to where she was standing and raised up on my toes to give her a kiss. When the heels of my feet returned to the ground, she nestled her nose in my neck, deeply inhaling.

"You always smell so wonderful, Amelia." Her lips returned to mine suddenly, and she held my hips tight. "If you smell that good," she purred, "I wonder how you . . ." She lightly shook her head. "Never mind." She let go of my hips and backed away. Fire spread through my cheeks while I watched her go, and I felt dazed. She sashayed to her room, picking up my duffle along the way, and carrying it with her inside. I fumbled with removing my outer layers and shoes then I rushed to meet her there.

By the time I stepped inside—she was busy trying to stuff two thick, fuzzy blankets into her arms. I chuckled as I grabbed one of them to help.

"Thanks. I was thinking we can have hot chocolate today and watch this romantic movie my friend, Nova, told me about." She hugged the blanket in her arms and sat on the bed. "You remember her, right?"

"Yeah." I nodded. "She's the gay rocker chick you met in grad school that studies stars and planets, right?"

"Right." She smirked proudly. "She's an astrophysicist."

"That sounds cool, but also like it's *way* too complex for me."

"Definitely," she agreed.

We both returned to the living room and set up the blankets. I then looked through Alena's bookshelf while she prepared the hot chocolate for us. "You never told me about that dinner party you went to with your friends on Halloween," I said, mindlessly scanning through a hardcover romance novel on the shelf.

"I didn't? Maybe it's because we've both been so busy." Her voice faded for a moment. "It was really fun though! My friend Carter and her boyfriend, Will, hosted the dinner. They can't help but jump at any chance to throw a party. And you should've seen the food, Amelia! It looked grotesque because of the theme, but it tasted wonderful. I'll show you some pictures once we're all cuddled up," she promised.

"Okay." I dropped my hand from the shelf and turned around.

"How was that basketball game with *Sarin*?" She exaggerated the syllables of the name.

"Why'd you say it like that?" I playfully questioned.

"Mya seems to think you two are an item." Both of her brows were raised when she looked back at me.

I stepped closer to her. "And we both know that Mya's wrong about that." I crossed my arms and scowled, lowering my voice. "Not that it's her fault or anything."

The corner of her lips turned down. "I'm sorry for bringing her up like that, Amelia," she exhaled before she briefly brushed her fingers along the curve of my cheek. "So, how was the game?"

"It was nice," I had to concentrate hard to formulate my words. Every time she touched me, I felt a spark of electricity. "They won of course, and Sarin even has scouts watching her this year."

"Isn't that something." She nodded before turning and quietly garnishing our drinks with marshmallows and whipped cream.

After Alena set our cups on the coffee table, she yanked me onto the couch. I was closely tucked into her and couldn't resist the urge to tickle her. She laughed and begged me to stop as she unsuccessfully dodged my advances. She still somehow managed to climb over me, and when she did, she promptly pinned both of my hands down at my sides.

"Are you done?" she asked sweetly.

"Oh, so you think you're in control now, do you?" I taunted from underneath her.

She looked me up and down and said, "It looks that way." She then smirked as she loosened her grip on my hands. I rested them on her thighs while she put her curls up into a ball on her head. I was utterly spellbound as I lay flat in the middle of the couch staring up at her.

"You look *so* cute. I love it when you put your hair up like that."

Her hands positioned themselves on either side of my head. "I look *cute*?" she questioned in a suggestive tone. She then leaned in, but instead of kissing me she began teasing me tremendously by making it hard for me to grab a hold of her lips with mine. She kept inching herself just far enough away from me while I tried to no avail to pull her in closer.

"Alena, what are you doing?" I whined in frustration.

"I'm keeping this civil. You know . . . because I do have control."

"No, you just enjoy teasing me," I complained.

Her eyes gleamed and a sly smile covered her face. "So what if I do?" Her lips finally met mine, her tongue quickly getting involved as she damn near took all the air out of my lungs. She leaned much of her weight on me, and both the pressure and proximity had my body aching for more. I felt myself losing my sense of control, and I knew that I needed to retreat. I used my palms to push back on her shoulders which prompted her to stop.

"Oops. I'm doing too much, aren't I?" she said, moving away from me and sitting up.

"No, I uh . . . it's just harder for me tonight. Don't ask me why," I managed to stutter out, slightly embarrassed.

"Don't worry about it. Let's watch the movie." She passed me my mug of hot cocoa and covered the both of us up while the movie *Carol* began to play.

Although the classically filmed movie piqued my interest, I began fading away in Alena's arms with my head comfortably nestled into her chest. The last thing I remember of the movie was the ringing work bell at the young girl's job.

I later awakened to the sound of a pan sizzling, but I didn't smell any food. When I opened my eyes, I was able to comprehend the reason behind the sound. Alena was stroking my back slowly while her eyes were fixated on a cooking show on the television. I grinned sleepily as I squeezed her with my arms, which were already wrapped around her.

"Are you going to make that for us?" I asked in a hoarse voice.

"Oh, you're finally awake." She brushed her hand over my forehead.

"I didn't even know I was asleep. I thought the movie was good so far, but I guess I still faded away."

"It *was* interesting, but I couldn't keep watching it while you were sleeping. I want us to finish it together." She idly rubbed my left cheek. "You must not have slept much last night, though, because you were out for hours. It's almost seven-thirty now."

"Damn." I lifted my head from her lap and scooted backward on the couch. "You're right, I barely slept. I was studying for my philosophy test most of last night." I yawned. "I'm hungry, did you eat anything?"

"Nothing other than a few strawberries since you came. Do you want to order something? I don't really have anything to cook tonight."

"Yeah, let's do that. What do you think we should eat?" I stretched out my arms.

"How about I surprise you?" She smiled coyly. There was a rush of excitement in her voice that made me giggle.

"If it makes you happy, Alena."

"It does." She kissed my cheek.

I stood and dragged my feet to the window and looked outside. "It's raining?" I smashed my nose to the glass as if it weren't already clear that it was. "It wasn't even that overcast when I got here."

"I know, it came out of nowhere." Alena stood and grabbed her phone off the counter.

"That's probably why I slept so long," I concluded, scratching my side.

I stumbled over to the hall bathroom while she quietly ordered our food on the phone.

"Do you think I have time to take a shower before it gets here?" I asked, exiting the bathroom.

"You have plenty of time," she assured me before directing me to the fresh towels in her bathroom closet.

Warm water rained over my naked body inside of the tiled shower. The cocoa-brown painted walls were covered with teal decor and accented with splashes of purple to match the bedroom. I always enjoyed a shower in this room as opposed to my apartment because the water pressure was iffy there, as were the water temperatures. I liked my showers long and hot.

The lights flickered from the rumbling thunder as I continued to bathe, and I started thinking of what Alena had said to me earlier about how I smelled. She stopped herself before saying more, and the only thing she might've been hinting toward was of how I tasted. The mere thought of that set my heart beating fast, and I felt the area below my belly pulsate in return.

The idea of Alena wanting to devour me made me feel somewhat nervous, but it aroused me even more than that. I began to question if I was ready to go deeper with her, and I wondered exactly what I was feeling for her at this point.

I knew that I enjoyed the softness of her breathing at night when she was deep in slumber. I relished the way the right side of her mouth twitched a little every time she held back a smile that inevitably reared its head. Her lithe movements throughout the auditorium at school matched the eloquence with which she did nearly everything—from the way she yawned to the way she cooked or laughed or poured tea. I treasured the freedom of her spirit which flowed throughout her presence. I adored the way her voice lulled me to sleep whether I was here or talking to her on the phone at my apartment. I loved the honesty of emotions shared between us concerning anything and everything; she was even open about her feelings regarding the divorce.

I knew that I was willing to risk so much just for a morsel of her time and energy, and I would drop everything to be with her if she needed me. The sudden awareness of what I had unknowingly been feeling for Alena was disorienting. There's only one term that could encompass all of what I felt. One word that could make sense of why I would be so self-sacrificing for this woman and why I would invest my emotional energy into her so freely. The same word also explained why doing all of this left me with a sense of peace.

I love her. My breathing faltered as I repeated the words in my head. *I really love her. I love Alena. Oh, shit! That means I love my profess*—with a sharp and shuddering rumble the lights flickered off. The water continued to pour onto my glistening body, but I was now trapped in complete darkness.

Not a minute later, I heard a gentle knock on the door. "Amelia, the power's out in the complex. I'm coming in with some candles so you'll be able to see, okay?"

"Alright!" I called out as she opened the door. The shower curtain was pretty thick, so I didn't worry about her seeing my nude form. But would it matter if she did? Maybe I wanted her to . . . I felt at ease once I could see again in the darkness.

"Are you okay?" she asked through the curtain, a smile apparent in her voice.

"Yeah, thanks. I'm not afraid of the dark," I laughed. "I'll be out soon."

"Take your time," she advised as she left the room, closing the door behind her.

I ended my shower and wrapped a plush, purple towel around me before I crept into her bedroom that was now filled with candles. It was such a beautiful scene. I sat on the bed in my towel for a moment before getting dressed and putting on an oversized tee with fuzzy pajama bottoms. Upon stepping out of her bedroom, I could see candles on nearly every available surface of the main room in her apartment.

"The power may be out, but at least it's beautiful in here with all these candles!" I declared cheerfully.

Alena was lounging on the left side of the sofa with her eyes closed. "I know, right?"

I lay on my stomach in the middle of the opposite side. "I guess we can't finish that movie then," I muttered.

"We could always just make one." She opened an eye and glanced at me.

"*Ha-ha*," I let out sarcastically.

"You know that was a good one!" she defended herself.

I shook my head disapprovingly as she crawled toward me, grabbed my hand, and curled up next to me. "You must not know how beautiful you look in the candlelight," I whispered to her, placing a kiss on the top of her forehead.

"Not as beautiful as you," she stated in return.

A loud growl from my stomach immediately dampened my mood. "Are we ever going to eat tonight?" I whined.

"Yes, have some patience. Our food is scheduled to be here in approximately two minutes," she guaranteed after checking her phone.

"I guess I finished my shower in perfect timing then," I remarked, and she nodded.

Exactly two minutes later there was a knock at the door, and we both stood to retrieve our dinner. Alena had ordered us steak with mashed potatoes and salad from Russel's Steak House. She tipped and thanked the driver while I spread the food out on the table, and we sat down together for an impromptu candlelit dinner. She had also taken out two wine glasses and a bottle of Chardonnay. The food was amazing, and our conversations went deep as the wine soothed us.

"What did Mya have to say about our plans this weekend?" Alena asked me as I lay down in her room after dinner. She had already changed into some gray sweats and a white long-sleeved top with a fabric that was notably thin. I couldn't help but stare at the outline of her nipples every time she faced my direction.

I watched as she discarded her clothing into a black, crocheted bin in the corner of the room between the closet and the bathroom. She then moved around some shoes and placed my duffle on a chair instead of the ground. It would've been freezing in here by now if she didn't have two large and powerful heaters blasting in both the living room and bedroom. They were powered by a portable backup generator her father had gotten her for unpredictable situations just like this.

I sighed. "She doesn't understand why I would want to go to

Charlotte without her. I told her it was a solo trip, but she thinks I'm secretly going with Sarin."

Alena sat on the edge of the bed. "And you're upset because she's partially correct—because you're secretly going with *me*?"

I nodded, feeling defeated. "I just wish I could tell her about you." I was proud to be growing a connection with Alena, but nobody else in my life knew about us, and I hated that.

She climbed toward me in the bed, her lofty figure swirling shadows in the candlelit darkness. "Amelia, why don't you . . ." she paused for a moment, "why don't you just tell her?"

I scowled. "You're kidding, right?"

"She's your best friend. Don't you trust her?"

"Yes, but I don't know if she would take this well . . . scratch that—I know she most definitely wouldn't."

"Okay." Alena looked away as she sat cross-legged in front of me. She extended her shoulders back for a moment. "I don't know what else to say. I can see that this upsets you, but if you don't think it's a good idea . . ."

"Have you told anybody?" I didn't even think of the question before because even that felt like a secret best kept silent.

"I have, actually," she answered softly. "Of course, Teresa knows, and Jess. I told my best friend Desirée about you too. Nova knows, and the friends from the dinner party know about my interest in *someone*, but not that you're my—"

"Your student," I finished for her.

Alena placed a hand on my cheek and traced my lips with her thumb. "It won't be like this forever," she said. She then extended her back and shoulders once again and her face showed an obvious discomfort.

"Are you okay?"

"I'm just tense, that's all. I ran yesterday for the first time in a while. Maybe my posture was off. My back wasn't really bothering me before."

"Do you want me to massage it?"

Her face lit up. "You would want to?"

"Of course!" I smiled. "Where's your lotion?"

"Here." She slid off the bed, walked over to a chest beside her closet, and grabbed it for me.

"Thanks." I snatched it away. "Go lie on your stomach, please."

"As you wish." She obliged after first giving me a once over that made my body tingle.

When she lay flat on the bed, I straddled her back and sat on my knees. I smoothed the fabric of her shirt with my hand but caught myself before I lifted it up. "Shirt on or off?"

"I want the full experience, Amelia," she said. "Take it all off."

I swallowed hard as I carefully slid the shirt up her smooth body, and I admired her back which had clearly been perfectly crafted by God. The muscles along it were strong, and the candlelight only heightened the beauty of her brown skin—so much so that it made me shiver. Her curls were in a tousled bun on her head, out of the way of her perfect form. When I thought about the bare nipples just beneath her, a flutter from my chest reached my throat. I took my time warming the lotion in my hands before I spread it across her back in purposeful, rounded motions. I started with her lower back, where the line of her spine made its way down to her butt. I desperately desired to move my nose along that ridge and kiss every inch of her back, but I refrained.

As I moved upward, I noticed how Alena's disposition was slowly but surely shifting. Her previous quietness was replaced with a soft grunt that escaped from her mouth every time I loosened a knot. I reached her strong shoulders and nearly died when I was able to emit a moan from her. I stared in shock, though I should've expected it, but my hands didn't slow while I struggled to steady my breathing. It sounded like she whimpered a bit toward the end as well, and I somehow felt like I had received the massage myself.

"Oh my God, Amelia," she crooned, turning her face to the side to look at me. "I didn't know you were so good with your hands. I feel like my back is brand new." She continued making an arching motion with it that made my stomach sink into my crotch.

"Mind turning around?" she asked. "I need to stretch before I put this shirt back on."

"Okay," I sheepishly and reluctantly turned from her.

Another moan exited her mouth after what I presumed to be quite a good stretch.

"Thank you, thank you." I felt her lips kissing me and opened my eyes to her clothed body once again. The only difference was that the once relaxed nipples now protruded sharply through her shirt. This made me struggle for air.

"Do you feel better now?" I asked anxiously.

"*So* much better, baby." The smile did not leave her mouth, and even in the candlelight I could see a flush of red in her cheeks. Maybe it was more than just what a good massage could do for her that I had done.

"Do you feel anything else?" I continued, unable to control my curiosities.

"With my back?" she asked as she cocked her head to the side. I shook my head and let my eyes fall to her chest. She followed my gaze to her swelling nipples, and the redness in her cheeks grew. "How could I *not* feel something else?" she asked in a sultry tone. "Especially when your hands are all over my body like that."

My mouth began to water. "You make some interesting sounds." I leaned back onto a pillow with a face full of satisfaction—yet my heart was pounding, and my stomach was churning.

"*You* make me make interesting sounds, Amelia" she corrected, crawling toward me. She leaned over me and lightly nudged my nose with her own. I was finished with words once her mouth crashed into mine. We kissed wildly and passionately, and I could feel a light layer of sweat from the both of us mingling together as we pressed against each other.

Eventually, one of her hands began caressing the bottom of my stomach from underneath my shirt. Her lips stayed soft and languid on mine as she inched her hands up before she abruptly slid them back down. "Sorry," she whispered.

I pulled my lips away. "It's okay, Alena. I'm okay with it."

"Are you sure?"

"Yes." I grabbed her chin and urged her back in my direction.

"Just tell me if you want me to stop," she whispered into my mouth before kissing me again. Her hands slowly retraced their way back up my stomach until she finally reached between my breasts. "Do you want me to stop?" she asked, her fingers softly grazing my skin.

"No," I breathed out with a feeling of anguish. I *needed* her to touch me. I held in a moan from the pleasure of feeling her hands in places they hadn't been before. She paused again and looked at me with intense eyes, then she shrugged my shirt upward. I helped her remove it before nearly snatching hers off her body in return.

Breathing was hardly a factor now as she pulled me into a deep kiss and her soft skin met every inch of my upper body. She moved from my lips to my neck, slowly and intentionally. The burning inside seemed unquenchable. I wanted her lips to travel to the innermost depths of my body and her tongue to lace itself around every nook and cranny.

I heard a moan escape from my mouth when she began sucking on the lower area of my neck. She wasn't being gentle about it either, yet all I felt was pleasure. A flood rushed beneath me as she traveled down and brushed her lips along one of my breasts. I then watched as she delicately took a nipple into her mouth. Her eyes were closed, but the enjoyment on her face was unmistakable. More sounds I didn't know I could create flowed out of me, and I held my hands to her curls.

When she glanced up, I knew death was surely awaiting. How could I live another day after seeing her look at me as if she were famished, parched, and everything in between—and like I was the cure to it all. In the moment our eyes were locked, she took her tongue and slowly dragged it across my nipple. I gasped, and she gave the most devilish grin I'd ever seen in my life.

She began sucking on the nipple while twisting the other one, and she continued watching my reactions. As I looked into her eyes, I sensed something in her demeanor that had previously been concealed. There seemed to be a frustration rising from inside of her the more intimate we became. She appeared to desperately need release, and maybe only because I observed her so closely could I notice that at all. Her breaths were becoming more and more shallow, she kept moving her hips forward as if she craved friction, and every now and again she let out a low moan as she explored my body.

"I want to watch you touch yourself," I huffed out suddenly, again breaching my usual limitations. If I ever shocked her before, it was still never quite like this, but I didn't stop there. "You look like you want to come, Alena. I want to see."

There was a mix of desperation, distress, and determination in her response. "You want to watch me?" She stammered out, maneuvering herself so that she was facing me. With her body mounted over me, her breasts hung so close to my face that I almost forgot what we were even talking about.

"Yes," I whispered, moving my gaze from her chest to her eyes. She leaned in and kissed my neck and lips then settled herself beside me, facing me before she looked down. I followed her eyes and watched as she slid down her shorts and placed a hand between her thighs. Her eyes glinted with need as she sucked her bottom lip into her mouth and moved her fingers over her slit. My lips parted at the sight, and I released a shaky breath.

"I'll make sure to come for you, Amelia," she murmured. She took a single finger and traced it around her clit in a slow, circular motion. I was entranced as I watched her pleasure herself. "Kiss me," she whimpered in a guttural tone after she slipped two fingers inside.

The feeling was indescribable as she tongue-kissed me while she simultaneously finger-fucked herself. I felt the movements from her arm on my clit, and I rubbed up against the motion. While she was touching herself and I was kissing her, my knee reflexively pushed between her legs, and she moaned. I was new to this, so I didn't at first understand the power of this movement. Her eyes flew open, and she stopped kissing me. There was a question in them that I didn't understand.

"Do you mind that?" she asked breathlessly.

"What?" I asked in return, and she answered by moving herself against my leg once again. She exhaled sharply, and I quickly understood what she meant. "I don't mind," I said.

My hands glided across her back as I kissed her while she repeated the motion, growing more and more impatient along the way. I felt a sense of power and control over such an intimate encounter. I pushed myself closer to her in tandem until she gasped and shuddered against me. Her quiet cry of pleasure sent a rippling through my own body, though it was not nearly as strong. I held her as she trembled from the aftershocks.

I was mesmerized, dazed, and starstruck. This stunning, self-possessed woman had put herself at my mercy. She had opened herself up to me in a vulnerable way, and she was so sexy in doing it. I tightened my grip on her as we cuddled since she still didn't feel close enough to me.

After this experience with her, my appetite was merely whetted. I was not fully satisfied. I wanted her to moan more, buck wilder, and have her way with me—but I also enjoyed the unbroken momentum in me, and the fact that my release was still imminent.

"Amelia," she sighed. "Do you want me to . . ." She let the rest of her words hang in the air. I thought about it as I began caressing her body. Of course, I wanted her to. I even needed her to. But I could also wait.

"Not tonight."

Chapter 13 Do It for Me

I woke up early, the sun just peeking in through the curtains of Alena's bedroom windows. My eyes opened to a wonderful view of the gorgeous woman sleeping next to me. Her arms were securely wrapped around me as I lay on my back admiring the statuesque beauty. Her curls were sprawled across the satin pillowcase, and she was snoring lightly.

How do I deserve such a blessing? My waking thoughts were serene and blissful—that was until a more passionate memory surfaced. Alena was once again clinging to me and moaning. Her erotic scent permeating the air around us. Her lust filled eyes trained on me as she licked my skin.

A heat now surged within me, and the pace of my heart accelerated as I began to sweat. Or was I already sweating? I paid more attention to my surroundings, soon pinpointing the actual cause of my perspiration. I saw a light through the crack of the closed bathroom door then looked up at the ceiling vent where I could feel heat pouring in. I gradually pieced together that the power had returned during my slumber, and the combination of that and the heaters made for an overly steamy environment.

I quietly slid from underneath Alena's grip and went to turn off the heaters and lights—but I had apparently forgotten that I was topless and that Alena was too. Her skin appeared golden in the sunlight, her softened areolas were a shade lighter than her eyes, and she looked like an angel that swooped in from heaven to save me. I gazed distractedly at her figure but soon had to tear myself away to complete the task at hand.

By the time I reentered the room, she was feeling around the bed for me with closed eyes. "Amelia?" she called out sleepily. I slipped back into the bed where her arms took me captive and crushed me against her breasts. The only way I could describe the feeling of lying there with her was of a sweet and utter bliss. She resumed snoring and I closed my eyes, listening to the countering rhythms of her breath and heartbeat.

Half an hour passed before she began to stir again, and this time she slowly opened her eyes and blinked at me. "Good morning, beautiful," she greeted me, a grin emerging.

"Good morning, gorgeous," I cooed while nudging my nose against her forehead.

"Why the hell is it so hot in here?" she asked in a sleepy voice that I found adorable.

"We forgot to turn down the air, and the power came back some time this morning. I turned off the lights and the heaters when I woke up, but it was already pretty toasty."

"Ugh, I feel gross." She sat up in the bed, inadvertently shedding the covers from her body. I struggled to even swallow as she shook out her curls while topless and uncaring. How much more could I take of this? She continued to stretch and yawn before she acknowledged how still I was. "Are you okay?" she asked idly.

"*No.*" I shook my head desperately, and she laughed.

"Is it my hair?" She placed her hands on the curls which in turn shook her breasts.

I bit my lip and groaned. "Why do you do these things to me, woman?" I moved from underneath the sheets and slid toward her perfect frame.

"Damn," she murmured. "The candlelight did not do you justice." She licked her lips as she studied my breasts.

My pulse quickened, and I pulled her toward me and held her close. We were chest to chest, and I could feel her heartbeat speed up significantly. When I pulled away from her, I searched her expression for anything other than her usual calm.

"Your poker face could put anyone to shame," I said.

"How is that?"

"Your heart is pounding, but looking at your face I couldn't tell."

"That's good. You wouldn't be ready for me not to keep some composure," she remarked matter-of-factly. She stood up and strutted toward the bathroom door. "My shorts are also soaked, but you didn't know that either, did you?" she added before stepping into the bathroom.

She left me there, a pile of melting flesh. I could never predict her sensuous remarks, so they always took me by surprise.

I soon heard the noisy flush of the toilet followed by the sound of the shower turning on. She opened the door and asked, "Are you interested in conserving water this morning, or should I be quick so it doesn't get cold for you?"

We were half an hour from Charlotte when the sky broke open and unleashed a mélange of thunder and rain.

"Dammit," Alena groaned, turning on her windshield wipers. "There goes our stroll in the park," she grumbled sadly to herself. "And probably the stargazing too."

"We can always just dance in the rain," I offered sympathetically.

"I don't think that's such a great idea," she sulked, but she immediately perked up once her head turned in my direction and our eyes met.

"We're still going to have a great time." I grabbed her free hand and brushed my thumb against it. "At least we can do *this* in the restaurant and the museum and wherever else we decide to go." I smiled peacefully as the car now approached a lofty building in the city center. I couldn't tell what it was until Alena drove toward the entrance and I saw the name: *The Abbey's Hotel.*

"Alena, where's our hotel? Is it behind this one?" The structure looked nothing like the one we had chosen together when we officially set the date a week and a half ago.

"No, this is it." The corners of her mouth lifted.

"*This* is the hotel?" I repeated, astonished.

"I wanted to surprise you." She beamed proudly. "I think I was successful."

I nodded wordlessly as I studied the building.

"I wanted to get a place we could both get lost in. I know you appreciate the artistic styles of any and everything, and I love places with a classic aura. This was the perfect blend."

Once we made it to the front of the valet parking line, we swiftly gathered our bags from the trunk of the car. Gorgeous paintings and chandeliers decorated the lobby, along with a thoughtfully planned color scheme. The cedar floors were shiny, and some of the walls were patterned with circular arches and hanging plants. An elongated spiral staircase was wrapped around the side by the front windows that framed the gray day.

So far, the hotel looked exactly like what I imagined the inside of Alena's head to be. Standing here, it was almost like I could touch her thoughts and I loved it because it felt like another realm.

After Alena checked us in under her maiden name, we made our way to the elevators with a welcome gift bag in hand. There were mints, chocolates, and two water bottles inside of it. As we ascended to the sixth floor, I felt a bubbling up of emotions. It was difficult for me to comprehend Alena booking us such a beautiful stay. I wasn't used to things like this at all; I was used to being forgotten. I was practically my older brother's understudy before my younger siblings came into the picture, and I wasn't very popular in school prior to college. I had people in my life now like Mya and Gabe who no doubt made me feel special, but I still never experienced treatment quite like this.

"You're awfully quiet. How are you feeling?" Alena asked me when the doors opened to our floor. We began rolling our luggage across the beautiful wood in the main hallway, and I briefly got sidetracked by the artistic décor on the gray-and-pearl-white walls.

Once I met her brown, discerning eyes again—I immediately recalled the question she asked me. "I feel special," I told her with my lips pouted.

"That's because you are, my love." She leaned down to kiss the pout off of them.

My first instinct was to internally scream because she referred to me as "my love," but my second one was to scan the hall. It was empty, but even if it had been occupied it wouldn't have mattered. No one knew a thing about us here. We were strangers in the somewhat distant land of Charlotte, North Carolina.

I returned my eyes to her. "I'm sorry, Alena. I don't mean to be paranoid."

"I understand." She stroked her fingers along my cheek. "We both have a lot of new things to get used to. Now come on, we're almost to the room." She took my hand and led me down the hall.

Our room was tucked away near a huge window at the end of the hall, and when I looked down at the city from the window, happiness struck me at my core. Satisfaction was apparent on Alena's face. When I finally tore myself away from the view, she urged me to scan the key card and open the door.

We both entered an elegantly decorated room. I placed down my bags then explored nearly every crevice of the room while Alena watched with delight. The room was quite spacious and in pristine condition. The white paneled walls were gorgeously layered with Victorian-style lamps. The furniture flourished the same style. The Channel tufted bed frame was upholstered with a soft, tan cloth. The bedsheets were white, with a purple running board and purple accent pillows on top of them. Across from the bed sat a gray sofa—a glass coffee table in front of it, a glass floor lamp beside it, and a bronze barrel chair opposite it. There was a massive window overlooking the city, and I was captivated by everything about the room just as much as I was by the view.

"It's even better than the pictures," Alena commented as her arms surrounded me from behind. She laid her head on my shoulder, and I reveled in the silent exchange. It was nice to be with her alone in a different city with full privacy and no restrictions. I was thrilled about the date soon to come, with the food and museum, but I was even more excited about returning here with her for the night.

Once she loosened her grip on me, I escaped her arms and planted a firm kiss on her lips. The smell of warm vanilla and marshmallows entered my nose and dizzied me. Her lips were always so soft, and I never wanted to leave them.

"Alena, this is amazing. Thank you for the surprise."

"Did you look at the bathroom yet?" she asked with a lifted brow.

"Oh!" I pushed past her dramatically and rushed into the room. My heart leapt as I stared at a bouquet of yellow roses that had been placed on the marble sink.

"Where did you get these from?" I whispered. The tears, once safely tucked in their ducts, now watered my eyes and threatened to release.

"I had them delivered so you wouldn't see them until we arrived."

"Why would you give me flowers?" My voice cracked as I spoke.

She laughed. "Why would I not get flowers for the most beautiful woman I know?" I embraced her as my tears now fell, and her chest shook lightly from remnants of her laughter as she held me securely in her arms. "It's okay, Amelia. You deserve good things." She grabbed my chin and kissed my tear-stained lips.

"Thank you so much." I wiped my eyes before turning back around so I could finish examining the room. "I love this bathroom. It's so bright and chic!"

"*My* personal favorite is the tub," she stated, walking toward where it sat beside the window.

"I like *this*." I slid the glass door of the transparent shower open. "Isn't it sexy?" I teased, turning back to face her.

"Indeed, it is." She brusquely pushed me in and followed behind. "And it fits two nicely," she chanted into my ear as she held me firmly to the wall. I couldn't move, and she had seized me so quickly that I was completely disoriented. Her lips brushed the side of my cheek as she nudged her nose on mine.

"I—I . . ." I tried to speak, but I was unable.

"Maybe we should save the water this time around?" she continued temptingly as she held me fast to the wall. Her lips now grazed my neck before she kissed me slowly on the mouth. Her tongue swirled gently inside, and I still couldn't free myself so I'd have the ability to touch her in all the ways I wanted. Hours could have gone by with us behaving like this—and I wouldn't have cared—but she eventually pushed her hand into my chest and backed away. "We have plans," she said, almost to herself.

Fuck those. I impatiently tried to rejoin our lips together, but I still couldn't escape her grasp.

She watched my futile efforts with a laugh in her eyes. "I'll let you go when your heartbeat slows down," she promised.

Ari Lennox, Snoh Aalegra, and Mac Ayres played loudly from Alena's cellphone while we unpacked our bags and settled into the room. I hung up my emerald-green dress for dinner, and she hung up her black one. We put our heels by the couch and spread our toiletry items across the twin sinks of the bathroom. The rain began to pick up outside, and the methodical pattering was the perfect set-up for a nap. Unfortunately for me, it was approaching two-thirty and we had reservations at the museum set for three-thirty. Alena entered the bathroom and minutes later emerged wearing a glittering burgundy jumpsuit. I could only gawk at her as she spoke.

"Do you want to grab some tea and pastries from this coffee shop nearby before we head to the museum? Or should we get sandwiches instead?"

"Umm . . . I can't hear you," I said as I walked toward her and stood on my tiptoes to get a better look at her flawless cleavage. "Damn, Alena. Don't you think you should wear that to class sometime?"

"Absolutely not," she reproached. "Pastries or sandwiches?" she repeated firmly.

I reluctantly chose the pastries and tried my best to concentrate on getting dressed in the bedroom while Alena applied her makeup in the bathroom. I put on a pair of slick black pants and a golden button-up blouse with flowing cuffs. I could've sworn that my outfit would do absolutely nothing in comparison to what Alena's outfit did to me, but the hunger in her eyes told me a different story.

By the time we were both ready, I was mesmerized by the woman who currently looked like a runway model and smelled like a dessert I wouldn't mind eating right then.

The coffee shop wasn't far from our charming boutique hotel. When we walked in, we spoke to a barista named Ryan who was both very kind and very gay. He had short straight black hair, and his square-framed glasses did little to age his youthful appearance. His shirt was the reason I distinctly knew of his sexuality because it literally read: *I am both extremely caffeinated and very gay.*

I glanced around the room—at the stucco walls, quaint light fixtures, and overall unorthodox style of organized chaos. The tables varied in material, shape, and size. Every set of seats had differently colored cushions. There was a lot going on, and it was a bit gaudy, but it worked.

We waited for our drinks and pastries at a small seating area by the front door. I took it as an opportunity to ogle my date while she spoke about the best coffee shops in California. The aroma of rain was heavy in the room as it began pouring even harder than when we'd first arrived. It didn't take long to get our orders, so we soon exited the shop with Alena holding a large transparent umbrella above us.

"I like that place. It seemed very open and welcoming," I said in between sips of my tea once we were in the safety of her car. Before knowing Alena, I would've probably ordered a coffee—but she was primarily a tea drinker, and by now it had rubbed off on me. She didn't believe in constant caffeine but was still a proponent of consuming hot beverages to keep the systems clear.

"It was definitely cute," she agreed. "I loved the décor too. It was a bit erratic but in a good way."

We arrived at the museum fifteen minutes before our set appointment time. I'd heard good things about Blanchette's Museum of High Arts, but I had never visited before. Alena said that when she'd looked it up, it reminded her of this place she had been to in California some years ago. Both places regularly showcased rare artwork from various galleries. She wasn't into the arts quite like I was—but she had gone with her friend, Desirée, who appreciated it just as much as me. It was one of the reasons Alena had apparently mentioned me to her friend much earlier on in our budding romance. She told me that she often gushed over her favorite students and with seeing me in her office so often, it was hard not to mention me.

The museum was full of gorgeous paintings and sculptures, and there was also a room for live arts that I knew Gabe would've loved. I made sure to take plenty of pictures so I could scrapbook them and show them to my friends once I was back in town.

Alena and I held hands as we took in the beauty of the museum's art. There were a lot of abstract works, and I even saw a painting that reminded me of the piece that hung on the wall of her office. It was like a wanderer in a foreign place that brought light into the darkness.

"The canvas in my office came from Nadine, a friend of my mother's," she explained to me while we paced the exhibits. "She was the first one to help me realize that I wasn't messed up as a kid—I was just gay. She even helped me hide it from my mother until I was ready to tell her."

"That must've been hard for you." I frowned and squeezed her hand.

"Not as hard as it would've been if I had no one. Nadine was really an angel in my life then."

"Do you still keep in touch?" I asked curiously.

Alena smiled to herself. "We speak almost every month. She's one of my favorite people to see during the holidays. I can't wait to tell her all about you. I already told her a little, but there's plenty more where that came from." Her eyes crinkled as her smile widened, and I joined her with a joyful smile of my own. I was glad to know that she had people in her corner, but I also felt a tinge of sadness because I longed for that same sense of safety she was able to find in her family and friends. I wondered if what I desired was even possible in this lifetime.

We made it to a special exhibit at the end of the museum featuring a painting called *Les Nombreux Femmes*. It was a large, breathtaking piece: Several powerful women encircled a fire. The fire blazed in different color tones of green, blue, pink, purple, red, and black. Some of the women ran, others danced, several kissed, and one pair did quite more than that.

My jaw hung agape as I studied every inch of the painting. I wanted to reach out and touch the smudges of hardened oil, but of course that was impossible to do. I felt a light squeeze in my right hand, then looked up at Alena who had a contented sparkle in her eyes. She knew *exactly* what this massive painting meant to me.

I told her about *Les Nombreux Femmes* maybe the second week of school. There was no way she should have remembered how badly I wanted to see it, especially since we weren't even at the friend stage back then. My only dilemma in seeing it so far was that I could never find a showcase that was both nearby and set for a date when I was free. I'd only mentioned it that once, and even I had honestly forgotten about it at this point. I had settled for finding it sometime next year. Yet here we were . . . and here it was.

"You knew this would be here," I stated in a weak voice, squeezing her hand in return. We stayed there for nearly twenty minutes before Alena guided me away. It was the end of our time at the museum, and she had apparently found us a slot for wine tasting that we could possibly make it to before dinner. We needed to make our way back to the hotel so we could change.

The rain slowed as we walked to the parking lot. I didn't speak much after seeing the painting because I'd been left in a state of shock and felt another urge to cry.

"How'd you like the museum?" Alena questioned me once we were seated in her car with the warm air blasting on us.

"I didn't like it." I leaned my head back on the headrest and turned to her. "I *loved* it—wow, I loved it so much, Alena!" I could barely contain myself. I wished that I could see deeper into her than just her eyes. I wished I could somehow read her mind and know why she was such a thoughtful person or at least know why I was the one who deserved this thoughtfulness from her.

I traced my thumb along her cheek and without thinking I said, "Almost as much as I love—" She waited, and I quickly corrected my next words. "The first one I ever went to as a kid." I leaned over and kissed her cheek, now avoiding her eyes. I hoped that she hadn't caught on to what I'd nearly revealed. "I'm afraid to even attempt to plan a date for you now. How could I ever do for you what you've done for me so far?"

"Amelia, you don't understand." Her head shook as she pulled out of the parking lot and drove toward the hotel. "Everything you do for me and *with* me is enough. You smile and it's enough, you complain about your classes and assignments, and it's enough. You walk into my apartment, rubbing your hands together because you're always too cold and it's enough. You sneeze and it's enough, you snore like a bear in my bed and it's enough, you laugh and it's enough, you breathe... even that's enough."

The entire way up to our room I couldn't help thinking about how much I loved her. I wanted her to know this, but I didn't want the revelation to alarm her. The romantic situation between us only continued to make interesting curves and turns, but it was impossible to forget that she was still someone else's wife. I was, however, finally getting over the label because Alena was undoubtedly crafted for *me*; she had to be. Teresa was just holding on to something that was no longer there and to someone who didn't have the capacity to give to her anymore.

We neared our room, hand in hand, and I could feel my heart begin to race when we finally stood in front of the door. My love for her spread through my veins and a fire lit inside of my soul. I desired to do exceedingly more than just tell her how much I loved her. I needed to show her.

"Do you have the key?" Alena's question interrupted my thoughts.

When I dug into my jacket to find it, I felt a receipt which reminded me of a gift I had purchased for her. I had even brought it with me because I wanted to give it to her, though I thought it might be too much for just a *first date*. Clearly, we were far more familiar with each other than your typical pair on a first date, but I was still trying to be careful in my approach. I'd bought the gift two weeks earlier and stuffed it into my luggage absentmindedly, along with another gift that I was more certain about giving her later on in the night.

"Here it is." I opened the door.

Alena headed straight for the gray sofa where she collapsed. "That was a lot of walking in these heels," she muttered tiredly before taking out her phone and scrolling through it.

"But you do it so well," I praised her and set down my purse on the coffee table.

"Damn, the wine tasting is fully booked now." She clicked her phone off and threw it onto the bed without getting up. "Which means we have approximately two hours before dinner . . ." She let her words hang in the air, and I wished to swallow them whole then devour her next. "What shall we do?" she continued enticingly.

"I don't know about you," I began unbuttoning my top, "but I am going to go run a bath." I walked away from her as she lay there with a baffled expression on her face. I snagged a large plastic bag out of my suitcase before I reached my destination and shut the door.

The bath that I began to run was not for me at all; I tended to it like a soup as I added bath salts and soap until bubbles began to form. I then frantically fished through my bag for the gift and smiled when I finally found it. I held a silver bracelet carefully between two fingers, and it shined brightly as it swung in the air. I'd gotten it engraved with her name and middle initial which she had thankfully told me before I discovered the jewelry: *Alena H. Moore.*

A knock at the door startled me, and I pocketed the bracelet and its box before hurrying to turn off the water. The bubbles were at perfect height, but the water was too hot. "Before you take your bath, may I pee, Amelia?" she inquired through the closed door. I opened it, now only wearing my bra and black pants.

"Yes, of course, my dear," I said, stepping aside to let her through. She was shorter than before, her heels now replaced with a pair of flats. Once I closed the door, I ran back to my suitcase to look for the card I had written for her two nights before. I didn't mention my love for her in it, but I did share my deep appreciation and excitement about our growing connection. I quickly took the box out of my pocket and placed it underneath the card. I then waited in front of the bed with my hands behind my back until she emerged from the bathroom.

"What are you doing, Amelia? You look suspicious."

"Nothing." I quietly stepped to the side, revealing her gift and card on the bed.

"What is this?" she questioned uneasily. "I know you didn't get me a gift." She was clearly taken aback.

"Of course I did—and you got me flowers, so don't be like that."

She slowly approached the bed and reluctantly lifted the card from it. I watched her tear open the envelope and read my words, stopping twice to give me a look of gratitude each time.

"Amelia." She threw the card down and pulled me tightly into her. "Thank you," she murmured. Her head shook as she picked up the red box and stared at it curiously. "I have no idea what this could be," she admitted. "I don't want to open it."

"Go on, Alena. It isn't going to bite you," I joked.

She lifted the top of the red box and pulled out the silver bracelet encrusted with small jewels from her birthstone. Her body stiffened as she examined the jewelry. She held it up in the air, eyes wide. "No, Amelia." Her voice cracked. "This is *gorgeous*!" She turned to me with furrowed brows. "You didn't need to get this for me."

"As soon as I saw it, I knew it was yours," I assured her.

She flipped the jewelry around and finally saw the engraving, prompting a tear to slide down her cheek. "Thank you so much." Her lips turned up in a smile before she kissed me, which immediately reminded me of my previously rising passions.

My natural instincts took over as I firmly grabbed her hips and pulled her into me. Her desire must have been consistent with mine because she hurriedly backed away and ripped the covering off the bed before laying me flat on the clean sheets. As our lips locked together again, I hastily unzipped the back of her jumpsuit. I worked at moving the gown over her shoulders and sliding it down all while exploring her mouth from the inside out.

She stopped kissing me long enough for us both to remove the rest of the jumpsuit. She then unhooked my bra in a swift motion. I started to remember the bathwater that was waiting for her but instantly forgot about it when her mouth surrounded one of my nipples. There was a flutter deep in my chest as my body welcomed the warmth and wetness of her mouth. When I looked down, I could see the cheeks of her ass hanging out between the thin line of a black thong. My hands followed my gaze so I could feel on the soft flesh.

She licked and sucked on me hungrily while her hands worked on my pants zipper. It was far too easy for her to loosen the pants and pull them off. I knew where things would be headed from there, and this time I was ready. The entirety of my skin buzzed with excitement as she moved higher and pressed her lips onto my neck. I sighed and relished the feeling of her tongue grazing me there.

"Where can I touch you?" she whispered longingly into my ear. The way her lips lingered on my neck coursed a strong current downward. I was more than ready to receive all she wanted to give to me. It was finally time.

"Wherever you want to."

Chapter 14 Prime Time

Anticipation would apparently be my disposition for the night. I had finally given Alena permission to do whatever she wanted to do to me, and though her eyes lit up and she seemed ready to oblige, she retreated from me. She had suddenly insisted that it was important to make our dinner reservations on time despite the fact that we still had another hour until then. I knew that getting ready for dinner was about to be an impossible task because I was far more interested in making love to the woman of my dreams.

It became inconsequential that the bath I'd previously drawn for her wasn't warm enough by the time we started getting ready. After she drained the water from the tub, she glanced at me with a question in her eyes then looked toward the shower.

I couldn't help but stare at her wonderful frame as hot water rained over both of our bodies. It was to the point where she was actually blushing as she stood in the back of the shower. But this was our first time seeing one another completely naked—in bright lights at that—and Alena was the most stunning woman I had ever seen.

"Sorry." I turned around and continued scrubbing my arms with a loofah. "I just can't believe how gorgeous you are. I can't even believe I'm the one who gets to see you or that I'm the one you want."

I felt her wet body press up against me from behind, and she kissed the side of my neck and shoulders. "Thank you," she whispered into my ear as her hands slid down my thighs. I soon noticed a wetness that wasn't coming from the water.

"How could I possibly see anybody else when I'm so busy looking at you?" Her voice began to grow louder above the pouring water. "I love everything about you, Amelia." Her open hand unexpectedly came to my ass. "Including these cheeks!"

I whimpered and turned around, rubbing my backside with a scowl on my face until we both began laughing. She then clutched me again as we locked our dampened lips together.

For dinner Alena took me to Zatinya's, a Mediterranean spot downtown, and the entire time she toyed with me. From the moment we sat down to when we finally walked out of the restaurant, I couldn't help but think of her naked body and how much it deserved my praises. I was only yanked out of the fantasies through our banter and conversation but was once again distracted whenever she purposely said or did things to further arouse me.

Her foot caressed mine underneath the table, she made sly remarks and commentary, and she gazed at me amorously. I was utterly captivated by her black split-sleeve dress. It had a sheer V-neckline that made it just as sexy as it was classy. I also adored the silver crescent moon necklace she debuted tonight. She told me it was a gift to herself in honor of her liberation and that it represented new beginnings. The bracelet I had given her was securely bound to her wrist, and it gave me a form of pleasure I couldn't describe.

Alena and I drank Chateau Musar Lebanon Blanc '14, and it was better than I expected. I was glad we began sipping the wine before our meal because I had previously been so stimulated and anxious that I couldn't even fathom eating. Regrettably, as much as the wine eased my frustrations enough to eat dinner, it also heightened my desire for Alena.

"I think I want to try a red wine next time," I mentioned in between sips of my drink. It wasn't the only new thing I wanted to try.

"You should," she agreed. "And you know what? We should go wine tasting in California," she proposed.

"Really?" I asked excitedly, and she nodded with a smile.

"I can show you where I grew up, and we can visit different art centers there. There are plenty of beaches around too," her eyes lit up, "and we can meet up with Desirée! She and I can show you some of the hiking trails we used to climb as kids. And I know she would love to talk art with you."

"Ooh! Yeah, I love how that sounds, Alena! I'd love to meet her." I beamed. "Maybe when we go to the beach, we can take surfing lessons too!"

"I don't know about that," she chuckled. "But it *would* be nice to see you wet." I choked on the wine that was making its way down my throat, and Alena leaned back in her seat looking pleased. Just in the nick of time our waiter, Donnie, arrived with our meals and placed our entrees in front of us. I'd ordered the Beef Soutzoukakia, and she chose the Lamb Baharat and a Fattoush salad.

My food tasted absolutely delicious, but I managed to only pick at the dish once the calming properties of the wine subsided. I kept thinking about the hotel room and the bed that awaited us. Alena had more than primed my body by attending to every love language in the book, and she was now incessantly poking at the overwhelming anticipation building within me. She had me open in the best ways, and I wanted her in the worst.

"Why aren't you eating?" she asked as she finished her salad. "Do you need some help with that? I'm hungry tonight, I can definitely eat you out—*help you out*, that's what I meant." She batted her eyelashes innocently while she smiled derogatorily.

"*Alena*, why do you keep doing that?!" My eyes were bulging as I wiped my mouth with a napkin.

"It was an accident. I misspoke." She returned to her lamb dish between bites of her salad. "You really should eat more though. You're going to need the energy for when we get back to the room..."

I pressed my lips tightly together, unimpressed. "You're taunting me on purpose," I said, sounding more distressed than I would've liked.

"So are you, Amelia," she replied languidly.

"How?! I'm being extremely civil," I protested.

"Have you seen what you're wearing?" she asked tenderly. "It's hard for me to even concentrate while looking at you." Alena had endlessly raved about my green dress the entire night. It was a fitted one-shoulder ensemble that I had paired with a small golden necklace and matching heels. Green was her favorite color, and the dress made my ass look good, so I knew it was the perfect choice for our first official date.

"Oh..." My cheeks warmed, and I averted my eyes from her while sipping my drink.

"Did you wear it for me?" Alena continued as she finished her second glass of wine.

"Wouldn't you like to know," I countered defiantly. "Did you wear *yours* for me?" I nearly lost myself in the beauty of her black dress once again.

"Yes," she answered assuredly. "And do you know what I *didn't* wear for you?" Her eyes penetrated me.

Donnie approached us yet again with his wet-looking curls falling over his brows. "Were you able to save enough room for dessert?" he asked before he began grabbing our empty plates.

"I surely did," Alena spoke with her eyes still securely on me. I was ready to leave immediately, but she took the menu he offered when he came back from clearing the table and reviewed it meticulously. She inquired about two different desserts before deciding on a third one that interested her.

"I can think of something a lot more delicious back at the hotel to eat," she said before her eyes flew up to meet mine. She then turned to Donnie and returned the menu to him. "But I think we'll have the Galatopita." She smiled elegantly, and a certain heat pulsated throughout my body.

▼

"Alena," I breathed out as she rhythmically pushed her naked body against mine. We had hardly made it into the hotel room before I could snatch her black dress off quickly enough or before she could rip off my green one—along with anything I wore underneath it, apart from my panties.

There was no more caution between us or subtleties. We were both ready to receive what we had been craving as we finally bared our all with one another.

"Breathe, Amelia," she reminded me as she kissed on my thighs. I was panting still as one of her hands clutched at my chest and the other began sliding over the front of the lacy fabric. My head was propped up on a pillow at the edge of the bed while Alena was bent over me, skillfully working my body.

"You shouldn't have left me so keyed up before dinner," she said. "Now that I've had to wait, I'm going to move painfully slow for you. Sorry about that, darling."

I knew for a fact that she wasn't sorry at all, and we both knew it was her idea to wait in the first place. Lucky for her, I enjoyed the long game, so I didn't argue with the devious woman.

An eternity passed as she explored the lower half of my body with her fingers, lips, and tongue. She applied just enough pressure to make me feel weak in the knees. I wanted her to focus on the most sensitive parts of me, but she somehow knew when I was appreciating the attention a little too much for her slow and deliberate teasing. I was only able to catch my breath when she shifted back toward my stomach and laid gentle kisses up to my breasts. I quite enjoyed having her there because her scent was stronger than when she was farther below. I could also better see the angular curve of her jaw as well as the beautiful brown eyes I was so in love with.

She soon kissed her way up my neck and sucked on the sensitive skin there. Pleasure consumed me with her in my arms—and as I watched her naked body work over mine, I witnessed a growing tension in her eyes. Much like the night before, it was apparent that she was stuck between wanting to please me and wanting to find release herself. I was all too ready for the opportunity to satisfy her needs, but it was clear that *she* was the one in control.

Our lips collided, and I reflexively moved my hands down to massage her ass while her left arm disappeared somewhere beneath us. I soon discovered exactly where once she resumed rubbing the top of the lace. I was losing my breath again, as well as my resolve to keep a morsel of my composure. I wanted her to quicken her pursuit, but I also wanted her to proceed with my pleasure on her own terms. When I finally felt her cool fingers hook around one side of my panties, I heaved a sigh of relief into her mouth which smiled in return. She slowly slid the garment down and off my legs. Her hand grazed my thigh and her mouth retreated from mine as she lifted herself above me.

She didn't say a word or look away from my eyes as her hand crept up my thigh even more. Her thumb trailed over my entire opening before she dipped the tip of one of her other fingers inside me. "Fuck, Amelia. You're soaking wet." She sighed before placing the same finger into her mouth and moaning. I should've dropped dead right then and there, but I was somehow still alive. "Are you okay?" she asked in a considerate tone.

"Mm-hmm," was all I could manage to get out. I was by no means okay, but in the sense of consent I was exceptionally more than that, and I didn't give a fuck what it was she wanted to do with me next.

When she grabbed me by the chin and kissed me on the lips, I could feel her bracelet tickle my face. The woman then backed farther and farther down until she disappeared between my thighs. She hadn't bothered to tuck her curls away either because we had moved so fast from the car to the lobby to the hotel room to the bed. She kept shaking them back with a whip of her head to move them out the way, but I thoroughly appreciated her unbridled appearance.

I was deeply thankful that she didn't waste any time—her lips did not wander around my slick folds for too long—because she was apparently finished with getting me primed and ready.

I gasped sharply when her tongue very gently slid across me. It made me want to cry and thank God for making me a woman. I lost everything after that: my train of thought, my wits about myself, and my fear of sharing my body with the wrong person for my first time. I knew this was right and that *she* was right in every way.

The slow beginning shifted as she switched speeds of licking both around and inside of me. It was hard not to shove my hips into her face because of how good it felt and because of how it simultaneously made me crave more. Her hands didn't roam my body but instead held fast to my thighs, keeping me in place as much as it was possible. I was wriggling with pleasure as she feasted on me as though she hadn't eaten a meal in a thousand years.

It didn't take me long to feel a rise from deep within my core. It was one that I was familiar with from my late night self-stimulating pleasures, but the fact that I was not the one satisfying my body made the experience all the more enjoyable. The aching for release grew as she divided her tongue movements between long strokes and a steady flicker on my clit. It caused me to inch myself into her and instinctively hold tight to the beautiful curls.

Her head nodded faster, and I couldn't catch myself quick enough to warn her of my approaching orgasm. The cry of pleasure that came from my mouth was crafted especially for the way that Alena was using her tongue on my pussy. A whining sound followed as she persisted, and my eyes watered as I struggled to catch my breath while my body continued to convulse. She didn't stop even as I grew more sensitive.

"*Fuck*," I breathed hoarsely, feeling something unknown surging inside of me. "Alena? What—" Again I shook even more forcefully than the first time.

I never thought it was possible to return to the earth once you entered heaven . . . and maybe I didn't. I did not truly know or care where I was anymore after Alena whipped my body into submission. I counted four orgasms before she even let me give her any form of release—which she hardly let me do. She told me the night was mine for my first experience, and what a fantastic one it was. It was more than the physical pleasure. It was everything she did before that too.

It was the hotel, the dinner, the art museum. It was the way she read me poetry nearly every time I visited her just because she knew how much I enjoyed it. It was the way she cooked for me knowing that I was missing some of my favorite meals from home. The way she prepared tea, promising it would both cleanse my body and keep me warm. The care and gentleness in every action and word was all that I needed. She had undoubtedly made love to my mind for weeks before she even touched my body.

Hours later, the night came to a wonderful and satisfying end as we embraced in the dark. She asked how I was feeling and if anything had made me uncomfortable. She also wanted to know what I enjoyed the most and if there was anywhere she could improve. I protested when she left the bed to go to the bathroom, but she returned with a towel that was warm and used it to soothe the now overly sensitive area between my thighs. Once she finished, she curled up next to me and almost immediately drifted off to sleep.

I wish that we could've stayed up the entire night talking with one another. It would've been nice to listen to her voice, her laugh, and her heartbeat. Thankfully, I saw her in my dreams when I fell asleep.

♦ ♦

We were in a grass field and Alena rode a bike, her hair flying in the air. There was a rainbow in the sky, and I could feel that my face was sore from smiling. She pointed up where there was a bird soaring high in the distance. It sang the most beautiful tune as it roamed freely through the sky. I ran toward her when she got off the bike to stare up at the bird. As it disappeared into the sunlight, she looked down from it and smiled at me.

"I love you, Amelia," she said.

Chapter 15 Flashbacks

It seems that Alena made it her mission to further spoil me as soon as we left Charlotte. A few minutes into the drive, she directed me to search for a gift bag that was hidden somewhere in her backseat. After several moments of my blind fumbling through the thick, unused stargazing blankets that had fallen to the floor, I finally found it. Inside of the bag lay a handwritten letter as well as a miniature painting from the same artist of *Les Nombreux Femmes*. Women were once again the theme of the painting, but this time there was no fire; there were flowers and birds and grassy lands that reminded me of the dream I'd had the night before. I described it to her, forfeiting the part where she proclaimed her love for me, and she found it fascinating.

Once we arrived back at her apartment and made our way to the front door, I discovered yet another bouquet of roses that had been delivered to her doorstep. They were red this time and they came with a bear and chocolates. When we finally got settled inside, I opened the letter she'd written for me and read it out loud—as was her request—with a shaky voice.

It was a poem about us, but most of all about how I made her feel. It was endearing and even slightly sensuous but overall incredibly sweet. The letter ended with a *will you* at the end of it, which made me look up at her in confusion. She flashed me the most attractive smile, and I thought my heart might shatter from the pace it leapt to.

I held up the card for her to see, "It just says 'will you' at the end, what does that mean?" I asked her.

"*Will you* be my girlfriend?"

My breath caught in my throat, and I swallowed hard. "Are you sure?"

We were standing between the glass table and the sofa, closely facing one another. She stepped even closer. "One hundred percent." She looked simultaneously nervous and triumphant as she awaited my response.

"Yes, of course." I threw my arms around her neck, and she kissed me hard. We soon ended up naked once again in her bedroom, sharing the pleasure of ourselves with one another.

Throughout the next week and a half, I visited Alena almost daily. I was enthralled whenever I would catch her scribbling thoughtfully in the leather-bound journal I'd gifted her the morning after we first made love. The green journal was indented with a pattern of leaves and flowers, and she thought it was more than fitting for her.

I had spent most of my nights during this time cuddled up in Alena's arms—only after I'd finished all my assignments, volunteering, and whatever studying needed to be done. It was her single condition for me because of how seriously she's always taken education. She told me that it was her duty as an academic, or even just as a caring partner, to make sure that I stayed focused.

Despite the blissful moments with my new girlfriend, I still had difficulties with school's swiftly approaching end and my growing distance from my friends. I didn't neglect them for the sake of Alena, but the guilt from my lies weighed so heavily on me that it was extremely hard to face Mya or Gabe for too long.

I discovered that attending Alena's class after we'd had sex introduced yet another difficulty. My heart would race as I entered the room, and my body tensed as I waited to see the object of my affection. It didn't matter that every day since the trip I had seen her mere hours before class—smiling and laughing in her bed or gasping for air as she gulped down her orange juice in the kitchen after an early morning run. My eyes would search the room impatiently as Mya and I made our way to our usual seats—and when Alena finally entered my view, the world seemed to stand still. Every student in the class disappeared, including Mya, and all I could see was her: Alena in all her glory with her flowing head of curls, her sharp nose, full lips, and brown eyes.

I watched her elegant movements at the center of the auditorium and admired the way she took control of the class. When she pointed to the screen behind her, I examined the plethora of rings that always lined her fingers. She wore different rings on different fingers on different days, but I never quite figured out her formula for it. The longer she spoke, the deeper I got lost in the abyss.

I was stuck on the soothing rhythm of her voice, which all too easily brought me back to the sound of her moans of pleasure. I could almost feel her warmth and wetness on my fingers once again, could almost taste her succulent flavor on my tongue as I observed her, right there in the auditorium. I began seeing less of whatever elegantly planned outfit she had on and more of her rich, caramel skin, her brown areolas, and the soft folds below that I wished I could live between.

I had to look away during her lectures so I could keep my composure, though I still managed to innocently admire the crescent moon necklace above her breasts. A new sense of pride grew within me as a result of the silver bracelet I had gifted her, which was securely wrapped around her wrist during class.

Its anonymity held a charm to it that was both tantalizing and demoralizing in its own way. No one knew that it was from me. No one knew that I had likely seen, smelled, and tasted her before she walked in with a smile. No one knew. But she knew, and I knew.

Our final presentations for Alena were set to start the week after Thanksgiving break, and Mya and I would be one of the first groups to present. It was a daunting task to deal with my best friend, who had thankfully abandoned her relentless questions about my "strange moods" or "weird, distracted behaviors." Both of our workloads had kept us busy enough to not have much opportunity to visit one another off campus more than a handful of times in the last few weeks, but we still met in the library on occasion.

The weekend before break, she came over to my apartment so we could finish our final project. Neither of us wanted to work on it over Thanksgiving, so we were committed to getting it done by the end of the weekend.

We'd worked determinedly for two hours straight, and I didn't think anything of it when Mya told me she had to use the bathroom. I was so accustomed to her being at my place and walking through it like it was her own. The problem was that there was only one bathroom in my apartment, and to get to it you had to go through my bedroom.

When Mya walked back into the living room minutes later, she held my thriving bouquet of flowers in her hands and a challenge in her eyes. I'd left the yellow roses with Alena and had kept the red ones in my own apartment. Though I made it a point to hide them away in my room before Mya came—along with the bear tucked under my bedsheets—I had completely disregarded the possibility of her seeing them if she had to use the bathroom.

"Who are these from?" she asked daringly.

Shit! I jumped up from my spot on the mocha-brown couch and snatched away the bouquet. I then ran into my bedroom, slamming the door behind me. "Don't worry about who it's from, Amayah! You don't have to be so damn nosy all the time!" I roared through the door. I almost never used her full name, but I was particularly flustered from letting this slip past me.

"Amelia, I'm trying to be patient with your secretive ass, but I think you should tell me who you've been *fucking*!" she shouted in response.

I was too preoccupied to even entertain her further until I properly calculated any possible movements of the letter Alena had written me. I'd kept it in my room, fawning over it every single time I set foot in the apartment. I even gave it an air kiss before I left.

"It's gotta be someone—I know it!" Mya wailed through the door.

The letter was laying on the computer desk next to my bed where I had left it, and thankfully, it didn't appear to be tampered with. The flowers that Mya had found were previously placed by the windowsill on the opposite side of the desk, so I was still worried she might've seen it.

"You've had that look, Amelia," Mya said. "I can't believe you're trying to pretend that what I'm saying isn't the truth."

I trembled as I tucked the letter away in my drawer and repositioned the flowers next to the window. I had to take a few steadying breaths before I opened the door and faced my best friend.

"Mya, I am owed my privacy, okay? I told you it's complicated." I walked past her, my breath still faltering.

"That isn't fair!" she huffed, nostrils flaring. "I'm your best friend. Don't you trust me?"

"Yes, I do." I sat on the sofa and sunk down into its cushions. "I just . . ." My head lowered. "I'm not ready for you to look at me the way I know you will when I tell you."

She sat beside me, grabbed my hand, and looked me in the eyes. "Amelia, you're like a sister to me, and I love you. Whatever you're worried about won't matter enough to change that. Even if I might not like it, you can trust me with it." Her eyes idly traveled off to the side and back. "You really can't blame me for already not liking her though. Whoever the hell this is has clearly had you bugging out all semester." Her brows furrowed as she thought for a moment. "Actually, not the whole semester—but still most of it. Anyways, Amelia, you know me." She squeezed my hand. "You can tell me."

I don't know what possessed me to finally give up my secret or to do so without checking if Alena was still okay with it; I guess I just couldn't bear the pressure any longer. "Her name is," I paused and took in a breath. "Her name is Alena."

Mya's hand promptly dropped mine, and she backed away. "No, wait." Her hand came to her mouth. "You don't mean the only Alena that we know, right?" she asked with a smile that eventually faded due to my silence. "*Alena?*" she questioned again, believingly this time. "*The professor?*"

I nodded warily, wondering how many more titles she would've used if I didn't answer. She stood up and turned from me, staring into the kitchen. The hair from her messy bun fell idly onto the nape of her neck. She connected her fingers together on top of her head and lifted her chin toward the ceiling.

"She's my girlfriend," I murmured.

This revelation prompted Mya to whip her entire body around with her mouth hanging to the floor. "*Professor Hutchinson is your girlfriend?!*" she squealed out. She paced the room now, eyes closed. "Wait." Her eyes flew back open, and she stepped toward me. "Isn't she *married*, Amelia?!" she shrieked in what I assumed to be a sudden remembrance.

"Yes." I stood and held out my hands in surrender. "She is, but I promise you it's not like that."

"How could you do this to her wife? That poor woman," she whispered.

"Mya! I can explain it if you just give me a chance." I tried my best to deescalate the situation. Mya, of course, had a strong disdain for any type of cheating and rightfully so.

"Does she know about you?" she asked critically.

"I—I don't know. She knows that Alena has been seeing *someone*. I don't think she knows that it's me because at Beck's—"

"You saw her at Beck's?!" Mya interrupted.

I really should've measured every word more carefully before they exited my mouth. Unfortunately, I was now telling it all, and it wasn't coming out the way I intended.

"Yeah, I did—but it was by accident, Mya! This whole thing really was." I stepped closer to her. "Please just sit down so I can tell you everything. I feel like you're about to walk away, and I don't want that."

"I really don't understand this, Amelia," she started. "But I know—or at least I hope I know—you wouldn't be as messy as you sound right now." She momentarily resigned and settled onto the couch. "How long has this been going on?" She folded her arms. "Whatever this is . . ."

I remained standing. "I didn't know I had feelings for her until the middle of September." I played with the fabric of my pants as my teeth tugged at the bottom of my lips.

"So, you two didn't know each other before the school year started?" she questioned.

"No, of course not. I would've told you that."

"Would you have?" Her brow raised and skepticism remained on her face.

It was a fair remark, given the circumstances, so I didn't dispute it. "I had this dream about . . . her and I. And I accidentally told her too much about it one day when I was in her office." I left out the part where I didn't tell Mya about the dream either, even when I wanted to. "She was shocked, but we both ended up sharing a mutual attraction."

"Her wife be damned," Mya curtly interjected.

"I'm getting to that, Mya! It isn't Alena's fault that her wife won't sign the divorce papers. She still wants to be with Alena, so she won't do it." I huffed and sat down on the sofa.

"That's what she told you, huh?" she said, leaning away from me.

I tried not to react adversely to my friend, but I also didn't like her questioning the morals of the woman I loved. "Yes, and I know it for a fact," I declared. "Alena's *been* unhappy with her wife and has tried leaving her for nearly a year now. She just refuses to give up and sign it."

Her eyes narrowed. "Professor Hutchinson can take further legal action for that you know." I winced internally at her use of the formal name.

"She can, but she doesn't want to if she doesn't have to. She already doesn't like anyone else having to be involved as it is."

"Yet she involved *you*." Mya's voice was as sharp as a sword.

I blinked at her wordlessly, considering the accuracy of the implication.

Mya stood back up. "Why didn't you tell me anything? You could've said something instead of keeping this bottled up all semester." Her scowl would've cracked the bridge of her nose in half if it were any sharper.

"I was scared," I admitted silently. "I wanted to, Mya. I just didn't know how." If looks could kill, I would've been buried alive by her glare. "Alena could get in so much trouble if anyone said anything," I continued. "I didn't know—"

Mya scoffed. "Do you honestly think I would snitch on you? Do I really seem that judgmental?"

"Notice how you reacted to her still being married when you always talk about how well you know me."

"How the hell else should I react to that, Amelia?"

"How would you react to any professor dating their student while the student is still in their class? What's your first instinct, Mya? Tell me you don't think it's wrong. Married or not."

Her lips stayed pressed tightly together, and she nodded. "You know, you're right about that." She maneuvered toward her laptop and books, and my heart dropped. She seized the bookbag that hung on one of my bar stools and began furiously packing.

"Mya," I muttered weakly as I stood again.

She didn't speak until she was finished packing. When she turned around to face me, her eyes were watery. "I'm trying to understand why you would lie to me, Amelia, because that's exactly what you've been doing." She spoke with a strained voice.

I was frozen in place and my lips were parted, but I couldn't speak.

"You've been distant and weird and defensive, and it's all because of our *professor*?" She wiped a tear that seemed to fall without her permission. "I feel like such an idiot."

The blood in my body went cold and still. "Mya, you're not an idiot," I protested.

"But I believed you," she whispered.

There was an ache in my chest as I stepped toward her, but she stuck out her hand to stop me.

"We can finish the project another day. I don't want to talk to you anymore right now." She kept her head down as she walked to the door. I watched her as she left my apartment, and when she was gone, my eyes finally squeezed shut.

Tears trickled down my cheeks as I stumbled my way back to the sofa, and my body shuddered as I cried. I had finally told my best friend about my relationship with our professor. The damage was done.

Chapter 16 Turkey Talk

Thanksgiving break was finally here, and I was absolutely dreading returning to my hometown for the week. My desire to damn near be living inside of Alena's skin was the greatest disadvantage of the break—but as if being away from her were not enough, I would also have to endure four and a half days with my stern, judgmental mother.

I reclined on my favorite side of Alena's plush sofa while she moved around the kitchen fixing a bowl of chips and salsa. Like several other professors, she had canceled her classes tomorrow, which was the Tuesday before our break. As a result, I had no reason to prepare for school again until we returned the next week.

"I don't want to go back to South Carolina," I whined pitifully to Alena. "I wish I could just stay here for Thanksgiving."

"There won't even be anything to do here, Amelia." She shook her head. "Your friends are going home, and I'm going to Colorado. Mostly everyone is going somewhere for the break," she reminded me level-headedly.

What friends? I wasn't sure Mya even considered herself as my friend anymore, and perhaps Gabe wouldn't either, whenever I was able to brave telling him about my secret relationship with Alena.

"Regardless, it's good for you to be with your family once in a while. I'm sure they miss you a lot." She placed a small dish of salsa on the coffee table before plopping down next to me. Her perfume filled the space around us as she lounged beside me with the large plastic bowl of tortilla chips in hand.

"My family hardly even likes my gay ass," I further complained, before inhaling deeply so I could cover my lungs with her scent. I grabbed a chip from the bowl.

"Correct me if I'm wrong, but no one in your family even knows that you're gay in the first place," she commented. "Especially not your parents."

"Not definitively, but it should be an easy guess at this point." I grabbed one of her curls and kneaded it between my fingers. "Besides, they don't have to know that I'm gay to not like me," I continued solemnly. "Ever since I left for college we've had issues because they don't really like the person I'm becoming."

"Do *you* like that person?" she asked.

"Mostly." I shrugged, dropping the curl.

"Then it doesn't really matter what they think about it." She finished one more chip before offering me the bowl. When I declined, she placed it on the table. "How you feel about yourself is more important than how anyone else feels about you, Amelia," she stated firmly.

"Thanks." I gave her shoulder a squeeze. "I know you're right, but it's still hard for me. I used to care so much about their approval, and I guess it's just hard to let that go."

She sighed lightly and caressed my cheek. "It's just one of those things, Amelia."

"Yeah . . . I just wish it didn't have to be." I frowned for a moment before forcing myself to perk up. "But enough of my complaints. Tell me all about Colorado! Have you been before?" I clasped my hands together and cast aside my somber emotions. I wanted Alena's good fortune to be front and center instead of my discouraging family issues.

"I've only been once or twice. They were small hiking trips when I was much younger, so I don't clearly remember them." A wide smile took over her face. "But my brother just mentioned this train ride through Royal Gorge Canyon that he got us tickets for! There's going to be beautiful mountain views and wine—and did I mention the train ride already?!" she cheered as she leaned closer to me. "I'm so excited for it. If it's good I'll make sure to book us a trip sometime—maybe next year," she added. Alena spoke with so much certainty about a future that existed for us beyond my time at the university, and it made my heart beat with an extra pulsation of joy.

"I'm sure it'll be beautiful." I smiled. "Make sure you send me pictures, okay?"

"I wouldn't dare forget!" she declared with a vigor in her voice. "I want pictures of you and your family too," she cooed, sinking back into the couch.

"Okay. For you I will." I sank back too. "I think I may finally tell them though. I always said that I would do it once I had a girlfriend." I took her hand casually and played with her rings.

"If you're ready to do that, Amelia, I stand by you one hundred percent. But if you aren't, you should wait."

"I'm pretty sure I'm ready." I brought her hand to my lips and kissed her soft skin. "The quicker they get over it, the quicker I can show you off to them." I smiled cunningly. "I'm going to give them the 'turkey talk!' It's like the birds and the bees except it's the *shes* and the *shes*."

Alena erupted in laughter. "Where the hell do you even come up with this kind of stuff, Amelia?"

"I don't know." I giggled alongside her.

She leaned her head on my shoulder, and I wrapped both of my arms around her body. I pretended to accidentally catch one of her breasts along the way. "Oops, I'm sorry," I murmured.

"No you're not," she countered, still leaning lazily into me while I gently rocked her. "I'm going to fall asleep if we stay like this." She yawned. "Have you spoken with Mya again?"

The mention of her name sent an involuntary rippling through my body that prompted Alena to sit straight up. I immediately felt the urge to cry like I had already done an embarrassing amount of times since I released my secret to Mya.

"We finished the project earlier today," I lamented. "Then she canceled our friends' dinner for tomorrow evening that we planned over a month ago." My lips quivered.

"Oh, baby, I'm sorry." She held me close to her.

"I don't think she'll even talk to me until after the break," I added with a weakened voice. "She won't even text me back."

Alena sighed. "She just needs some time, Amelia."

"I shouldn't have lied to her." Alena had heard me say these words at least a hundred times now, but they continued to reign true.

She wiped the tears that slid down my cheek and kissed my forehead. "It'll be okay," she promised.

I nodded and drank in a deep breath, exhaling slowly. "So, are you ready to watch that 'seductive-lesbian-killer show' that you said was good?" I asked. I desperately needed something to both distract me and cheer me up, and nothing was better for that than cuddles and a good plot with Alena.

"You mean *Killing Eve*? If you are, then yes." She stood up, pulling me with her. "I'll get the popcorn. You get the wine." She flashed me a warming smile.

The popcorn exploded wildly in the microwave while I fumbled with the wine opener and cork, cursing underneath my breath. Alena watched me for a moment with her arms crossed and her head shaking before finally taking over. She popped the cork with ease and set the wine back on the counter with a clank. "I *must* teach you to do better with opening that," she said.

I turned in her direction, sporting a charming grin. "I'm sure there are *plenty* of things you can teach me." I turned from her before I could see the expression on her face. I imagined shock or, better yet, intrigue. Alena usually one-upped me in the flirting game, but I still liked to play.

I retrieved two wine glasses from the cabinet and set them down before I scooped the wine bottle off the counter. I carelessly swung it around as I danced to a nonexistent tune before Alena hastily snatched it from my hand.

"Amelia, you're going to drop the bottle acting silly like that," she censured, pouring the wine into the glasses while I jumped up on the counter. When she was finished, she set the two glasses on either side of me then opened the microwave and placed the bag of popcorn nearby.

"Let's make a toast, shall we?" I exuberantly suggested, thanks to my random burst of energy.

"What to?" she asked smugly, cornering me where I sat on the counter.

My heart paced faster, and my energetic confidence momentarily faltered as I looked at her soft lips only inches from me. "T-to our beautiful new relationship," I barely managed to get out. "Also to Thanksgiving because I am *very* thankful for you," I added, a lot more clearly.

Her head moved forward, and my lips grabbed hers with fervency. "I'm thankful for you too, Amelia." The *a* at the end of my name rolled off her tongue as if it were a feather floating in the sky. "Mmm," she moaned. "I love the smell of fresh, hot popcorn. I'm not sure what I want to eat more right now," she continued softly. "*That* or *you*." Her eyes held a challenge in them.

I wanted to say, "Por qué no los dos?" but I wasn't sure how much she knew of Spanish, and I also didn't know how forward I felt like being tonight. "You can have whatever you want after the show," I assured her.

Her head nodded, and she backed away. "After the show," she purred. "Right. I have to stay focused, don't I?"

"Precisely," I agreed shakily.

"Before we get to that though," she leaned back toward me, "I need you to tell me what you think of this wine." She picked up the glass and swirled the wine. "It's red but it's sweet, the way you prefer things to be." She put the glass to my lips, and I drank. "How does that taste?" she asked in an even tone that still managed to stir me. There was something unsettling about the question because of her close proximity to me as well as the underlying quality of her words.

"It's good. What's it called?" I aimlessly tried to look past her body and hair to the bottle.

"It's Lambrusco. I haven't had it in a while, so I'll have a little taste too."

She tipped the glass back in my direction, and I was fairly confused as I sipped and swallowed it again. She then set the glass down and slowly traced her tongue across the entirety of my lips. A familiar tune of urgency continued once again in my heart.

"That *is* good," she agreed, picking up the glass and popcorn before sauntering back to the sofa.

I stared after her before I slid off the counter, grabbed my wine, and followed. I set my glass on the coffee table and couldn't help but stare at her, although she had already turned on the television and started the show.

"What?" She finally acknowledged me a few minutes in and smirked knowingly. "Did you want some?" She held up the bag of popcorn.

What I wanted was to pounce on her right then and there, but I somehow maintained my composure. "No, I'm fine. I'm going to get changed though, I'll be right back."

I returned to her in a pair of shorts and a brown crop top, but she didn't acknowledge me. She kept her attention focused on the show.

I knew it had to be a good one because Nova recommended it to her, but there were currently far more important things on my mind.

This craving surging through my core had not left me since the first time I became aware of it. The emptiness after being filled was enough to make me damn near beg for it. I knew I needed to feel it again. I needed Alena back inside of me.

"You're going to get cold in that," she cautioned, setting down the popcorn and pulling me close to her with a hand on my ass.

"I'm actually pretty hot," I countered with the slightest tinge of impatience in my voice.

She chuckled and turned in my direction. "Isn't this the show *you* wanted to watch tonight?" she asked mockingly. "You might want to pay attention to it."

"That's definitely not what I want right now." The tone of my voice surprised even me.

She lifted her brow and looked at me, her eyes perceptive. "What *do* you want then?" she asked seductively.

"I want you inside of me, Alena."

It was all I needed to say to her. Hardly any time passed before she pulled me onto her lap and kissed my mouth and neck while needily clutching at my sparsely covered body. Apparently, I still had on too much clothing for her liking. She quickly removed the brown top and hooked her hands around the shorts as her tongue parted my lips.

Her hand slid down my back to my bare skin underneath the thin fabric of the shorts. She reached between my thighs and easily made contact with my delicate flesh without the nuisance of any undergarments. As she lightly pressed her fingers against my sensitive nub, I could feel my body melting. I was malleable like putty when I was in her hands, and the drip from between my thighs was like hot candle wax.

Her lips pulled away from mine, and she determinedly slid off the rings from two of her fingers. "Sit down, Amelia," she ordered, but she didn't wait for me to follow her request. She gripped my hips and pushed me down so my legs were opened on her lap. Her left arm braced me around the back and her right hand caressed my neck, massaged my breasts, then carefully thumbed my clit through the leg-opening of my shorts.

I wriggled on her lap as her fingers trailed over my slit. "So wet for me," she purred contentedly. She entered me slowly, delving deeper and deeper—then thrusting at a steady, rhythmic pace. As she continued, I began impatiently bucking my hips to meet her strokes.

"*No, no,*" she verbally disapproved. "Amelia, do *not* move."

I was surprised at her insistence, but I submitted to her immediately and fought the urge to continue my movements. I despised every brutalizing instant where her fingers were no longer inside of me. It seemed an eternity before they returned only to leave me empty again moments later.

I hadn't known just how painfully pleasurable such a simple thing could be. She denied me release, but the buildup was enticing. I wasn't allowed to maneuver my body over the edge, and she did little to help me over it herself. I was stuck in an orgasmic limbo, praying for some form of relief which finally came when she tucked her lips into my neck. Her warm breath tickled me as she spoke. *"Are you ready?"* were her words, but I don't remember much of what came after that once she sped up her pursuit.

She provided enough pressure for me to cross the threshold I had been longing for. In less than a minute my body trembled mightily, and I clung to her for dear life. I lost myself in the currents of my pleasure and began to think about how improbable my present situation was.

Alena was the woman I had found alluring since the second day of the semester. She was the woman whose office I had frequented countless times and who I had accidentally fallen head over heels for. She was my *professor* who should have only been giving me grades, academic advice, and recommendation letters. But here she was now, giving me a bounty of butterflies and a plethora of orgasms. Her power was infinite.

My eyes watered as I came down from an undeniable high, my body growing limp beneath me. I rested my head over her shoulders while still in her lap. I involuntarily clenched once more as she removed her fingers from me. They went directly into her mouth and then she kissed me tenderly, with none of the aggression previously ascribed to the encounter.

"Alena," I breathed out, spent from the pleasure.

She took my mostly naked body into her arms and held me close. "I love you, Amelia," she whispered into my ear, and for a moment I thought I was dreaming again.

My heart ached as I questioned her, "You do?"

"So much." Her hands rubbed the length of my bare back.

I pulled away so I could look into her eyes. "I love you too," I whispered with a smile before surrendering to my emotions. Alena stroked the coils on my head and wiped the tears out of my eyes.

In the softness of her face was an adoration that was different from before, and I knew without a doubt that this woman would go to war for me. She would stand by me, protect me, and love me.

"When did you know?" she asked.

"Right before the trip," I admitted timidly. "I didn't want to tell you right away because I knew you might not have been ready for me to say it. I just didn't want to add any stress." A shiver overtook my body as my bare skin began to miss the warmth of my clothes.

"Your love is far from stressful to me, darling," she cooed, grabbing a blanket and wrapping it around me. She kissed my forehead. "I knew I loved you when I was planning the trip, but I wasn't sure if I was moving too fast for myself. It's honestly even scarier now that I know you feel the same way."

"Why?" I asked delicately.

Her intense gaze did not falter. "Because I'm afraid to love again."

"Because of Teresa?" I asked, already understanding, and she nodded.

"I know you're not her, but I'm still wounded. I'm still holding back parts of myself from you, and it isn't fair that I am because of everything you've been willing to give."

"Things like that take time, Alena." I sounded sure but a wave of uncertainty slowly spread through my body. I knew that a failed relationship usually required a certain amount of healing before moving on to someone new, but I didn't have a clue about what was needed for a failed marriage.

"I know." She sighed. "It doesn't help that I've struggled to believe your feelings for me from the start. It's been quite the internal battle because I know the type of lover I am. I give my all, and I don't want to make the same mistakes right after getting out of one set of them. But I also know without a doubt, Amelia, that you are genuine. You've really allowed me to trust and to believe in someone again." She smiled even though her eyes were welling up with tears.

I lifted my finger up to stroke her cheek. "Don't doubt me, Alena. I love you, and I want to be with you." When I placed a kiss on her lips, the wonderful smell of her perfume began to distract me. Our bodies drew closer as I deepened the kiss, and I couldn't help but remember my nakedness. Alena's nipples were poking me through her shirt, and I much preferred to have them and the rest of her body on my tongue. I pulled away.

"God, Alena, I need to taste you." My face felt hot as I bit down on my lip and looked into her eyes. Going down on her was something I hadn't done before.

A wave of shock briefly swept over her face, but then she smirked as she tightened the blanket around me. "Are you sure you can handle such a delicacy?" she questioned boldly.

"I guess I'll just have to find out, won't I?"

She chuckled as she stood me upright. "Okay."

I kissed her lips and held her close to me. "You're still wearing too many clothes."

"We should do something about that, shouldn't we?"

The two of us made our way into her bedroom where she lit a candle on either side of the bed while I rid myself of my shorts. I then slowly removed every item of clothing she wore, down to the remaining rings on her fingers.

"That's much better." I licked my lips as I examined her naked body from head to toe. My eyes lingered on a wetness on her inner thighs that I only noticed once she was lying flat on her back. I wasn't sure if it had come from her or me.

I knelt above her and pressed my lips to her forehead and cheeks before traveling lower. My lips went from her neck to her shoulders then down to her breasts and nipples. I kissed a line down her stomach and roughly smoothed my hands over her thighs. She seemed to enjoy whenever I wasn't as gentle with her as I preferred to be, so I indulged her in that. I kissed on each thigh several times over and grabbed her legs, pushing them so her knees were bent and her feet were planted on the mattress.

I could see a quiet yet fiery anticipation in her eyes as I looked up at her from between her legs. After building my confidence for an entire week, I was all too eager to taste her—but it was important for me to ensure that she enjoyed receiving more than I enjoyed giving. The last thing I wanted to do was to be so enthusiastic that she didn't get enough pleasure from it. "Teach me what you like," I tentatively suggested.

"I want to see what you have in mind first," she replied. "Then I'll let you know as you go."

I nodded my head before leaning forward and inhaling her erotic scent. I realized then that the smell of her usual perfume meant nothing to me. My mouth watered as I nudged the nub hidden between her legs with the tip of my nose. I then planted soft, lingering kisses around the area and used my fingers to unfold her like the petals of a flower.

I wanted to take her in visually as much as I did in every other way, so I took my time admiring her. I had given her pleasure before, but never like this, and I was greatly anticipating having Alena at the mercy of my mouth.

Her breaths were heavy by the time I dragged my tongue across the crease of her lower lips. The sound she made encouraged me further, and I looked up to see her head tilted back and her teeth set to the bottom of her lips.

"Is that okay?" I asked softly.

"Just fine," she whispered in a ragged breath, tilting her head back down to look me in the eyes. "Keep going."

I kept my tongue flat as I traced her entrance again. I then began to focus my attention on her clit, softly lapping at the sensitive button. My movements were methodical, and it appeared to be pleasurable for her—but it was also clear that she was yearning for more.

Her gorgeous brown eyes stayed on me as she lay there, clenching the bedsheets and arching herself up whenever I dared to slow in the slightest. I did my best to keep up the pace while she writhed in pleasure—and I eventually had the inclination to feel the smoothness of her insides once again, but with both my fingers and tongue in succession.

To feel the slick, velvety wetness the first time was reminiscent of a miracle. She was warm and soft, and I loved every moment of being inside of her. I already knew that she enjoyed it tremendously as a singular action, but I wondered if she would appreciate it the same way in the midst of me devouring her.

I cautiously slid a finger across her slit, my tongue keeping focused attention on her clit. This prompted a coarse release of her breath. I kept grazing my fingers along the area and assessing her reactions which grew increasingly exasperated. Before I could even do it on my own accord, she took my hand and guided two fingers inside of her.

I created a new pacing between the flickering of my tongue and the thrusting of my fingers, and it wasn't long before she called for another. I was now three fingers deep inside of her, and I could feel that her walls had stretched to accommodate me. When she further tightened around me, a wonderful flood of wetness surrounded.

"Faster," she pleaded. Her hand hovered over my head, but she refrained from pushing down on me. I could tell that she wanted to be gentle just as much as she wanted me to feast on her with more conviction.

I couldn't get over the flavor of her, and though I was the one giving the pleasure, I began moaning. It was not purposeful at all, but it seemed to be just what she needed to make it over the edge. Her body shuddered harshly as she cursed aloud, and I was rewarded with more of her sweet juices as she shook into me. When she finished trembling, I licked her clean while her subsequent aftershocks and mini moans of pleasure satisfied me once more.

She lifted her head as I moved from between her legs—and once I knelt over her, she kissed me determinedly, licking my mouth empty of any traces of her. "You were absolutely wonderful," she commended breathlessly.

"You *taste* wonderful," I responded. "Did you really like it?"

"Yes," she assured me with a single nod. "And . . . I like it when you're a little rough with me, Amelia," she admitted.

A grin spread across my face as I lowered myself onto the bed, swiping her leg with my previously unrecognized wetness along the way.

"Is everything alright down there?" she questioned mischievously.

"Apparently not," I confessed between clenched teeth.

She looked directly into my eyes as she took two fingers and swiped them across my pussy; it caused me to tremble. "Do you like that?" she asked tenderly.

I answered with a kiss that knocked her backward onto the pillows. While we used our lips to exchange the many languages of our love, her fingers found my dripping entrance once again. She entered me and sent an instant wave of shock through my system. My body moved on her fingers involuntarily while my lips held pace with hers, and I moaned as she slowly decimated my walls.

The way that the candlelight glinted off her moon necklace eventually captured my attention. I lifted the moon with my finger before sliding the same finger across her chest. I then got distracted and couldn't help but wrap my hand around her perfectly contoured neck while I ground myself down on her fingers. I held her neck gently, my thumb caressing the soft skin, and I was utterly transfixed on the beautiful woman fucking me.

"Everything about you is perfection," I panted out, my body momentarily relaxing with her still inside of me.

A devilish smile emerged from her mouth. "Amelia," she sighed, "You're going to have to hold my neck tighter than that."

I stiffened my grip in response then smirked as I cocked my head to the side. At this her eyes shifted. I had unlocked a fierceness in her. She quickly exited me, lifted me up, and then slammed me onto my back with minimal effort. My hands now lay at my sides and my mouth was open wide in disbelief as I stared up at her.

"Did you want to try something else new tonight?" she asked in a sultry tone, holding a hand to my chest as she began to straddle me.

"If it'll take away the ache," I answered, grinning wistfully.

"For a little while at least," she said, kissing my forehead. "Bend your knees."

I followed her instruction, and she pushed my legs farther apart. My body swirled with anticipation as I watched her thighs spread open above me. I could see how wet she was again as she carefully lowered herself onto me, and I gasped once our bodies finally connected.

"How does that feel?" she asked, breathing heavily.

"God, you're so wet," I whispered, unable to speak any louder. My hands slid up her stomach and cupped her breasts. "It feels good." She rolled her hips against me then, and I moaned.

"You're so beautiful," she rasped as she moved her hand over and twisted my nipples before pushing her hips forward, again and again. I struggled to breathe as I rode the currents of deep pleasure coursing through my body with each of her movements against me. She didn't have any more words for me, but her eyes spoke volumes.

We grinded against each other for what felt like hours before we both met a nearly simultaneous release. I then held her naked body close to mine and wished not to dream this time. The truth of her presence was enough to satisfy me through the night.

Chapter 17 Homestretch

"Did you grab the eggs?" my mom asked anxiously as I made my way toward her with two bags of dinner rolls and a bag of sweet potatoes.

"Uh, my hands are kind of full, Mom." I swung the bag of potatoes over the cart and set the rolls as far away as I could from anything heavy.

"Amelia! That could've been tucked in your arms." She shook her head and hurriedly rolled the cart toward the cold section.

I followed her as she knowledgeably sped through the aisles, the small ringlets on her curly pixie cut shaking along the way. "Why are you always so last minute anyways?" I complained as she searched for a carton among the few egg crates left.

"I'm not! I got most of the supplies during the weekend, but you can never have too much when there's company." She frowned as she picked up another carton. "I think all of these are cracked."

I picked up a random carton and opened it, grinning when I noticed that every egg was perfectly shaped and unbroken. "Here." I held the eggs out to her.

Her eyes widened as she examined the box then her brows furrowed. "Of course you would find it on the first try."

We left the store twenty minutes later with an abundance of

groceries. After loading the car, I sank into the passenger seat and yawned with outstretched arms. I didn't want to be up this early making food runs with my mom, but she had whined about us hardly having any time to bond together. On top of that, I needed to butter her up because I was going to tell both her and my father that I had a girlfriend sometime in the next three or four days.

She looked satisfied as she exuberantly entered the car and slammed the door behind her. "See. I told you the early bird gets the worm." She started the vehicle, and heat blasted on us.

"The day before Thanksgiving is not early," I reminded her flatly.

"Oh, that doesn't matter!" She waved her hand to the side. "I think you might have the wrong holiday too—by the way. Christmas is next month, *Scrooge*."

"Hey!" I pouted my lips for a moment before we both erupted in laughter.

"Thanks for coming with me. I miss having one of my oldest children around. Your younger brother and sister are driving me mad."

"Don't be dramatic," I snorted.

"I'm not! Your brother hardly ever listens anymore, and you haven't seen little miss teen's newly developed attitude. It's horrendous."

"I'm sure they got it from somewhere," I muttered pointedly while gesturing at her.

"You're right." She smiled. "They got it from your father's side."

I thought of Alena as we bumped along the paved roads, watching the leafless trees pass by. She was likely sleeping peacefully right at this moment after another eventful day with her family. When she called me the night before, it sounded like she was having a great time with her nieces. She was watching after them while her brother and his wife were on a date, so they were up well past their bedtime, playing with their favorite aunt. It would only be around six in the morning now in Colorado, so I didn't expect a message from her any time soon.

"Amelia, I have to ask," my mom started. "Is there anyone special I should know about this holiday season?" Her curved, left brow lifted up as she awaited my answer.

"Am *I* not enough, Mom?" I asked in a dramatic, quivering voice.

"You know exactly what I meant, Amelia." She rolled her eyes and returned her attention to the road.

My phone buzzed in my pocket then—and I readily checked it, hoping that Mya might message me today. She hadn't spoken to me since we finished the project, and I felt helpless on how to better the situation between us. Gabe had, of course, heard about our dispute by now, but he didn't know the reason behind it. Since both he and Mya were from Florida, they were carpooling for Thanksgiving break. The last I'd heard from Gabe was that she was still upset and didn't want to talk to me, so all I could do was wait and continue to give her the space she requested.

It was Alena's number that popped up when I unlocked my phone. She had sent me two messages that made me perk up immediately. My cheeks warmed as I looked at the picture she'd sent of her sleepily smiling along with two other people, who I remembered was her brother and his wife. They looked unreasonably happy for the time of morning it was in Colorado. I scrolled up to her first message which mentioned that she was up early for a morning run with them and that it was freezing cold there. Another message then flashed across the screen:

Alena♥ (10:10 a.m.)
How is your morning going, my love? ☺

Instead of responding, my eyes were still transfixed on the image she'd sent before it. Everyone in the picture wore athletic clothing, but I was singularly fixated on the white, spandex top around my girlfriend's torso. I eventually noticed a chandelier and a regal staircase in the background of the picture as well. Alena had once described to me how nice her parents' home was, but I still didn't expect the level of regality that I spotted in the picture.

I began to text her back a plethora of heart eyes and fire emojis, but before I could send them, I heard the noisy sound of my mom clearing her throat. When I turned in her direction, her face was overly smug.

"There *is* someone," she said, now letting a smile wrap around the length of her face. "Please tell me about him, Amelia, I beg you!" she howled.

Here we go. I bashfully clicked off my phone and slid it back into my pocket. "Don't get your hopes up," I warned. "But just know that I'm happy, Mom." I would've undoubtedly been a vibrant shade of red if my skin was not as dark as it was.

She giggled like a schoolgirl and shook in her seat. "*Finally*! Bring him home for Christmas, will you?! We can have a—"

"Whoa, whoa! Slow down there, Mom. I'm not bringing anybody home this soon." I stopped her in her tracks. My excitement for my new lover didn't overpower my wits. This was something *new*. Meeting the family was currently far from my mind, and it had nothing to do with my fears of bringing home a woman instead of a man.

"Don't be a bore, Amelia," she sneered. "At least invite him. He may want to come."

She, I thought forcefully, *it's she*. I sighed and pinched the bridge of my nose. My saving grace was the forthcoming arrival at our home. I calmed down as my mom turned into the neighborhood, and I admired the beautiful houses in the brilliance of the sunlight. It had rained the entire day before—when I'd made it back home—so it was nice to see everything more clearly.

We pulled into an oversized driveway surrounded by freshly low-cut grass, trimmed bushes, and hibernating trees. The house was mainly covered in gray brick but also had splashes of white stucco on some of its surfaces. Pumpkins decorated the porch, along with the kind of lights you would see for Christmas, and the yard had two turkey flags pitched into the grass. It seemed highly unnecessary to me to have Thanksgiving decorations outside, but my mom was in love with the holiday just about as much as she was in love with Christmas.

Calling this place home still felt fairly new to me, although I had technically lived here during the summers since the beginning of college. Despite it not being the home I grew up in—it was probably three times the size of that actually—it was finally starting to feel homey.

My mom's red Hyundai Genesis was parked outside our three-car garage while my dad's car and my siblings' shared car were already parked inside. My mom pulled the family SUV into the final spot—and when she turned off the engine we both sat there, silently standing off with one another while the garage door slowly closed behind us.

"Promise me you'll invite him," she pressed with a serious expression.

"Not going to happen." I turned and opened the door.

"Now, here is the best dish of the holiday season!" I broadcasted, carrying a large pan of baked macaroni to the dining table. Cherene followed me with a serving dish of sweet potato casserole and Jordan followed directly behind her with the dinner rolls.

"That must be *so* heavy, Jordan," I taunted my older brother as I set down my wonderful creation. "He's making you do all the heavy lifting." I directed my words at his wife, Cherene, while rolling my eyes.

"Ha-ha, Amelia. You're so hilarious," Jordan snickered.

Cherene giggled and patted his shoulder comfortingly.

"That's enough," My mom said, walking in with the turkey—my dad behind her with a dish of gravy.

Guess I know where he gets it from, I scowled. But the men in my family weren't actually that bad. The previous day my mother's contempt over my nonexistent boyfriend was short-lived because my father and my "horrible" younger siblings had tidied the house while we were away.

My mom's precious kitchen was spotless which caused her to be jovial for the remainder of the day while she prepped stuffed peppers, greens, and her famous sweet potato pie. I'd spent most of that day catching up with my teen siblings and hearing their stories of sneaking out and going to parties with their friends. Evidently, my parents had loosened up far more than I thought from when Jordan and I were their age. Jordan and Cherene had arrived later that evening from Texas with their two-year-old, Ashanti. She was one of the cutest human beings I knew, and I was as proud of an aunty as I could possibly be.

Everyone situated themselves around the large mahogany table in my parents' luxurious dining room. All eyes were fixated on the display of food. Pinky lazily lay in the corner of the room, already knowing she would not get any of the food she was smelling. The light from the antique chandelier above the table shined on the auburn-colored tablecloth that had been hand-stitched by my grandmother. I was disappointed to hear that she wouldn't be coming for Thanksgiving since she was having a "destination holiday" with my uncle's family, but she would be visiting us for Christmas, so I'd get to see her soon.

"I am so thankful that we are all here together," My mom started. "It's just so wonderful to see all my children here in one room again. And my sole grandbaby." She wiggled a finger in Ashanti's direction. "Hopefully one day I'll be able to have some more of those." She glanced toward me with narrowed eyes.

"Let's say a prayer," my dad suggested, halting my mom's unnecessary musings. Afterward, we each uttered a specific message of thanks—one by one. The feasting then began, and time passed at a quicker pace amidst all the laughter, eating, and wine drinking for the adults.

"Amelia, you make a mean baked mac," my dad complimented me as we ate.

I smiled with a little extra emotion due to the wine. "Thank you."

"Yes!" my mom agreed. "Any man would be happy to have you cooking for him."

Fuck. My jaw went taut, and my heart began to beat faster while a slow-roasting anger filled my body. My younger brother, A.J., looked at me knowingly and smirked. Just about everyone at the table assessed my reaction because my mom had purposefully thrown out hints of my dating status throughout the entire dinner. I had *just* verbally asked her to resign, so this was the last straw.

I took in a deep, too-calm breath. "Well," I said evenly, "that would be a bit difficult, Mom. First of all, I'm nobody's chef. Second of all, it would be extremely hard for *me* to make *any* man happy."

"You have to be more confident than that, Amelia," she criticized, clearly ignoring the obvious fact that she had pushed my buttons one too many times.

My dad joined in—likely in an attempt to quell my impulsive mouth. "Justine, she doesn't want to talk about this."

"Alex, darling, she's fine. A mother knows."

"You don't know a damn thing," I spat out carelessly.

"Excuse you?!" my parents shrieked in unison.

My older brother exchanged looks with his wife and my siblings with each other.

"You must both be clueless," I continued, though my words were a little less impassioned now. "Don't you understand that there will never be a man for me?" I looked at them pleadingly.

Their previously angered response turned into full on confusion. "What are you talking about, Amelia?" my father asked.

"I never had a boyfriend. I'm never going to have a boyfriend, and it's not because I lack self-esteem."

Every eye around the table waited for me to make sense of what I was saying. Even the two-year-old looked from her parents to her grandparents to me, then she giggled and clapped her hands.

"I'm gay," I said.

The clatter of my mom's fork crashing onto her ceramic plate sounded loudly in the otherwise silent room.

Chapter 18 Resolutions

"Just like that?! *I'm gay.*" Gabe repeated my words, imitating my voice.

"Yeah, I gotta admit the delivery was pretty awful. And I nearly got thrown out of my house when I told my mom she didn't know a damn thing about me."

Gabe's eyes grew large. "You told her *what*?! Dammit, Amelia, I want to be invited next year. I could definitely help ease the tension between everyone. Just make sure to tell your parents that *I'm* not your man beforehand." He winked at me.

"I appreciate that, Gabriel, but *I* would first have to be invited next year in order to invite you," I joked, though the pain in my tone was noticeable.

"I'm sure this won't change your invitation status, Amelia." He patted my back soothingly, then his face grew serious, and his bushy brows pressed together. "I'm proud of you, my friend." He put his arms around me and gave me a hug.

An unexpected knock at my apartment door prompted our heads to snap in that direction. Our eyes met before Gabe stood up to check who it was. He peeked through the peephole before glancing back toward me with a smile.

"It's Mya." He opened the door to reveal her standing there with a plastic container in her hands. Her shoulders were hunched underneath her green puffer jacket, and she grimaced as she stood in the cold.

"Hey!" she greeted us in a frosty shriek.

"Come on in," Gabe urged, pulling the door back so she could pass.

I shakily stood and went to hug my friend.

"Amelia, I'm sorry I—"

Gabe quieted Mya's words with a slam of the door that sent a strong gust of icy air in our direction. She and I both shivered.

"Sorry," he muttered, rubbing the back of his head.

"It's fine. I was just going to ask—well, did you and Gabe talk yet?" She looked from me to him.

"We only talked a little bit but not about *that* yet." I took a step back from them and shifted uncomfortably from one foot to the other. "I really didn't think you would show." Mya texted me once on Thanksgiving, but I hadn't heard a word from her since.

Mya slid off her coat and stepped carefully around me before she threw it on one of my stools and jumped onto the other. "I've had enough time to process," she said with a sure nod of her head. "My mom sent me back with your favorite cookies—the Mantecaditos." She held up the container, which might as well have been a white flag, then set it behind her on the counter.

I grinned as relief flooded my face. "I'm glad we're okay. Thank you. And um, thank your mom for me too, will you?"

Mya nodded, grinning back at me.

I stood between Mya on the stool and Gabe who was now seated on my sofa, his arm on the edge and his right foot propped up on the opposite knee. He cleared his throat. "So, what's the big secret guys?" he asked frankly, crossing his arms and leaning back into the cushions.

I slammed my palms together and let it all out. "I've been seeing someone for a couple of months, and we're dating now. It took us a while to get to that point because there are . . . complications. That's also why I've had such a tough time telling you two."

"Complications? What kind of complications?" he questioned, sitting up straighter on the sofa.

Now my palms started to feel sweaty, my pulse quickened, and I could hardly get out an easy breath. "Uh, well she's . . ." For some reason my brain couldn't decide whether to first say that she was married, or that she was my professor. I got tongue-tied in my attempt and clearly needed help.

Mya graciously stepped in. "Her girlfriend is that woman you saw the night we went to the movies right after fall break."

"Oh?" Gabe raised his eyebrows "Yeah, she was beautiful. I guess you did get her number after all." He clearly wasn't registering exactly what this meant.

"She's also Mya and I's psychology professor," I more clearly stated.

Gabe's jaw dropped. "OH!" His eyes flitted from mine to Mya's. "Are you serious?" he asked determinedly.

"She's extremely serious, Gabe," Mya asserted in a surprisingly calm manner.

"Damn. How'd your parents take *that* one?" he asked.

"Your parents?" Mya's eyes widened. "You told them?"

"Yeah. I finally came out to them . . . at the Thanksgiving table. I definitely didn't have any time to mention my professor-slash-girlfriend after that," I murmured unhappily.

"Shit! I'm sorry for not being there for you." She slid off the barstool and hugged me tightly.

I felt a weight lift off my shoulders as the fear of losing my best friends finally began to dissipate. "I'm sorry for not telling both of you sooner," I said.

Gabe stood and joined the hug. "We stick together, Amelia. You know that. Nothing you need to share will ever be too much for either of us."

I nodded, tears now coming to my eyes. "I just wish it wasn't so difficult." My voice quivered. Mya dashed out of view while Gabe led me back to the couch and comforted me. "I hate not being able to be more open about the person I care so much about. I never wanted to have to hide somebody I'm with, but she's still married—and I know that makes me look like a terrible person because of how much I feel for her." I blew into a tissue that Mya handed me once she returned.

"We don't think you're a terrible person, Amelia," Mya said softly.

"No, we don't but... did you say she's *married*?" Gabe looked perplexed.

I nodded and Mya saved me yet again. "Gabe, she's getting a divorce, remember? And she hasn't been with her wife for like a year. Right, Amelia?"

I nodded. "I didn't even mean to fall for her, Gabe—we just *talked*. That's all we did for months, and it still happened." I knew I sounded pathetic, but I didn't care when I was inside the safe, protective bubble of my best friends.

"It's okay, Amelia," Gabe assured me. "That's literally how it's supposed to happen. Humans are social creatures. We don't create the structures inside our hearts the way we do external things. If you two were meant to connect, it was bound to happen regardless, and nothing's wrong with that. *Nothing*." He tightened his arm around me.

I felt relieved by the certainty of Gabe's words and the comfort of both his and Mya's reassurance as I sat there vulnerable and in tears on the couch. In this moment, I knew for a fact: I was safe with my friends, and I would always be safe with them.

Gabe pulled his gray Prius back into my complex with me sitting in the passenger seat and Mya sitting in the back. The three of us hadn't been together with so much free time in weeks, so we decided to have a "friend night" before returning to school the next day for the last two weeks of the fall semester.

Gabe carefully took a heavy bag stacked with Styrofoam takeout containers from Mya while I carried the lighter bag into my apartment. Once inside, Mya helped me collect all the blankets I had—and Gabe spread out the boxes of Japanese food on the countertop.

"When's the last time we did a movie night?" Mya joyfully asked.

"Not in forever with all of us, except at the theater a couple times," I replied.

"It isn't the same as this," Gabe chimed in. "Pajamas, covers, and drinks occasionally."

"Except *you* don't have pajamas here," Mya teased him.

"I'll be alright," he said, grabbing three large plates from the cabinet and setting them down by the food.

We were soon huddled together on the sofa under the blankets, eating and watching the movie. Mya had chosen *Home Alone* in honor of the approaching Christmas holiday. We laughed and joked throughout the movie, and by the time it ended, it was around nine o'clock.

Gabe stretched as he moved from the sofa. He slowly paced around the kitchen before clearing his throat and asking, "So uh, can I hear more about you and that professor?"

"Please just call her Alena," I said with an embarrassed frown on my face.

"*Alena*," he corrected himself as he opened the fridge.

"Yes!" Mya agreed, laying her feet out where Gabe had been sitting on the other side of her. "Tell us about your woman."

A rush of blood tickled my veins as my heartbeat shot up. There were too many emotions to count that surfaced. I still felt anxious by default in discussing Alena with my friends after hiding for so long, but I also felt nervous about their judgment of my girlfriend in the typical sense. At least it was nice that Mya called her my *woman*.

"Well, she's not nearly as intense as she normally seems in class. That playfulness that comes out every now and again is how she is most of the time, but even when you go to her office hours you can tell that."

Mya nodded. "Yeah, I noticed that before. But I've only been like twice this whole semester."

"She's really thoughtful and sweet," I continued dotingly. I suddenly remembered another fabrication I had yet to reveal to my friends. "She's the one I went to Charlotte with," I blurted out guiltily before clenching my teeth and waiting for their reaction.

Mya sucked her teeth. "I knew you took someone with you! See, I told you, Gabe!" she shouted in his direction. "Amelia, you're a horrible liar by the way—if I didn't mention that before." She threw a pillow at my face, and I barely caught it. "Where does she get all this time anyways? Isn't she busy—I don't know—grading papers or something?"

All three of us laughed.

"Yeah, sometimes she is, but you should see how fast she does that. Her time management skills are incredible. That's probably why she finished grad school so quickly." A sense of pride bubbled up inside me as I mentioned Alena's accomplishments.

"Do you know her friends or anything like that? How deep are you two in together?" Gabe probed while swallowing a newly opened beer. We'd picked up a four-pack from the gas station on the way back; it was meant solely for him since neither Mya nor I liked beer.

"No, I haven't met her friends yet. We only officially started dating two weeks ago so all of that'll come whenever it comes, I guess. But her closest friends do know about me."

Gabe walked back over to us and fell in between Mya and me on the sofa.

"Ouch!" she squealed, squirming to move her feet from underneath Gabe's body. He smiled and lifted his butt up enough for her to escape. She then pushed him, and he laughed before pestering her further.

In the meantime, my phone began buzzing. I checked it and saw that Alena had sent me a picture of her and several other messages in succession. An unrestrained smile flashed across my face as I read them all.

"What are you smiling at?" Mya was peeking around Gabe's body with a raised brow when I looked up. "Is that her now?"

"Yeah." I hid my phone away. "She uh . . . misses me tonight." My cheeks were on fire as I looked at my friends as best as I could through the hearts in my eyes.

"Too damn bad! You're ours for the night!" Gabe shouted, and I laughed.

"I am. She'll be fine. I picked her up from the airport this morning, and I already told her I was going to spend time with you two today. I did think that I'd make it back tonight to see her again, but she knows that we're bonding."

Mya chuckled. "We really are though." She exhaled a satisfactory sigh. "I love this so much. I'm going to miss this once we graduate."

"Me too," Gabe agreed.

"Me three," I joined in. "I'll especially miss being able to see you dance like a duck on the dance floor every time we go to a bar or a club."

"Excuse you," Mya admonished, nostrils flaring.

"I think she's a pretty good dancer," Gabe murmured quietly.

I bet you do.

"Remember that time you got blind drunk sophomore year?" Mya said to me. "Who was there to help you get home and to your toilet when you yacked? *Me.*"

"Hey! I helped too!" Gabe added offendedly.

"Yeah okay, okay, no need to bring all that shit up. But I do appreciate you both. You've always been there for me. I'll love you forever for that." My chest was tight and my eyes burned as I spoke, but I didn't care that I was being sappy again. I stood on everything I said.

"I just know the three of us will be friends for eternity," Gabe proclaimed confidently, going along with the sentimental mood. "We just have to make sure to go on trips and visit each other every year—and once Mya gets on TV, she can invite us to all the celebrity parties."

"You two will be the first to know," Mya promised. "So, does Professor Hutch—" Mya cleared her throat, "Alena, already know that *we* know about her being your girlfriend?"

I nodded. "Oh yeah, she knows."

"How does she feel about us knowing?" Gabe asked.

"She's fine with it. She's happy I told you, but she's nervous about your critical-best-friend-scrutinizing of her."

Mya laughed. "Oh my God, that sounds so . . . normal. I guess she really is just a regular person, isn't she?"

"Not to Amelia," Gabe snickered. "*She lights up her world.*" He made an air-rainbow with his hands.

"You can definitely say that," I agreed with a sparkle in my eyes.

Chapter 19 Ring Finger

The first week back in school passed by much too quickly, and I hardly had any time to be with Alena. I had decided to spend most of the week away from her apartment so I could maintain my focus on the finals, but we still made sure to talk with each other at least once a day. Unfortunately, I ended up tossing and turning for about half an hour every night before I fell asleep.

I missed how she smelled and how her hair spilled across her satin pillowcases—how she would hold me tightly in her deep slumber and snore very quietly when she was exhausted. I ended up having to imagine she was there with me so I could drift off.

By the time the weekend came, I was grateful to have plans to meet up with her. I stayed in on Friday night, spending some much-needed time alone, and I spent much of Saturday out shopping with Mya. After we finished, we checked out a new burger joint downtown before parting ways. It was seven-thirty before I returned to my apartment, toting several shopping bags with me. Once I was inside, I threw the bags on my bed then lit a candle and turned up the heat.

Alena had earlier told me that she was using her Saturday morning to prep the final grades and upcoming exams for her students. She then had an afternoon luncheon planned with a couple of her favorite coworkers. I didn't know if that was done yet, so I texted her to call me whenever she had the chance and left my phone on the dresser across the room.

My eyes now focused on a black shopping bag laying on the bed. I hesitantly pulled it toward me, slipped my hands inside, and removed a velvety lace set. Mya had forced my hand in purchasing lingerie for Alena, but I wasn't adamant about wearing it any time soon.

The sound of Alena's ringtone startled me. I flung the undergarments on my bed, feeling as if she could somehow see them through the phone. I rushed over to it and answered.

"Hey, Amelia! I just got in," Alena announced joyfully. I could hear the sound of something plastic swinging through the air.

"Yeah, me too . . . sort of," I said.

"Would you like to come over tonight? I wanted to do a little movie night, but only if you're not too busy."

"There isn't enough busy in the world, Alena," I jeered, and she laughed on the other end.

"I do have one request though, darling."

"Ooh, a request." I laid down stomach first on the bed and swung my feet in the air behind me. "What is it?" I asked sweetly.

"That you let me pick you up for the movie."

I chuckled. "Why?"

"Because I want to," she answered decisively.

"Sure, I guess so. Do you need my address?"

"Yes, please," she cooed.

I moved my ear from the phone and shared my location. "Just sent it to you. When should I get ready?"

"Now. And make sure to wear something warm too, okay? I'll see you in about twenty minutes. Goodbye!" She hung up abruptly.

I removed the phone from my ear and stared at it. *That was weird*, I shook my head. I sprung out of the bed and prepared myself for her arrival. I thought about putting together an overnight bag, but I had no reason to. I already had extra clothes in her apartment along with several options of her satin bonnets or pillowcases to protect my hair. There was also a toothbrush that she had bought for me over a month ago.

I jumped in the shower and got dressed in some warm clothes before throwing on a fur-collared coat. When my phone buzzed again on the bed, I promptly picked it up.

"Are you ready?" Alena sounded eager on the other end.

"Almost!" I chanted into the phone. By now I had grown properly excited about my escort tonight.

"I'll be in front of your building in four minutes."

"Okay." I hung up and rushed to spray on my perfume and pik out my hair. Before I knew it, I was jumping into the passenger side of her Cadillac and greeting her with a quick kiss on the lips.

"Hello, gorgeous." She smiled in my direction before pulling off.

We chatted idly for about ten minutes before I noticed her merging onto the interstate. I already figured something was up, but that's when I knew for sure that we were definitely not headed toward her apartment. "Alena, are you kidnapping me?" I asked with false astonishment.

She laughed. "Yes, and no."

"Where are you taking me?"

"I'm taking you to see a movie."

It took me several moments to comprehend what she meant while I looked at her with my brows furrowed. "Oh, so we're going to a *theater*?"

"Yes."

"Why?" I asked anxiously.

"Why not?" she responded with sass.

"I could give a few reasons." I sank into my seat next to her.

"The theater we're going to is forty-five minutes away." She kissed my hand. "We can go in separately if you're still worried about anything," she suggested.

"What time does the movie start?" I asked, still feeling uncertain.

"Nine-thirty, so we'll be there in time." She glanced at me nervously. "Do you want me to turn around?"

I took in a deep breath and slowly exhaled. "No, I just—I could've picked a better outfit," I complained lightheartedly, looking down at my thick jogging suit.

She laughed again, resting a hand on my thigh. "You look great."

The dine-in theater was considerably upscale from the looks of it. Thankfully they didn't have a strict dress code. We walked in closely together, but without holding hands.

I didn't let Alena pay for the tickets since she had already covered our last date, as well as the many unofficial ones at her place. I would have to plan something really nice for the upcoming holidays and definitely something extravagant for her birthday next August. Regardless of what I did though, it was unlikely to compare to everything she had done for me so far.

We walked into the theater for the last showing of *Creed 2* for the night. The commercials were still running when we arrived at our seats, so Alena and I spoke in hushed tones while they played.

"I think this date night was a nice idea, Alena," I whispered pleasantly.

"Wasn't it?! I know we both like the movies, and I figured it was time for us to see one together. Are you hungry?"

"Not enough for a meal." I shook my head. "Mya and I ate burgers a couple of hours ago, but I could use a drink and maybe popcorn."

"Okay, they have water and soda . . . and wine." Her brows pressed together as she studied the menu.

"I could go for some White Zinfandel," I suggested, using my finger to trace her brows.

She looked up and grinned heartily. "Great choice. I'll order you a glass."

Alena ended up ordering me two glasses of wine, a soda for

herself, and a large bag of popcorn to share. Our drinks and popcorn were brought to us right as the movie began, and we settled comfortably into the reclining seats. For the duration of the movie, Alena's foot nudged against mine and she held my hand while gently stroking my fingers. My cheeks felt warm and fuzzy, but I couldn't tell if it was a result of my euphoric feelings with Alena or the wine.

When the film ended, we exited the theater and talked and laughed our way all the way back to her car. We sat inside of it debating the best scenes of the movie. It was just after midnight now, and I was tired from my recent travels and from being out all day with my best friend. The engine was running as we waited for the vehicle to warm before heading back.

"Alena." I spoke softly. "I had a great date with you tonight."

She turned to me with a smile on her face. "Me too."

I stared into her eyes amorously for a moment before grabbing her hand and kissing it. Raveena was playing in the background which made the night feel even dreamier. I leaned in and captured her lips—and though she kissed me gently, I kissed her with urgency and strength. Fire seemed to chased the blood in my veins as my fingers twisted in her hair. I moaned and put my hands on her chest before her lips suddenly pulled away.

"Wait," she whispered with a smile. "Are you trying to get lucky in the car right now?" She sounded amused.

"Mmm... I don't know—I just—I don't know." I leaned back. My body throbbed, and I felt a tingling sensation underneath my skin. It didn't feel right for us to be clothed in her car when we could be naked in her bed instead. I wanted to feel her warmth from the inside out, and I wanted to feel it right now—but all I could manage was a longing stare since her returning gaze leveled me.

I thought it was obvious we weren't on the same page until her lips abruptly seized mine. Her tongue's meticulous movements inside my mouth reminded me of the things she did when she was using it in other places. I moaned again, and she pushed her hand between my thighs. I extended my hips forward to deepen the pressure, and she drew in a sharp breath then laughed into my mouth.

Oh no. She usually laughed like that when she was making the decision to take a brutalizing amount of time teasing me and denying my release. I loved it when she did that. I also hated it.

"I think I should get you home," she whispered before moving her hands away and planting one more lingering kiss on my aching lips.

"If by that you mean *your* place, sure," I said.

"Just say the word, and I will," she responded, placing her foot on the brakes and shifting the car into reverse.

As she drove away, I held her hand and wondered to myself why my desire for her was so persistent.

"Aha! It's the wine," I exclaimed loudly.

"Amelia, what are you talking about?" she asked in a startled voice.

"I was wondering why I felt like jumping your bones so much—not that I don't always feel that way. But it's the wine making me hor—*romantic.*"

She chuckled as she shook her head and stroked my hand with her fingers. "Just can't get enough of me, can you?"

"Never," I stated firmly, beaming at her with a happiness that also made me sad. "I wish we could do this more often." I sighed disappointedly.

"One day, and sooner than you think," she promised.

Alena gently nudged me after some time. "We're here, darling." She was looking down at me from the driver's side.

"Where?" I asked, sitting up and yawning, momentarily confused.

"My apartment."

"Oh yeah," I chuckled as I unfastened my seatbelt. I only meant to rest my eyes for a moment, but I had completely fallen asleep.

Alena kept me steady as we ascended the stairs since I was drowsy and unstable. When we made it to the door her face suddenly dropped, and she moved me aside. "I didn't leave any lights on."

"What? Are you sure?" I asked tiredly.

"One hundred percent. Just wait here." She cautiously opened the door. "Hello?" she called out before stepping inside.

I heard a chair scrape across the floor, and when I peeked around the corner—I noticed Alena standing frozen in the living room, staring toward the kitchen. I followed her glare and the piercing green eyes that met mine instantly roused me.

"What the hell are you doing here?" Alena growled menacingly as she stepped closer to the woman.

I crept after her and shut the door behind me, closing out the cold weather but not the ice in the room. I was almost afraid to look back toward the woman seated at Alena's kitchen table, and I cursed to myself when I did. She was still staring at me with her pale, freckled face, disheveled hair, and bloodshot eyes. It was easy to tell exactly what mood she was in, just like on the first night I had met her. She was perceptibly cheerful and confident then—but now she seemed unkempt, frail, and tired. Her glare was only partially menacing and was more suggestive of some deep calculations going on inside.

Teresa stood and finally looked back toward Alena. "Is this her?" she asked with a sharp accusation in her voice.

"You aren't allowed to question me here," Alena boldly deflected the woman's words.

My eyes darted from my girlfriend to her wife and even the knowledge of that prompted an unnerving churn inside of my stomach.

Teresa's eyes fixed on me once again, and realization stirred within them. "I remember you," she said.

Alena looked in my direction with dread in her eyes.

"You never called me," Teresa said. "And I guess this is why." She gestured toward her wife.

"Teresa. Why the *fuck* are you here?" Alena questioned her irately.

"What have you been doing, Laney?" Teresa responded, again ignoring Alena's questions but asking several of her own. "Picking up young girls from the bar? Is that your new hobby?"

"Apparently that's yours. But you didn't do such a good job of that, did you?" Alena was fuming, and her face was as red as it could get. The ice in her tone and demeanor almost froze me. I'd never felt such an uncomfortable atmosphere in this apartment before—not even the times when Alena got into one of her rare sour moods, which were usually the result of her mother or Teresa.

The arrogant woman let out a single, fake laugh. "Aren't you going to introduce me?" she continued but didn't await Alena's response. "I'm Teresa, Alena's wife." She spoke directly to me.

"She knows who you are," Alena snarled.

". . . She does?" Teresa's face looked like it had been struck by Alena's fists instead of her words, and her arrogance faltered. "Okay, apparently you know me, but who are you?"

Alena didn't let me answer. "She's my girlfriend, Teresa."

I could tell that it was another verbal fist to the mouth for her, and I didn't know how to react to any of it. Teresa stood silent for a long time as she and Alena locked eyes with one another. Her voice cracked when she finally spoke.

"Umm. Jess wanted me to check to see if she left something when she was here last week. That's why I'm here."

"I live here, Teresa. I know for a fact that she wouldn't ask you to do that. What did you tell her?" Alena demanded.

"That you had something of mine," Teresa weakly admitted before looking down at a large box on the floor. "But I was actually bringing your old journals, and I thought that maybe . . ." She looked to me with softer eyes reminiscent of retreat.

"Why did you lie about that?" Alena's tone was still harsh.

"I don't know," she confessed soberly. "I guess I never really understand that about myself," she almost whispered.

Alena looked sympathetic but simultaneously impatient, and the way she positioned herself in front of me showed that she felt a need to protect me.

"I brought you this too." Teresa held up a shining diamond ring.

Alena looked blankly toward the beautiful ring and pushed her curls back with one of her hands. "I don't need that anymore." She spoke gently for the first time. "I think you should go now, Teresa."

The woman exhaled deeply while looking down and stuffing the ring into her coat pocket. "Okay." She glanced at me with an embarrassed expression and cleared her throat as she walked toward the door.

Alena stepped in front of me as she passed. "Teresa," Alena spoke before the redheaded woman walked out. The beautiful figure in the doorway turned around. "Please don't come back here again." Alena's tone was soft yet forceful.

Teresa nodded dismally. "I won't," she said quietly before she walked away into the dark, freezing night.

I might easily have slept away my troubles of the night had Alena not had such a hard time getting over it. She cursed for nearly an hour straight after I'd shed my clothes, put on a smaller pair of her pajamas, and lay beside her in the bed. She was on the phone with Jess, and they discussed what had actually happened with Teresa.

I couldn't hear the entire conversation, but it seemed that Jess accidentally left a spare key when she returned for Thanksgiving. It was underneath the mat outside, and she didn't want it to be a safety hazard for Alena. Jess realized this when she happened to be on the phone with Teresa who said she was nearby and could handle it for her. Jess did think to call Alena first, but the calls were unsuccessful, which she now knew was because of our date at the theater. Jess hadn't considered the possibility of Teresa pulling such a stunt on Alena, so she apologized profusely. She also didn't object to listening to Alena erupt on the phone about it. Even in the midst of her impassioned phone call, Alena rubbed me very gently and didn't so much as shake my half-sleeping frame.

When Alena finally finished her conversation with Jess, she apologized to me a million more times than she had already done before the call. She felt horrible about our breach of privacy and yet another encounter with Teresa at the apartment.

"I can't wait to move out of here, Amelia. I've narrowed down three places—I'll even choose at random at this point! Anywhere is better than here."

I had a difficult time responding to her now, as I had fallen asleep and woken up more times than I could count. "As long as the place is safe," are the last words I heard myself say. Alena said something else that my tired brain couldn't comprehend, then I heard her click off the light and felt her arms pull me into her chest. My face was buried in her breasts, and I could feel her heartbeat thrumming on my nose. This was the way I loved to sleep with her, although she didn't understand how I could even breathe in this position.

"Goodnight, my love," I heard her whisper before I was fully unconscious.

◆ ◆

My dream that night was a horrendous continuance of the evening. The difference was that Alena and Teresa had decided on making amends. The way they looked at each other made me feel like I was dying inside. I was asked to leave the apartment, and I could only imagine what they were doing inside of it after I left.

Time skipped—as it often does in dreams—and I was in class again. Alena looked elated as she wore the ring Teresa had brought with her, but my bracelet was nowhere to be found. The ring gleamed brightly, and I broke out crying, right there in the auditorium. There was no one there but her and I. "I'm sorry, Amelia," she said. "Our love was just too strong."

The words repeated in my head when I was awakened by Alena's kisses up the side of my neck. "I'm sorry to wake you so early, Amelia, but I think if I take you back before my run it'll still be dark out."

I stared at her hollowly, the feeling of betrayal still tainting my system.

"You okay?" she asked softly.

I gathered myself together as I looked around the room, and I began to realize that nothing I had just experienced was real—at least the parts about Alena and Teresa reconnecting.

"Yeah, I'm fine." I rubbed my eyes and sat up. I decided that it was best not to tell Alena about the dream. "That's a good idea, I'll get dressed."

I slipped from under the sheets that smelled of her and walked into the bathroom. I washed my hands after using the toilet, and as I did, I studied the toothbrush that Alena had bought for me.

The morning after the first night I purposefully stayed over, she noticed me wincing when I brushed my teeth. She asked what was wrong, and I told her about my overly sensitive gums and the specialized toothbrush I used at my apartment. Without mentioning a word, she researched it and bought an exact replica. By the third night I stayed at her place, the toothbrush sat in a box on the sink until I'd asked her why it was there, and she said it was for me.

I found solace in this memory because it reminded me that the woman in my dream was not the Alena I knew. *That* Alena loved Teresa more, but *this* Alena loved me more. Perhaps both versions, though, still loved Teresa in some capacity.

Chapter 20 Destiny

The sound of heavy snoring ruptured my eardrums as my eyes flitted open. I was lying on my back, now staring at the popcorn ceiling above me. I groggily sat up and yawned as I rubbed my hands over my bare forearms. My apartment was chilly this morning, but it didn't seem to bother Mya, who was knocked out on the tail end of my bed.

Today we would be taking our final exam in Alena's class, and the excitement that had been brewing within me over the past week now spilled over. As I stood and stumbled toward the bathroom, I thought about what I might do with Alena to celebrate; I already knew what I'd be doing with Mya and Gabe.

The three of us had long made plans to head down to Charlotte the weekend after our exams so we could commemorate the end of the semester as well as celebrate my upcoming birthday. We had split the cost of a downtown hotel not far from the one where Alena and I had stayed. We all wanted to drink and stay at least one night in the city so that we could club and do brunch the next day. I planned on having a good ass time with my friends, but I was equally excited to later spend some time with my girlfriend before Christmas.

As I brushed my teeth in the bathroom, I reveled in the fact that I would finally be losing my title as a student in Alena's class. The quicker I took my exam, the quicker I could put that dynamic to rest forever—or maybe not *forever*. I'm sure it would make for interesting roleplay down the line.

Mya shuffled around in the bed before she sat up and yawned loudly. "Shit. I can't believe it's Wednesday already." Her voice was unusually deep and raspy.

I spit into the sink. "I know, Darth Vader," I teased before rinsing my face with cold water.

"Shut up."

When Mya slid off the bed, I unfortunately had the perfect view of her shorts clinging to the crack of her ass. "My eyes!" I turned away with a shriek.

"Ugh, you're so annoying sometimes," she groaned as she walked past me while carelessly picking it out. "Are you ready to get this exam over with?" she asked, sitting on the plush toilet seat cover.

"Yes," I exhaled exhaustedly. We had both faithfully studied for our exam over the last week and a half and reviewed for several hours the night before.

"I bet you're super happy now, though. You're even closer to being with Professor Hutchinson without all the secrecy."

I turned to her, a smile reaching half my lips. Instead of correcting her with Alena's first name, I said, "It's Professor Moore."

Mya and I drove separately to a popular sandwich shop near the campus. She had another test two hours after Alena's, and I had one later that evening. We decided not to carpool because neither of us wanted to be stuck waiting for the other throughout the day. It was eleven twenty-five when we arrived at the restaurant. We were seated ten minutes later and promptly received our hot sandwiches. Our exam wasn't until two o'clock, so we had a good amount of time to eat and still arrive early enough for a little last-minute studying.

We spent most of our lunch discussing plans for the holidays.

Mya wanted me to come down for New Year's since both her and Gabe would be in town, and we had yet to celebrate one together. I thought it was a fantastic idea, though I also wondered if Alena and I would want to plan something for that time as well. And what about a New Year's kiss?

"I know you said you don't want to go home, so I was thinking you could just come to Florida with me when I leave," Mya offered. "You can drive or fly up to South Carolina for Christmas then come back before New Year's. My Abuelita misses you, and so do my parents."

"Aww, I miss them too. Especially little Lettie." Lettie was Mya's three-year-old niece, and she was adorable. She loved flowers, and she'd shown me all around their garden when I was there during the summer.

"Oh, speaking of Lettie." Mya rifled through her purse and pulled out her phone. "She drew another picture for you." Mya held her phone across the table, and I looked at the photo of Lettie's drawing.

"Aww, she's the sweetest! Tell her I think those are the most beautiful marigolds!" Marigolds were Lettie's favorite flower, and she was the one who first taught me their name.

Mya beamed and enthusiastically nodded, texting the message immediately.

"Shorty?!" I heard a familiar voice call from across the room. I looked up and spotted Sarin waving at me from the restaurant's entrance.

Mya glanced in her direction before she looked back at me with widened eyes and flashed a nervous smile. She was convinced that Sarin wanted me, though I didn't think that was the case. We had chemistry for sure, but I believed friends should have that regardless.

Sarin swaggered over to our table. "I almost thought you switched schools or somethin. I barely saw you after the last time we kicked it." She raced over her words as she spoke. Her attention then politely shifted to Mya. "Hey, Mya." She waved, a scar-raising smile on her lips.

"Hi, Sarin," Mya spoke with a stiff jaw. "I uh, left something in my car. I'll be right back." She excused herself from the table, and as she walked out of the building, she gave me a cynical look.

Sarin slid into the seat across from me and made herself comfortable. Her cologne permeated the atmosphere around us. She smelled like the ocean today—with a hint of cedar trees—and the intensity of her scent matched that of her dusky eyes.

"How're things going with you?" I asked in a pleasant tone before nervously taking a sip of water.

"Shorty, I'm booked as hell. The scouts love me. Ya girl's about to be famous out here!"

"Really? I'm happy for you Sarin," I commended her with a smile.

"Thanks." She sunk back into the seat. "And you? How are you?" Her left brow raised, and for the first time I noticed a small scar that was hidden there too.

"I'm excellent," I said truthfully. "I'm happy."

"You look it. Somebody must be adding to that happiness too, huh?" she asked casually.

I nodded while my stomach filled with butterflies just from the thought of Alena.

"Damn shame for me," she remarked. "Amelia B. off the market. I thought I might catch you at some point."

"I'm sorry?" I questioned, my cheeks feeling flushed.

"It wasn't obvious that I was feeling you?" she asked skeptically.

I jerked my head back in surprise. "I . . . guess I wasn't paying that much attention." *Okay, Mya was right.*

"Damn, shorty!" she gripped her chest dramatically.

"Sorry." I stifled a laugh. "It's been a really complicated semester for me."

"Nah, it's cool. I understand that." Sarin shifted in her seat then clasped her hands together and set them on the table. "I gotta ask though. Was there ever a chance for me?"

I immediately shook my head. "I was already in pretty deep with the person I'm dating now back when we spoke at the club."

"Ahh, you seemed locked in, I must admit. You weren't dancing with anyone. That's why I ain't even try it." She smiled. "But I still think there could be something here between us if you ever had the capacity for it." She held a smoldering gaze on me that caused an uncomfortable stir inside.

I didn't respond for several moments, trying but failing to understand that stir until I decided it didn't matter. "I want what I have now to last, Sarin, and I believe it will," I said.

She nodded slowly, looking away.

"Are you okay with that?" I asked guardedly. "I think we'd make really great friends if we keep in touch."

She blinked at me quietly for several moments before she finally answered. "Yeah," she said decisively. "What sense does it make to throw away a growing friendship. Life's too unpredictable to mess up a connection like this." She nodded. "Friends it is."

"Aye, Sai!" Her burly teammate with glasses called in Sarin's direction while the host stood next to them with menus. Sarin rotated her head and nodded when the woman gestured for her to follow them.

"What's the deal with *Sai* by the way?" I asked once she turned back to me. I'd meant to ask her after seeing her play in a few games and hearing her teammates yell the name.

"It's a nickname of sorts." She began to slide out of the booth. "My teammates came up with it."

"Why not *Sare* or something? Why *Sai*?" I watched her friends walk to a table on the opposite side of the room.

"Rumors," she said stiffly. "It's on some Greek, mythological shit or something though. They say I have 'powers' with women. Like a Siren."

"Oh, I get it now." I nodded and she chuckled.

"Yeah. If that were the case, it would've worked on you." She was now standing with her hands in her pocket. "Damn, my bad shorty. Don't take that to heart," she apologized.

I sighed uncomfortably. "Alright, Sarin. It was good seeing you." I gave her a polite smile.

"Aight, Amelia. Same to you." She placed her hand gently on my shoulder and squeezed. "See you later, shorty." She winked.

Not long after Sarin crossed the room to her friends, Mya came strutting back toward me.

"So umm, how was that?" she asked, plopping back into her seat and leaning forward on the table.

"How was what, Mya?" I asked nonchalantly.

"The tension I can feel in the air right now is *thick*."

"There's nothing there," I countered defensively.

"My ass!" Mya said. "She wants you."

"So, what if she does?" I said in too sharp a tone.

"Umm, you have a *girlfriend*."

"I know that, Mya! Sarin and I are just going to be—"

"Oh God, please don't say friends. She doesn't want to be your friend."

I rubbed the back of my neck. "I don't know what to say, Mya. You know I'm loyal."

"But there's no reason for unnecessary distractions," she huffed.

"I promise you no one has enough power to do that, Mya. And we hardly see each other anyways. I doubt we'll even get to hang out that much next semester."

Mya held up her hands. "Alright, Amelia. I'm just warning you. Don't be surprised if her 'friendliness' alters at some point."

"Heard." I leaned back in my seat and exhaled. I fidgeted with the receipt from the bill we had already paid fifteen minutes ago. "We should get going."

▼

As Mya and I stepped into the auditorium for our psychology exam, I felt a strong sense of nostalgia. The first day I walked through these doors, I never would've expected to have fallen for the professor, or that the professor would've also fallen for me. In hindsight, it seemed like everything moved so fast—but in reality, it was a slow process. Week after week our relationship grew, and we became closer and closer. It now looked like we were meant to be, and I fully accepted it.

I eyed Alena bravely as I walked through the room and flashed a smile in her direction. She wore a creamy-white blouse freckled with navy-blue polka dots. This was paired with slim-fitting trousers and a pair of glossy black heels. Her large tan peacoat hung over the podium and her black and gold purse sat on the desk. Curls peeked out of her usual bun. She looked joyful today, and she looked beautiful as always.

I sat down alone on the fourth row since we all had to spread out for the exam, and Mya sat three rows behind me. We both reviewed our notes while more students trickled in. Alena sat quietly at the front of the room, shuffling through the tests. Once two o'clock came around, she announced her instructions for the exam—and she had us come up one by one to retrieve our papers.

I studied her features as I approached the front to grab my test. When our fingers accidentally brushed during the exchange, I felt shivers up and down my spine. Alena's face looked unperturbed—but if my memory served me correctly, that didn't mean shit. The exam was effortless for me, and once I finished my test, I handed it in and left the auditorium. I waited patiently but energetically for Mya in the hall, but she didn't join me until about ten minutes later.

"Whew, that was tough!" she grumbled as she walked toward me.

"Are you serious?" I asked, supposing that she was exaggerating as usual.

"Most of it was alright, Amelia, but the freakin essay questions got me! Dammit!"

"Mya, I'm sure you did just fine." I squeezed her arms suddenly. "But you know what? It doesn't matter either way!" I shouted, my excitement now bubbling over. "We're finally finished, Mya! After Friday we only have one more semester to go!" I hugged her tightly.

"Relax, Amelia!" she laughed, hugging me back then pushing me away. "So, what are you going to do now? Go back home until your next exam?"

I glanced at the door of our class contemplatively. "I don't know. I really want to tell Professor Hutchinson goodbye first."

"Of course you do." She smirked. "That can't wait until later?"

"I won't see her again until Friday," I whispered. "But I'll probably go up to her office after the exam is over." I sighed lightly, looking around the mostly empty hallway. "I'll come with you to the library for a little while to pass the time and get some fresh air," I declared.

When we arrived at the library, Mya studied for her next exam in between discussing my upcoming birthday plans with me. Fifteen minutes after the end time of our exam, I decided to walk back and visit Alena. I was so giddy that I could hardly contain myself as I rushed over to Province Hall. Strangely enough, I decided to hop on the elevator which I almost never took anymore since I now preferred the stairs. For some reason I thought it might help me calm down, but when the doors opened to the second floor, I realized that it didn't make much of a difference.

I used every ounce of control I had not to barrel down the hall into her office. I knew she didn't have another test scheduled until an hour and a half after ours, so I pre-planned bringing her a small token of my appreciation. It was my parting gift from student to professor, the signaling of the end of an era.

I skipped cheerfully down the hall and crept near the opposite side of the door where I usually approached her from. When I peeked in— ready to proclaim all my joy—I caught a glimpse of bright red, curly hair.

It stopped me in my tracks. *Teresa.*

I stood there as frozen as a statue watching them from outside the room. They spoke affectionately with one another, and there was a tone of deep familiarity that I hadn't detected the other night. Alena's hand pressed down on what looked to be a piece of paper on the desk, and her face was soft and kind as she spoke to Teresa. I suppressed my initial shock enough to concentrate on what was being said between them, and I immediately regretted the decision. The next thing I heard was Teresa saying, "I'll always love you, Laney." She placed her hands on Alena's, stroking the skin with her thumb.

My heart fell further from its place in my chest—down to the floor, shattering into pieces. I was astonished that neither of them could hear the deafening sound of it. I nearly dropped my bag and the gift I held in my hands as I hurried away, holding back tears.

Their love was just too strong, I thought wretchedly. I guess it was just their destiny.

Chapter 21 Before I Let Go

The exams I had to take over the next couple of days were especially difficult for me to endure. I pressed through despite my distress, and in the end, I still managed to feel confident about the results. The confidence about myself and my new relationship, however, was a different story.

Alena had reached out to me over the next two days, but I brushed off her calls along with the subsequent messages she left. I told her I was too busy studying to talk and that we would catch up on Friday since we had already made plans to meet then. Now as I stripped myself of my house clothes and prepared to go to her apartment, I felt awful. Seeing her was the last thing I wanted to do because encountering her would mean having to face a harsh truth: it was the end of the semester and probably the end of our whirlwind romance.

I worked hard to make myself understand that I was only a placeholder for Alena until Teresa corrected her behavior. I wondered if I had known it all along. Maybe I didn't ask enough questions. I didn't know about the frequency of Alena and Teresa's communication—I just assumed. Alena had convinced me that things could never work out between them, but could she really be in the place to know that if she was actually still in love with her? At the end of the day, Mya had been right all along—and I was wrong. Now I had to suffer the consequences.

I cursed to myself and sighed as I walked to the mirror and studied my unclothed body. I realized just how uncomfortable I was then, and I pressed my palms over each of my breasts. I felt vulnerable and naked—inside and out. A despondent feeling hovered over me as I rummaged through my drawers for a pair of sweatpants. I threw on a gray pair as well as my school hoodie and a coat over that for good measure, then I drove to Alena's place.

Both my heart and my head pounded as I pulled into the dark parking lot near her building. It was the first time ever that I wasn't excited to see her. I dreaded this visit with every ounce of my being. I didn't want to discuss what I had seen. I didn't want to acknowledge what it meant for us. I didn't want any of this to be real.

Unlike my first visit, I didn't linger in the warmth of my car. I embraced the cold, wretched weather which mirrored the current state of my heart. This would likely be my last time here, and I was already doing things differently. I mechanically trudged up the stairs and toward her door, working extremely hard to keep my emotions under control. I had fallen somewhere between devastated and numb over the past two days. A small part of me thought I was overreacting, but my eyes and ears didn't lie. Teresa's words didn't lie. It made sense that two people who were still married would want to get back together. There was still a love between them that couldn't be ignored.

The shiny, brass number 212 signified I was at my love's door . . . or heartbreak's door. I didn't know which as I held up my hand to knock. The door opened quickly, and I was greeted by the breathtakingly beautiful woman I loved so deeply, dressed in a silky robe and slippers. She was glowing as she pulled me into a tight hug. I instinctively inhaled the fragrance of almonds, shea butter, and gardenias that radiated from her body. I could feel that her hair was dampened too. *Is the robe all she has on?* I couldn't help but briefly get distracted by the thought of it.

"Oh, Amelia! I've missed you so much!" She shut the door behind us.

"Umm, you have?" I asked confused.

She paused before a single chuckle escaped her mouth. "Yes, of course!" She yanked my jacket off and pressed her lips to my forehead. "I'm so proud of you! You finished another semester strong! How was your last test today?"

"Good," I said plainly.

"Great! I got you something," she announced, tipping her finger on my nose then rushing into the bedroom.

I was completely unprepared for her enthusiasm in seeing me, and I didn't know what to make of her behavior at all.

I had imagined her cordially sitting me down with a look of deep remorse in her eyes. *I made a mistake,* she would say. She would hold my hand and tell me the news. She and Teresa were afforded a second chance—one that she wanted to take. She would then apologize to me profusely and beg my forgiveness, and she would give me the space I needed when I left her apartment in tears. I already had tissues in my pocket and a pack in the car as well. But she wasn't at all like I pictured. She was giddy and happy and congratulatory. She had even kissed me!

Alena emerged from the room with a small green gift bag in hand. "Here." She handed me the bag, her eyes twinkling.

I held it away from me and frowned at her, perplexed. Her joyful expression immediately shifted.

"What?" She stepped closer to me. "What's wrong?" She instinctively grabbed my empty hand and I flinched away from her touch. "Did I do something?" Her brows were pressed together, and she looked concerned.

"I don't understand why you're acting like this." I dropped the bag on the coffee table.

"Acting like what?" She laughed nervously. "Happy? Shouldn't I be? The semester is over—and shouldn't *you* be?!" She pointed in my direction accusingly. "What's going on? Did something happen . . . with a test or with Mya or Gabe?"

"No." My body tensed. "I went to your office after the exam the other day. I wanted to see you." I spoke in a dull tone. "I had this whole spiel ready about how special you are and how much I love you and even how great your class really, really was—my crushing on you aside—but when I got there, I saw the two of you." My low voice trembled, and tears welled up in my eyes. "You and Teresa want to get back together, don't you? Just like that."

Alena's eyes bulged. "Me and *Teresa*?!" she exclaimed. "Amelia, *no*." Her head shook furiously. "Absolutely not!"

"You don't?" I whimpered out pitifully with a single tear rolling down my cheek.

She exhaled and smudged the tear with her thumb. "No, Amelia." She pulled me by the hand and sat me down on the couch. "Why didn't you say something when you saw me?" she questioned, her face serious.

"I didn't know what was going on. When she came here the other day you were so harsh and angry with her, but you spoke so peacefully together in your office. I don't know, you both just seemed. *Happy*." My voice was nothing more than a weakened whisper.

"I *do* know how to be cordial with people, darling," she snarked. "Even Teresa, believe it or not. She came to me respectfully and—" Alena cursed under her breath. "Wait. Is *that* the reason you didn't answer my calls?" she asked. When I nodded guiltily in response, she huffed and frowned at me. "So you've been thinking I wanted to leave you for Teresa since you saw her in my office the other day?"

"Kinda. Because you two were talking and her hand was on yours and I heard Teresa say that she'll always love you." I stumbled over my words.

"Amelia," Alena breathed out. "She can love me all she wants now, but she lost the privilege of having me love her back." She shifted uncomfortably on the couch and looked worried for a moment before she spoke again. "I still do hold a kind of affection for her in my heart—I won't lie about that," she began, "But it's more like a memory of what we shared in that time of my life, and I don't dwell on it.

"People change and people reveal themselves. I decided that I don't like what I see in her. I wouldn't end my marriage if I had any hopes of growth between us." She grabbed my hand. "And I most definitely wouldn't start a new relationship with you if I wasn't certain that what I see in you is golden and is absolutely everything I desire to have in a partner."

My heart convulsed inside my chest, and I felt an aching passion rising from within me. I vehemently refuted my previous beliefs and in turn craved Alena intensely. I leaned in and hugged her, nestling my nose into her neck and pressing my lips to her skin. She exhaled a pleasure-filled sigh as she tightened her grip on me.

"I love you so much, Alena," I whispered as I trailed my kisses down to her collarbone. I then reached inside her robe and brushed a hand across her bare breasts. Her hand instantly moved to my ass in response. "I'm sorry for overreacting." I spoke softly as I reluctantly pulled my lips away from her. I knew I would quickly get past the point of no return, and I needed to verbally reconcile with her first.

"I forgive you." She smiled, her hand still massaging my ass. "But in the future, I need you to confront me if you're ever concerned or worried about us."

"Of course." I nodded while rounding my thumb around one of her nipples, which perked up in response.

"We're in a relationship," she stammered out between increased breaths. I stopped my movements to be respectful. "More than two days without hearing your voice is too long, and ignoring me is *never* okay," she continued in a more even tone. "Whether you're mad or

I'm mad—we *always* need to communicate openly with one another. I can't deal with anything like that again, okay?"

"Okay, Alena. I'm sorry." I grabbed her free hand and kissed it.

She gazed into my eyes and said, "I love you too, by the way." Then her lips took over mine.

As soft as a cloud. Wet like the rain. My heart was the thunder that roared inside of me.

"*Mmm*, it feels so good," I crooned. Steam was rising from the floor of the shower.

"Yes, but save some of it for me," Alena murmured.
She stood behind me in the shower looking exhausted, as though *she* wasn't the one who had just worn *me* out.

"You're so damn beautiful," I declared as I ogled her.

"Uh-uh," she reproached. "Turn around and finish washing up." She swung my shoulders forward. "This may be hard to believe, but I'm actually tired."

I grinned to myself. "We can just sleep after we go another round."

"That would work if I didn't have the ceremony to prepare for in the morning. *And* I'm helping host the department breakfast, remember? I have to be up super early."

"Oh yeah." I frowned and turned around to rinse off the remaining suds on my back. Alena had dark pouches underneath her eyes, and she looked zapped of most of her energy. "Yeah, let's get you to bed."

After we finished our shower and dried ourselves off, we made our way to the bed. I lay flattened on top of her while she smoothed her hand over my back. "I'm proud of you, Amelia," she congratulated me once again.

"I'm proud of you too, babe. Teaching isn't easy." I spoke languidly, enjoying her strokes along my back.

"Definitely not, but it's still worth it." I heard a click at the side of the bed, and I could tell that Alena had turned on the lamp even through my closed eyelids.

"I can't believe it's over." I kissed her soft skin. "I never thought anything that happened this semester would, but I'm so glad it did."

"Amelia, I don't think anyone could've predicted this," she noted. "But I'm happy it happened too." She gently kissed my forehead and began kneading my ass. "Do you think you can handle opening your gift now?" she asked accusingly.

My cheeks burned. "Yes, I can handle it." I opened my eyes and lifted my head in time to see her amused expression.

"I'll get it," she declared, moving from underneath me and slipping out of the bed before I could even blink. I watched her perfectly crafted figure stride lithely out the room. All she wore was her necklace and bracelet, and that was more than enough for me. I was grinning ravenously when she returned.

"Amelia," she sighed my name out. "Why the hell do you look like that? Haven't you satisfied your . . . hunger for the night already?" Alena sounded tired and looked flustered as she met my gaze.

I chuckled, laying on my side. "I don't think I'll ever be satisfied in the case of you."

She sat beside me with the green gift bag and an envelope.

"What's that? Another card?" I reached for it, but she briefly held it away.

"No, but it's something you might want to see." She handed it to me then. My brows came together as I looked from her to the envelope. I opened the flap and pulled out a cream-colored paper. The first words I noticed were in bold: *Petition for Dissolution of Marriage.* Then I saw *Teresa A.H* loosely scribbled at the bottom, opposite Alena's signature.

My jaw dropped as I looked up at her relieved expression. "She signed it?" I gasped.

"Yes. *Finally.*" A smile slipped through the cracks.

"Oh my God." I shook my head and read it over again. "I can't believe it," I said.

"I almost didn't believe it myself," she agreed.

I hesitated. "Is that why she came to see you?"

"Yes, it was. I was a bit irritated when I first saw her, but she told me she tried calling—and that she didn't want to pop up here again even though she knew I'd be pleased with the information she was bringing." Alena's eyes wandered for a moment before she looked back at me. "Our conversation was definitely cordial and not as tense as it's been since I moved out, but it certainly wasn't loving or whatever you thought before." She shook her head. "I think Teresa's only signing it because she knows it'll make me happy and . . ."

"Making you happy might also make you want her again sometime in the future?" I guessed. A single nod from Alena confirmed that my assumption and her beliefs coincided.

"But despite her motivations, I'm happy. I won't have to worry about this for much longer. I can just live freely and do what I want without the legal weight on my shoulders." She took the envelope from me and set it on the side table along with the gift before she tipped my chin up and kissed me.

"Thank you for always being there and supporting me every step of the way, Amelia. You've listened to me and comforted me and given me advice—and I know it couldn't have been easy. I understand that it's been difficult for so many reasons, but I can't imagine not having you in my life."

"Neither can I." I grinned wistfully.

Her naked body pressed against mine as she embraced me, and I felt an ache between my legs. "Okay, let me see the gift before I get distracted," I shakily muttered.

She bit down on her bottom lip. "Your weakness is adorable." She grabbed the bag and handed it to me.

When I unwrapped the tissue and reached in, my hand bumped

into a jewelry box. I slowly opened it, and my eyes grew wide as soon as I saw what was inside. Alena had gotten me a silver sun-shaped necklace.

"This is gorgeous, Alena," I smiled broadly as I held it up to the light and examined it further.

"Let me put it on you," she suggested when I lowered the necklace. I turned so she could unhook it and fasten it around my neck—and once it was secure, I placed my hand on it and rubbed the tiny rays.

She then lifted the necklace with her fingers. "You're the sun," she said and leaned forward. I thought she was going to kiss me, but she moved her other hand to her neck and picked up her own necklace. "I'm the moon."

Chapter 22 Don't Apologize

I froze in the bathroom, panicking as the sound of clacking boots made their way back toward me. The scowling figure that appeared behind me in the mirror was so beautiful—so much so that I almost stopped fidgeting with my hair to properly appraise her.

"Amelia," Alena groaned, folding her arms.

"I'm almost done!" I shrieked.

Her expression told me that she didn't believe it for one second. "If you don't stop playing around with your hair—and what outfit is this now?!" She stepped forward and lifted the bottom of my dress. "Baby, you do know that we're going to view the apartment first, right?" She sounded a little too judgmental for my liking, but I still felt a thud in my chest from her choice of words.

"I love it when you call me, baby." I turned around and gave her a sultry grin.

She grasped my hips and leaned down to face me. "And I love it when we get to places that we're supposed to be *on time*."

I couldn't resist placing a kiss on her nose before pulling away. "I was ready, but then you made me look underdressed, so I changed." I frowned as I looked from my dress to her outfit. I then walked past her to where my clothes lay in front of the bedroom closet. "Now I'm starting to think that I'm overdressed," I said, scratching the back of my head.

"I don't believe in being overdressed." She trailed behind me. "But I also don't know how comfortable you'll be wearing that when we tour the apartment and go for drinks before dinner. We'll be doing a lot of walking in the city too, and it's *cold*."

It was adorable just how concerned she sounded. I observed her in her plain jeans, cream sweater, and brown boots then frowned again. "I guess I should try one more outfit."

"Whatever you do, please just hurry. We need to leave here in the next ten minutes so we can meet Nova and Kevin at the complex."

"Okay, okay!" I unzipped the dress and ripped it off, paying no attention to her as I searched for the hanger and hung the dress up in the open closet.

"On second thought," I heard her murmur from behind me. "Maybe we *can* be a little late."

"What?" I spun around to find her eyes fixated on my body.

"I don't think I've seen you wear this before." She stepped toward me and traced a finger from my shoulder down to my lacy bra.

"I uh, put it on after my shower." I had completely forgotten about the lingerie I'd finally decided to wear. I figured it was enough of a gamble as to whether she would see it or not, so there'd be no harm in trying it out.

"It's new?" she asked, bringing her other hand down to the lace of the panties. She brushed against the fabric and brought her thumb to my sensitive bud tucked underneath. She then moved closer to me, her fingers now tracing around the area in a circular motion.

My heart pounded in my chest while my clit throbbed beneath the underwear. I too easily gave in to the urge to roll my hips into her gentle, satisfying touch. My breathing faltered then, and I stifled a moan while a surge of pleasure rushed through my veins. It took me a moment to regain my senses, and when I did, I firmly grasped her hand.

"Don't keep doing that unless you really want to be late," I sputtered out a warning as best as I could manage.

"Right." She removed both of her hands from my body and stepped back, shaking her head lightly. Her face was flushed. "You have three minutes!" she declared, stamping out of the room and slamming the door behind her.

Alena's fixation on being timely made it so that even being late was early. We pulled up to The Burberry for the set time of three-thirty and patiently awaited Nova's arrival.

I was stunned when Alena first invited me to tour the apartment that Nova had found for her. I would be there enough to warrant at least an opinion on it, she had pointed out, but more than that—she was eager for me to meet her close friend.

The apartment complex was the same distance away from me as the Brookfield Apartments, but it was a bit farther away from the university. We were set to meet Nova here, and she would then introduce us to the subletting tenant, Kevin, who was "a friend of a friend." After the apartment tour, we would all head downtown to take in the sights of the city before dinner.

The Burberry was located on the edge of Greenwood's downtown center. It was right on par with the Brookfield Apartments in terms of pricing, but there were certain structural differences that Alena preferred here. One was that the apartment door was located on the inside of the building which was only accessible from the locked lobby and a keycard elevator. Teresa stood no chance of popping up here if that was still something to worry about, and it likely was. I held very little faith in the idea that the fierce and riveting redhead would actually stay away. Her personality was too persistent for me to believe she had so easily given up a fight she had yet to win—especially when "the prize" in her eyes was Alena.

"I should've let you stay distracted before we left," I grumbled. I was growing bored waiting in the car, despite being seated next to my favorite person in the world. Nova was running late because of traffic on her way up from Raleigh.

"I don't know," she sighed. "We might've had to cancel this meeting altogether if you didn't snap me out of it."

"Exactly the reason I wish I hadn't," I complained.

"There's always later . . ." She licked her lips as she stared at my chest. I'd chosen to wear a tan, long-sleeved sweater with a deep V-neck, purely for her satisfaction. "But for now, I'll just enjoy the view." She intertwined our fingers and set our hands on the center console.

"How much do you know about Kevin?" I asked, leaning my head back on the headrest. My skin was buzzing from her touch.

"Not much yet. Just that he's an extremely talented software engineer that's looking for someone to rent out his apartment for a few months while he's in another country."

"Good for him," I said.

"Mm-hmm," she agreed. "Apparently, Nova and Kevin are best buds now too. She's always making instant friends with people." Alena laughed. "Or enemies."

Enemies? My jaw tightened. "What were you two when you first met?"

Alena shifted toward me looking slightly perplexed. "I uh . . ." She cleared her throat. "Enemies, I guess. But it's not important."

"Yes it is! If *you* were her enemy, then nobody's safe. You're one of the nicest people out there."

"Not everyone sees me in that light, Amelia. It'll be fine." She kissed the back of my hand.

"I was excited to start meeting your friends, Alena, but I don't know. Nova sounds terrifying."

"She's great, I promise. She's different . . . which I love, and she's very blunt." Alena grinned as if she were recalling Nova's candor at that very moment.

"Blunt can be scary."

"I wouldn't let her do anything to you, Amelia." She released her hand from mine and brought it to my cheek. The thumping of loud music suddenly alerted us; it could be heard before we could even see the small blue car whip into the parking lot.

"Here she is!" Alena cried out, beaming with excitement. She dropped her hand and waved.

The pale figure in the car had an impassive expression that immediately altered once she noticed Alena waving at her. Alena quieted the engine, snatched her keys out of the ignition, and dashed to Nova's door, yanking it open and pulling her friend into a hug.

Nova was wearing entirely black clothing, from her aviator jacket and tight jeans to her shiny combat boots. The faintest sign of a tattoo could be seen at the bottom of her neck. Her short, spiky hair was a blend of jet black, magenta, and cobalt blue. She had winged eyeliner at the edge of her eyes and a dark shade of purple on her eyelids and lips. A silver piercing encircled her bottom lip, and an identical barbell went through her left eyebrow.

I opened my door and exited the vehicle just as Alena was setting her small friend back on the ground.

"Fuck, Alena! It's been too long!" she howled.

"I saw you a month ago, Nova."

"Still! I used to see you like every week, and I miss that. No one ever told you to move to *Greenwood*." She scrunched her nose, feigning disgust.

"Don't act like you don't love it here," Alena said.

"Only because I get to see *you*," she replied.

I shut the door behind me and wandered closer to them.

"This must be the girlfriend," she broadcasted animatedly, sticking out her hand. "I'm Nova, goddess of all things lesbian entertainment. It's nice to finally meet you. I heard you've liked my recommendations so far."

I shook her hand and smiled. "Yes, I've loved them! I can't believe I didn't know about all those movies and shows before."

"Not that we've actually gotten to *finish* any of them," Alena whispered under her breath. I looked up at her and playfully smacked her shoulder. She furrowed her brows but had a grin on her face when she grabbed my hand.

The shrill sound of Aerosmith's "Dream On" stole our attention. Nova reached back into her car and grabbed her ringing phone along with her wallet-sized purse. "Hello? Yeah, we're outside, Kev." She paused for a moment while the person on the other end spoke. "Because I just got here!" She slammed the door and walked toward the building's entrance, waving us to follow behind her. "Yeah, well I'm here now. There was just so much fuckin traffic. . . . They were already here waiting for me. Just come open the door. *Please.*" She hung up the phone then clicked the lock on her car. We now stood outside in the cold, waiting in front of a large glass door. Despite the chilliness of the day, it was sunny, and the sky was empty and blue.

"So it's Kev now, huh? You move mighty fast, Nova," Alena remarked.

She shrugged. "You know me. He's no longer a friend of a friend. Just my friend, however damned annoying he can be." She rolled her eyes.

A slender, brown-skinned man with a green and white Hawaiian shirt and faded jeans approached us from the lobby. He swaggered as if he had arms too big for his shoulders, but he was not very muscular at all. As he neared the door, I could easily tell that he was several inches taller than Alena. His head was shaved down and he wore an expensive-looking pair of square-framed prescription glasses.

"Hello everyone," he courteously greeted us upon opening the door. Nova entered first with Alena and me following behind. "Sorry to keep you waiting. I didn't know *Nova* would be so late." He narrowed his eyes at her, and she immediately wrapped an arm around his waist.

"I'm never late. Everyone else was just early," she reasoned.

Kevin scoffed. "Sure." He showed us around the lobby which had white marble floors and navy-blue walls. There was a large ball-shaped chandelier over a glass table in the main room. I counted at least five different Christmas trees: one large and green, another two that were frosty white, and a blue and pink one in each of the see-through leasing agent offices.

"It's extremely festive in here, isn't it?" Nova grumbled.

"Hold it in, Nova," Alena warned. "I know you despise Christmas cheer."

"Don't say that!" she protested. "They'll believe you. I love Christmas as much as your average person, but don't you think they did a little too much here?"

"No, I don't," Alena disagreed.

"I kinda feel Nova on this," I chimed in, which prompted Alena to look down at me with a muddled expression.

"Really? You're the art critic. Is this not a beautiful variety in decorations?" She gestured toward the trees.

"Yes, but there's no organization whatsoever. Not one common theme apart from Christmas. I hope they have someone coming in to spruce it up a bit." I pursed my lips and looked down.

"They do." Kevin finally joined the conversation. "The manager was out of town for a few weeks unexpectedly. He'll have a fit when he sees this, but I'm with Alena on this one. I like it."

"See?!" Alena expressed delightedly.

Kevin pointed down the hall past the elevators toward a large window at the end and two black doors. "That's the entrance from the garage. You'll of course have a reserved space there in lieu of mine if you decide to stay here. My mom is keeping my car with her while I'm away."

He led us to the elevators, and Alena put her hands around my waist as we all huddled inside. Kevin slipped a keycard into the slot above the control panel and pressed floor five.

"The complex is only six or seven years old so most everything is updated. I say *most* because I personally think that they could've gotten newer appliances when they first built the place."

"You're also obsessed with technology," Nova interjected.

He lifted his finger and pointed in her direction. "That I am." He turned back to us. "There's a washer and dryer in-apartment. The windows are remote controlled." He clapped his hands together. "My stereo and light systems are quite elaborate, and you'll be more than welcome to use them both."

"Which rooms do they go through?" Alena asked.

"The entire unit." Kevin grinned, obviously pleased with himself.

When the elevator doors opened, we followed him down the long hallway to unit 511. "The rooms have both keycards and keys." He held up a set from his pocket and jingled them. "I prefer the keycard when I'm coming back late or just feeling lazy, but there's something special about using keys." He opened the door. I might've thought he'd just opened the gates of heaven if it weren't for the lack of golden chariots and blinding lights—or whatever heaven was supposed to open up to. But it was only the stereo that he had previously mentioned now blasting opera into the hallway.

He grabbed a small control off the counter and lowered the volume. "My bad. I was coding, and it helps me to listen to something melodic."

"No worries," Alena said as we entered. "It was beautiful anyway." She tilted her head up to look at the hanging light fixtures.

There was a contemporary kitchen to the left of us with glossy wooden floors that layered the entire apartment. A glass dining table was tucked near the wall on the other side. A blue sectional sofa lay near the base of floor to ceiling windows, and a zebra-striped rug decorated the floor beneath a puddle-shaped glass table. The TV in front of the window was massive.

We shed our coats as Kevin slid off his slides near a shoe rack by the door. "You're all welcome to my beverages. There's alcohol, soda, juice, and bottled waters in the fridge. Whenever you're ready, Alena, I can give you a little overview of the place." Kevin moved toward the couch and Alena soon followed.

Nova stayed behind with me in the kitchen while Kevin and Alena discussed the details of a potential sublease. She poured a glass of some dark liquid from a square decanter on his counter.

"So," Nova began quietly, pouring more of the liquid into another cup and pushing it my way. "You're the one who's had my good friend in a frenzy all semester. Well, other than her dumbass wife, that is."

It seems we shared a disdain for Teresa. "I guess so." I palmed the glass cup as I sat on a cushioned barstool. "What's this?"

"Don't know." She threw back a large gulp of it. "Whiskey. It's good." She finished the glass then poured another one for herself.

"She was in a frenzy?" I asked uncomfortably, sipping the drink. It would've been better with ice, but it was still good.

"Oh, absolutely. Between me and her friend Desirée, she was acting like a madwoman." She stepped closer to me but didn't sit down. "Three-way calls and all. The only three way I've had in a while, unfortunately," she seemed to lament that fact as she sipped on her second drink.

I did well to hold in a verbal reaction to her unexpected comment but not so much a physical one, as my face clearly expressed my shock.

"I say the first thing that comes to my mouth. It's a habit. And I don't apologize for it either." She smiled. "But I guarantee you, I'm really nice. Mostly."

"I didn't mean to have her so worried." I frowned. "It's just a difficult situation."

"Damn right it is. I hope you've kept it under wraps. She loves teaching more than anything. I wouldn't want you to ruin that for her."

"Trust me, I wouldn't either." I quieted. "And we did keep things discreet by the way. No one really knows, even now." *Except my best friends, but that's not really important, is it?*

"Alena must really like you." She spoke suddenly and sharply. "She's never liked them young. *Ever.*"

My stomach churned as Nova finished off the glass and rinsed the cup. I felt like my heart was stuck in my throat when Alena and Kevin returned. "So . . . what are we doing now?" I asked, spinning around on the bar stool to face Alena and instantly feeling relief at escaping Nova's intensity.

"Kevin said we should look at the rest of the place now." Alena held out her hand. The two of us slipped off to a room on the right which was no doubt Kevin's office. It was evident from the desk and brown leather chair sitting in front of a large window. Two small potted plants were strategically placed on opposite ends of the desk.

"Ooh, what are these?" I asked, releasing Alena's hand and reaching for a plant.

She followed me and picked up one of the pots. "These are succulents," she declared confidently. "If I'm not mistaken, they're Aeonium Kiwis."

"Wow. You're really good with the plant names."

"I thought I proved that to you a long time ago." She set the plant back down and perused the other side of the office. "You asked me the name of every single plant you saw when I took you to that hotel in Charlotte. And the ones in Jess's apartment, and anywhere else we've gone that's had live plants."

"True. But it's still pretty incredible to me. Lettie's probably going to grow up to be just like you." I was now looking at a black Gibson guitar in the corner of the room.

"Who's Lettie?" she asked lightly, stepping beside me to examine the guitar as well.

"Mya's niece. She's really into flowers right now. Lettie's only three, but she taught me the names of plenty of flowers already. It's only a matter of time before she gets started on plants too."

"That's adorable." Alena smiled and turned around. "I like this room. It's perfect for grading papers with a view. Let's see the rest, shall we?"

I could hear Kevin and Nova's laughter coming from the kitchen as we left the room.

"Hurry up slow pokes, I'm ready to explore the city!" Nova whined when she caught sight of us.

"Maybe you should learn some patience, Nova," Alena countered.

We promptly toured the half-bathroom next to the office before we crossed to the other side of the apartment where Alena meticulously inspected Kevin's bedroom suite. I watched as she stood in front of the window with her hands on her hips, her head tilted up, and her eyes closed.

"Yes," she exhaled as she relaxed her position and turned around. "I can definitely see myself waking up to this view."

"Me too." I gave a sly smile as I stepped in her direction.

"Hopefully *we* won't be seen too clearly here then." She squeezed my ass as she walked past me. "I'll have to ask in case we want to take in the view naked."

My mouth fell open, and she smirked before giving me a quick once over that set my heart rate accelerating. "I'll have to make sure that Kevin's cool with candles too," she added, stepping toward the bathroom.

It didn't take us much longer to complete our tour after that. Lucky for Alena, the man was clean; his entire apartment was spick and span.

"It's perfect," she said, looking down at me as we stood in the bathroom. "What do you think, Amelia?" she asked.

"If you like it, I love it." I beamed.

"I'll take that in a good way." She poked my nose then dragged me by the hand back toward the bedroom door.

"I have one question, Kevin," Alena said, stepping just outside of the room.

Kevin and Nova both turned around from the kitchen.

"Do you mind candles?" she asked.

"Not at all," Kevin assured her as he sprung up and walked into the bedroom. He opened a drawer under a TV stand directly across from the bed, revealing a broad collection of color-coded candles. "You're more than welcome to bring any candles you have, but these candles are also at your disposal," he offered warmly. "I'm always buying more. The pots and pans are available for you too. Nova says your cooking is spectacular."

I instinctively grabbed my stomach. "Nova's right."

"I'll clear a space for you in the closet and drawers too of course," Kevin added.

Nova had peered around the corner of the room by now. "So are you gonna rent here or not?" she asked impatiently.

"As long as Kevin is still on board with everything we discussed, then yes!"

Kevin smiled and nodded. "Let's do it!"

Alena looked at me excitedly. "You'll have to get used to driving over here instead of Brookfield whenever you visit."

"I think I'm fine with that." I grinned as we walked back to the main room.

"I'm so glad you needed somewhere to stay, Alena," Kevin said. "I thought it would be impossible to find someone reliable willing to take it off my hands before I left."

Nova moved to Kevin's side. "You should buy Rianne and I a drink for it. Without us, you wouldn't have found Alena."

"Seems to me you've had plenty of drinks already." He motioned toward his decanter on the counter.

"Oh, please!" She slapped him on the shoulder. "That's nothing."

"Ouch." He rubbed the area. "Well, I'm buying everyone's dinner tonight, so I hope that'll be enough consolation."

"Kevin, you don't have to do that," Alena assured him.

"I insist." He held his hand to his heart and bowed slightly. "You're doing me a favor, really. I no longer have to pay double rent while I'm away."

"It still feels like an even bigger favor for me," she said, reaching behind her as she spoke and relaxing when I grabbed her hand.

"How long have you two been together?" Kevin asked, adjusting his glasses with a smile.

Alena blushed. "Not that long yet." She looked back to me and grinned. "Just over a month."

"You make a great couple." He nodded before clearing his throat and abruptly rushing to his room. "Let me grab a coat!" he shouted from the room. "Then we can take my car a little more central and walk downtown. I've already made reservations for five o'clock."

"Where at?!" Nova shouted in his direction.

"A Brazilian steakhouse not too far from that bar I told you about," he answered, walking back in with a large gray peacoat that hung down the length of his tall body. He held a brown pair of leather boots in his hands.

Nova tilted her head back. "Oh yeah, the one with the special old fashioned cocktails. Where have you been all my life, Kev? No one appreciates those drinks the same as us."

"Timing must've been waiting for us to meet." He was bent over, slipping on the boots while the three of us found our coats where they were draped over the sofa and put them on.

"Timing should've hurried the fuck up. I'll definitely have to visit here more often." She looked from Kevin to Alena.

"As long as you keep visiting once I'm actually back in the country," he said before standing tall. "I'm ready."

Chapter 23 Must Be

The outing that Alena and I had with Kevin and Nova was extremely entertaining. She and I spent the majority of time gossiping and flirting with one another while they were busy speaking a completely different language.

Kevin was overly knowledgeable about the city's architecture, as well as its upcoming developments—and Nova was equally adept in developmental intricacies far beyond the scope of our understanding. The unique pair seemed to talk in formulas and code for half the evening before either of them even noticed they were leaving us out. Aside from that, they made on like a married couple in the ways they joked and bickered with one another, so it felt more like a double date than anything. If it weren't for the fact that Nova was a raging lesbian and that Kevin was completely contented with a life of solitude, I'd choose them to be the perfect couple.

By the time dinner was over, everyone except me had become intoxicated, so I ended up having to drive Kevin's Range Rover back to the apartment. Alena and Nova had not only taken two shots of tequila before they left, but they then proceeded to drink several orders of cocktails at the restaurant as well. It had been a smart move for me not to drink after I had some of Kevin's whiskey. Alena deserved to have a carefree night and the proper opportunity to unwind—and I was happy she was having just that.

Once I'd driven us back to Kevin's place, we stayed there for over an hour while Nova and Alena drunkenly caught up with each other and Kevin drunkenly played video games. After one last round of shots, they finally crashed. All three of them were knocked out where they lay on Kevin's sectional, so I decided it was time for us to leave.

I drove mostly in silence on the way back to the Brookfield Apartments. A loud snoring erupted from the back of the car where Nova lay with her arm limp over the seat. She had decided earlier in the evening to stay the night in Greenwood before heading back to Raleigh the next day. Her snores woke up Alena who had immediately fallen asleep once we settled into the car. She now held in her laughter as she studied me, still in a daze.

"She always forgets how small she is," she whispered, looking back at her sleeping friend.

"I can understand that for her. But what's your excuse tonight?" I muttered, flashing her a daring grin.

"You think you're so funny, don't you?" she chuckled softly. "God, I love you," she cooed, placing her hand on my thigh.

"I love you too." I put my free hand on top of hers and ignored the pulsing between my legs.

"So, did you like it?" She was putting her words together well, but her voice was slurred enough for me to know that she was intoxicated.

"Did I like *what*, babe?" I asked, focusing on the dark road.

"Kevin and the apartment," she said, lowering her voice as she continued, "and Nova."

"Yeah," I nodded. "I did. The apartment's great, and I'm really glad that you'll be able to move in quickly. I know you didn't want to inconvenience Jess, and I honestly didn't like any of those other places you were considering."

"Now you tell me," she snorted.

I finally pulled into the familiar parking lot and found a space near the front. "Oh, and I like them both. Kevin *and* sleepy pants back there." I gestured in Nova's direction. It was true that I liked her, but it was also true that she concerned me. I had the faintest suspicion that she didn't particularly care for or trust me—and that she didn't want me to be with Alena.

She smiled at me drunkenly. "Good."

I turned off the engine and let out a deep breath while Alena's eyes stayed focused on me.

"So uh," she whispered as she played with my fingers, "would you like to finish what we started earlier?"

I froze and looked at her with wide eyes. "Nova's back there," I reminded her.

"Okay and?" She stared in my direction. "Answer the question." She slid her hands over my chest which prompted me to become even more flustered.

"Okay, okay!" I frantically whispered, shooing her off. "When we get inside though, alright?"

Her face lit up with a contented expression as she reached her arm over the seat to shake her friend. "Nova! Get up! We're at my place!"

I stared into the bathroom mirror as I shook my toothbrush and placed it in its holder. I was dressed in a pair of pajamas I had thrown on over the lingerie Alena begged me to keep on. I was surprised at my lack of fatigue. I had no worries of falling asleep anytime soon, although all I wanted to do for at least a hundred hours straight was to lie down and cuddle with Alena. She was still in the living room setting Nova up on the couch with a makeshift bed for the night and hopefully drinking some water while she was at it. I hopped on the bed to wait for her.

The door finally opened, and Alena slipped back into the room with a cup and a water bottle. "Good, you got water," I breathed out in relief. "But what's in the cup?" I sat up on my knees and leaned toward her to get a look.

"It's something for *Sober Sally* to get loosened up with," she quietly advertised as she shut the door behind her.

I shrugged. "Well, *someone* had to stay sober. I'm glad I did too. I like experiencing this new version of you while I'm in my right mind."

"Are you saying that I'm no fun sober?" Alena's lips were tightly pressed together as she handed me the cup. "Or when I'm only drinking wine, even?"

"No, I'm just saying that this kind of drunk looks good on you." I admired her from head to toe while licking my lips.

"And that *lingerie* from earlier looks good on you. You've been holding back, my dear." She opened the bottle of water and took a swig. She then set it down on a coaster by the bedside table and began taking off her jewelry.

"I had no idea that that's what you wanted to see," I murmured in between sipping the drink and catching glimpses of her undressing behind me.

"Don't get me wrong, Amelia, you look fantastic naked . . . I'm actually trying to decide which one I'd prefer right now." She stopped, mid-undressing, and tapped her finger on her lips. My body tingled involuntarily from the way she looked at me, and the pace of my heart quickened. "Let me see it again," she ordered in a soft tone that made me want to melt. I held out the cup to her and she took it, throwing back a gulp before placing it on a coaster on the nightstand.

"Damn, you haven't had enough yet?" I asked, sitting up and pulling the pajama shirt over my head.

"It's never enough," she said as I tossed the shirt on the bed and hooked my fingers around the pajama bottoms.

"You can finish taking your clothes off too, you know," I mumbled.

"You first," she urged. I pulled down the pants and she made a satisfied sound. "Now tell me again why the hell I haven't seen these before?" she mused, approaching me with the cup she had picked back up off the nightstand.

"I . . . wasn't sure." Blood rushed down to my core.

"Sure of what?" She handed me the cup. "You should finish that," she suggested with a smirk.

"Sure if we were doing things like that yet." I knew I probably wasn't making much sense at this point, but she had to have known by now just how nervous she made me when she spoke to me a certain way or did certain things. She had continued undressing while staring into my eyes which made me struggle to swallow what was left in my cup.

It wasn't long before she sported her own pair of matching underwear that wasn't necessarily lingerie and wasn't lace but was still very sexy.

"A little lingerie is nothing, Amelia." She grabbed the cup out of my hand once again and put it away. "But when it comes to what we're 'doing,' I'm willing to do just about everything except share you."

I remained silent as I sat perched at the edge of the bed waiting for whatever might be coming next. I didn't know what it was, but from the tone of her voice, I knew it was something I wanted. She came back to where I was, bent down, and whispered to me, "As long as you're comfortable that is." She then kissed me forcefully, biting and nibbling on my lips. This was not at all her usual style, but I surely did enjoy it. When she finally pulled away, she knelt on the bed and asked, "Will you help me with these straps, baby?"

I pressed my lips to her shoulder as I slid my hands over her back. I then captured her waiting lips and unhooked the bra while she simultaneously clutched at the lace covering my breasts. She tumbled on top of me before she could get my bra unhooked, and there was no way for her to pull it off while I was gridlocked by her body on the bed.

"Dammit," she whispered, clearly frustrated. "Take this shit off," she groaned in between kissing me, but I still couldn't move.

Her hands roamed my body and when she grazed the lace panties, she released a moan into my mouth. She pulled herself back enough for me to assist her in unhooking my bra, then snatched it away before she greedily brought her lips to the exposed flesh.

I had to admit to myself that I hadn't quite gotten used to her erratic sexual behavior. Most times she was soft, tender, and loving—but she was very aggressive sometimes, and tonight was no exception. I couldn't slow her down as she impatiently clutched at my naked body.

Liquor-drunk Alena clearly had a thing with using her teeth. She hadn't ever nibbled on my nipples quite like she did now, but she was using the perfect amount of pressure. When our eyes met again, I could almost see the licks of flames in them, and I could tell I was in for a treat.

"Don't forget Nova in the other room," I breathlessly whispered to her.

"I think that's something *you* need to remember," she arrogantly said. "You're going to have to keep quiet for this."

She slid her fingers right through the side of the lacy fabric, and I released a sharp breath as she entered me.

At the crack of dawn, I was awakened by the sound of a toilet flushing outside of the bedroom. My heart pounded violently out of fear before I recalled our unexpected guest sleeping on the makeshift bed for the night. As I calmed down, I rubbed my foot against Alena's smooth, long legs and sleepily studied her face.

My body throbbed from remembrance of the night before. I would definitely have to get some bottles of tequila to keep around her place because it made her absolutely insatiable. I nearly had to beg her to finally let me go to sleep, which had probably only been an hour ago now that I thought about it.

I squeezed my thighs together as I recalled her fingers and her tongue there, releasing all the tension of the previous semester. *Forget deck the halls, deck my walls.* My sleepy, unfiltered thoughts were swirling around my head, and I instinctively moved closer to her. I noticed that her coarse breathing had quieted, and I wondered if she was still sleeping. My eyes were fixed on her lips when she blinked awake and caught me staring at her.

She tilted her head to kiss me as she placed a hand on my cheek. She then rolled on top, propped over me on her knees with her hands on either side of my head. Even with how tired I was, my body yearned for her again. She quietly stared down at me for a moment before kissing my neck. She then nestled her head into my chest and maneuvered the weight of her body to the side. Moments later she was snoring lightly once again. I followed her lead and allowed her soft breathing to carry me out of consciousness.

Several hours later I awakened to the smell of freshly brewed coffee. I noticed the thrum of the vents pumping heat into the room as I grew more conscious, and I finally saw a brightness through the bedroom curtains after I opened my eyes. I could faintly hear the commotion of cars outside in the parking lot, but I could more easily distinguish the laughter now coming from my beautiful girlfriend and her friend in the kitchen.

I groggily sat up and stretched my naked body before shrugging off the bonnet that was already escaping from around my coils. I leaned over to the nightstand and grabbed my phone to check the time. It was half past noon. I walked into the bathroom and took a quick shower before slipping on a pair of Alena's sweatpants and a shirt of mine. As always, her clothes didn't fit me properly, but it didn't matter when I experienced such a comfort and pride in wearing them.

When I entered the front room, I saw that Nova's pallet had been tidied up; the extra sheets were folded and laying on the crease of the black sofa. Alena sat at the table with a steaming cup from Dunkin Donuts. She was typing away on her laptop while Nova sat beside her, craning her neck to see whatever Alena was working on.

Unlike what I would've assumed, Nova did not have on the same outfit that she had worn the night before. She had on a pair of latex leggings and a plum-colored biker jacket with the same black shoes. The jacket perfectly matched her lipstick from the previous day, although she didn't currently have on much makeup aside from a touch of eyeliner and dark brown eyeshadow.

"Morning," Nova greeted me as I made my way toward the sitting pair. Her bright hair was tucked underneath a black beanie.

Alena's head lifted from her computer, and she smiled at me so charmingly that I felt I might burst. Her captivating presence made it hard for me to find any words of greeting.

"I thought you laid her out for at least a full twenty-four hours, Alena? You're losing your edge." Nova smiled cheekily when Alena turned in her direction, a pinkish tint lighting up her face.

"Um. Good morning," I finally said, not knowing how to hide my embarrassment from Nova's comment. Perhaps she had heard us last night despite my resolve to keep quiet. Even thinking of that made me want to fade into the background and disappear. That was until Alena glared at Nova for the slightest moment before standing and quickly stepping toward me. She wrapped her arms around me before pressing her lips to mine. I tasted a strong coffee flavor on them, different from the usual hint of tea.

"Good morning, darling," she said before kissing me once again.

"Get a room!" Nova wailed from behind us. "And dammit, Alena, at least get your woman some coffee first," she continued. "She's going to pass out if you suck any more energy out of her." She burst into laughter. I don't think anything could've prepared me for her level of crudeness.

"Ignore her," Alena whispered, kissing my lips once more and grabbing my hand to pull me to the seat next to her.

"Were we... *loud* last night?" I asked shyly as I slowly seated myself.

"Nah, I was just fucking with you. I slept like a baby." Nova's chin lifted, and she glanced at Alena before throwing up her hands in retreat. "Okay, I'll cool it with the sex jokes."

Alena quietly collected one of the cups from Dunkin and a bag of donuts and placed them in front of me. She was dressed in a pair of high-waisted jeans and a long-sleeved floral top, her hair neatly tucked into a curly bun. "I didn't want to wake you, so I took Nova to get her car probably two hours ago now. She *just* got the Dunkin though. I was hoping you'd be up soon, so I made her wait until I heard you stirring in the room."

"Thanks for that." I smiled, opening the crinkling bag and pulling out a raspberry-filled donut. Alena must've remembered me telling her it was one of my favorites—who knows how long ago.

"I don't think I've ever seen you with coffee," I noted, biting into the doughy sweetness.

"It's about the only thing that helps me with a hangover which—as you know—I almost never get."

"Not anymore at least," Nova interjected with an unwaveringly smug expression on her face.

"Leave the past in the past, won't you?" Alena pleaded.

"Grad school almost took this one out," Nova continued anyway, gesturing toward Alena but directing her words at me. "She wasn't much of an undergrad drunk as far as I know, but she could *definitely* go as a grad student."

"I don't even know why I did that." Alena's lips pursed. "It was the first time I was ever so reckless with my education. But look at me now." She took a sip of her drink, seemingly her last as she shook an empty sounding cup. "Don't forget your coffee," she said, pointing toward my cup. "It's an Americano."

Of course she remembered what I used to drink before she got me hooked on tea. "Thanks," I spoke with a mouth full of dough since I was neck deep into my second donut.

"I heard you have a birthday coming up," Nova said.

I swallowed the piece of donut I was working on and followed it with several delicious sips of coffee. "Yeah, it's the twenty-second." I searched her for any hidden hostility, but I wasn't sure exactly what it was that I was seeing in her deep blue eyes.

"How old are you turning?" she asked, crossing her arms.

"Twenty-two." My eyes briefly flitted to Alena who had refocused her attention on her computer once again. I felt nervous about what Nova might say concerning my age.

"Golden birthday! Or year or—whatever the fuck they call it. You're getting up there just like us, huh," she snickered.

Well that could've been worse. I released my breath and finished my donut while Alena and Nova talked about their plans for the upcoming holidays.

Not a moment too soon, Nova slapped her hands on the table and stood. "Well! I'm going to head back to my rightful part of the state. I just didn't want to be rude as fuck and not say goodbye to you, Amelia. Even if I would've had to wait the full twenty-four." She grinned, and Alena looked from her to me with softened eyes despite the resurgence of sex jokes.

"I really appreciate that, Nova." Alena stood and hugged her friend.

I put down the third donut I was about to tear into and wiped my hands on a napkin before standing. Nova had never hugged me, so I figured we would part in a handshake just like when we met. But she pulled me into her arms instead and squeezed me tightly. "Take care of my friend, won't you?" she whispered before letting go.

Was this a peace offering? Was yesterday's attitude only a scare tactic to gauge my level of seriousness with Alena? Whatever it was, I was just glad it was over. Nova had damn near terrified me because she wasn't one to mince words. If I had done something wrong—or what she perceived to be wrong—she was sure to let everyone know. I was positive that she would speak openly against me if she hadn't liked me for any other reason as well. But here she was, hugging me and telling me to 'take care of Alena.' I had definitely succeeded in gaining my first ounce of trust from one of Alena's friends, and it made me proud.

Once Nova gathered all her things, Alena and I walked her out to her car. "Don't think it's lost on me that you two have hit the 'matching necklace stage,'" she said as she leaned between the open door of her car.

I looked up at Alena. "I'm part of a *stage*?" I asked curiously.

"No," she laughed.

"I don't know why I said it like that." Nova laughed too. "I actually haven't even seen her hit this stage once to be honest." She shrugged. "You must be special." And with that she climbed into her vehicle and slammed the door shut.

Alena and I waved as she sped away, music blasting. Alena then looked down at me and smiled. "You *are* special," she said as she grabbed my hand and led me back toward her apartment.

The second the door closed behind us, Alena pushed me backward and hemmed me to the wall with her hand. *God she's strong.* I'm sure my eyes were bulging out of their sockets, but she smirked as she looked down at me, hand on my chest. Her fingers trailed to my nipples which she pinched and circled gently.

"You know what? Nova might've had a point." She spoke lustfully.

"W-what's that?" My body quivered as her other hand slid toward my pants.

She raked her eyes over my body. "You *should* still be laid out right now." Her expression was smug, and her gaze was piercing. "But it's okay, darling, we can fix that." My heart throbbed in tandem with my clit as she grasped my hips with both of her hands. She pulled me to the sofa and sat me down. "Something about you wearing my clothes... and proudly in front of other people. It does things to me."

She got on her knees, and after she shrugged the sweatpants down, she leered at me. "No underwear?" She inspected me carefully, grazing her hands over my pussy. She then brought the pants down to my feet and lifted my legs over each of her shoulders. "I don't want to leave a mess," she said before lifting my ass off the couch and leaning her face in between my thighs.

"*Shit*," I breathed, my hands gripping the sofa.

"You're always so wet for me, Amelia," she hummed as she kissed around my center. I wanted to cry out, but I somehow kept my composure.

"Tell me what you want." I could feel her breath on me, her lips tickling my clit when she spoke.

"I want you," I puffed out.

"You want me *what*? Baby, be specific."

"I want you to fuck me. *Please*," I begged.

"Oh, you're so polite. I'll fuck you," she agreed. "But how would you like me to?"

I groaned as her lips brushed over my entrance and her fingers grazed my thighs. "Your tongue!" I cried out, in agony now.

She licked me slowly then—too slowly. My legs trembled involuntarily as I thrust my hips upward. I whimpered, and my eyes rolled back when she pushed her tongue inside me, her nose pressing up against my throbbing button.

"Oh!" I moaned. *"Shiiit!"*

Alena's hands gripped my ass, holding me up as her tongue explored me for what felt like a lifetime. "You taste so fucking good, Amelia," she said, finally pulling away. She then sucked my clit into her mouth and moaned.

I shook uncontrollably at her touch. Her mouth was warm and wet on me. My hands moved down to caress her face as she gave me the kind of pleasure I'd only dreamed of experiencing. At some point, she reached for one of my hands—and as our fingers intertwined, I began to feel a pleasant buildup radiating from my core. Alena didn't stop ravishing me until I came—and when I did, her tongue remained on me as she licked me clean.

My back hurt, and my legs were uselessly hanging over her shoulders when she pulled them down and slid the sweatpants back up. She then laid her head on my lap and rubbed her hands up my side for a few moments before she hoisted my body to a standing position and held me there until I was stable.

"I changed my mind. I think we should get lunch soon. You need more energy before we do anything else," she stated as she walked away, finally wiping her face which was glistening from my wetness.

"I know what I want to eat." My voice was weaker than I would've liked it to be, which made her chuckle as she washed her face in the bathroom.

"Maybe when you can at least speak in a normal voice, I can be on the menu," she said.

I didn't have the strength to contest her claims, so I moved on to something else. "I was going to ask when we got back here without Nova, before you . . ." When she shut off the water and stepped out of the bathroom, her beauty struck me once again. I lost my words for a moment. "What were you two looking at on the computer?" I finally forced out.

"Applications." She turned off the light and led me to the bedroom.

"For?" I raised a brow as we both sat down on the bed.

"Remember when I told you I wanted to start teaching somewhere new?"

"Yeah, since you want a fresh start away from Greenwood. I remember."

She nodded. "Mm-hmm. Well, that's where Nova comes in. She's amazing with resumes. She helped me get my job here, so I asked her to look over some of my stuff."

"Okay, well that's great." I smiled. "I'm sure every university you apply to will be salivating over you. You're literally the best professor I've had. Your lectures in the course were truly amazing. I'll make sure to leave an astounding review."

"Don't do that," she laughed as she moved to the middle of the bed and lay on her back. "You're far too biased."

"Fine, I won't." I crawled over her and lay flat with my head on her chest, feeling a dull ache in my core as our hips touched. "What're your top three places?" I asked earnestly.

"Wake Forest, NC State—Nova would be thrilled with that—and USC."

"Oh wow, *USC*?" I looked up at her from my current position. "Which one? The one in California?"

She nodded. "I thought it'd be nice to be back, you know? But honestly, I started that process before you and I even . . ." she sighed deeply.

I sat up and rested on my arm, keeping my other hand on her chest. "Alena, I don't matter in this decision."

"You what? Don't be silly, Amelia."

"I'm dead serious. If you want or need to move somewhere else for a fresh start, I understand that. I'll be here regardless."

"Yes, *here* in North Carolina for three more years at least, right? That's where you're planning to go for grad school."

"*If* I even go to grad school. None of my decisions are final, Alena."

"And neither are mine," she retorted. I could feel that her heartbeat had increased. This clearly put her on edge—but for some odd reason, I wasn't worried in the slightest. I felt comfortable being together even if distance was involved. I trusted our transparency with one another, especially after she had proved to me countless times that I was the only one she was interested in. She had shown no signs of pulling away from me any time soon.

"Apply wherever *you* want to go and the logistics for *us* can be handled later, alright?" I murmured gently. I tipped her chin with my hand and saw the fear in her eyes as she looked at me. "Alright?" I said once again, even softer, and she nodded.

Chapter 24 Delicate People

The sound of loud barking stirred me as a slew of random thoughts blew past. I blinked open my eyes and saw Alena on a beach. She wanted to swim with me, but I was afraid because the waves were too big. Still, I followed her into the water, and I waded there until a current struck me. I started to drown and was scared to death until I felt her hand grab mine. When she pulled me to the surface, I immediately gasped for air. I couldn't tear myself away from her horror-stricken face, but that's when everything suddenly faded.

◆ ◆

I shot up in bed as the barking continued—even louder this time—and I stared into the darkness. I heard a door alarm and then the sound of Pinky running through the house like it was a playground. She must've quickly settled herself somewhere because it soon became quiet again.

As my body adjusted to consciousness, I noticed a weak, rustling sound coming from my bed. I shuffled through the sheets and found my phone. On it, I could clearly see and hear Alena snoring. I smiled despite my confusion. She and I didn't usually sleep on the phone when we were away, and I didn't even remember calling her in the first place. Perhaps I had drunkenly dialed her before I passed out in my bed. Why had I passed out in my bed anyway? And what day and time was it? I looked for the answers on my phone. When I found them, I released a breath of relief. It was the twenty-third of December which meant that my birthday was over.

I didn't particularly dislike my birthday, but the usual celebration with my family had definitely changed its tone this year. I had almost decided to stay longer in North Carolina because of it. I even considered heading straight to Florida like Mya suggested, but in the end the idea was discarded. Each of my younger siblings had separately called and begged me to return home for the holidays. They understood my reluctance in coming back and had even told me they were punishing my parents in their own way for not being accepting of me, but it didn't completely change my mind. Ultimately, the voice of reason came from my grandmother, who not only convinced me to come home for Christmas but to also arrive in time for my birthday.

She had been at my parents' house since the second week of December, and she would remain there until New Year's. She knew there was tension between my parents and I, but I hadn't told her the reason why. She had gently urged me to at least spend my birthday with her and my siblings, even if I had to fully cut my parents out of the festivities—even if she had to shoo them away herself. The suggestion made me laugh, and I nearly laughed my way to the airport.

On my birthday, I'd awakened to a bountiful breakfast which included my favorite biscuits from childhood that my grandmother made from scratch. My mom had fixed me a special cocktail that wasn't too strong since she rightfully presumed I would be drinking my way through the day. I had become tipsy before noon, and I was having an excellent time.

My siblings took me to a gaming park that afternoon, and I enjoyed the feeling of being a kid once again. We later met with my parents and grandmother at a restaurant for a special birthday dinner—and there, I drank plenty of cocktails. It was easier for me to pretend with my parents when I was any level of intoxicated than it was to deal with them sober.

My favorite part of the day was looking at the racy pictures Alena sent to "keep me warm" through the night. I knew that it was only a sneak preview of what I would get to see when we reunited in the next week and a half. She had flown to California on the eighteenth, and she wasn't thrilled about not being able to spend time with me on my actual birthday. To compensate, she made damn sure I had a hell of a celebration before she left. We had enjoyed a "Christmas lights date" per my request—where the beauty of the lights, the warmth of the car, and the sweetness of our kisses blended perfectly with our hot chocolate. The night out with her had been just as magical as the early-birthday-sex that followed.

I missed her dearly, but we wouldn't be back together until the new year. In the meantime, we had to settle for phone calls and video chats. We'd spoken on the phone nearly every day or night since she left, and I even got the chance to speak with her friend Desirée. They had been drinking together with a group of friends one night when she FaceTimed me. Desirée had rich, dark skin and her hair was intricately braided down her back. I couldn't make out much of her facial features because of Alena's erratic movements on the video call, but Desirée spoke boldly and confidently—and she reminded me so much of Mya.

By the time I trudged to the bathroom and back, I was ready to return to my slumber. Instead, I scooped my escapee bonnet from the floor and dragged myself to the kitchen so that I could alleviate the incessant pain of my dry throat. One might've thought I was trying to drink myself into oblivion from the number of shots I had taken at the end of the previous night. It definitely wasn't twenty-two, but it was enough to make me stumble even after sleeping for several hours.

I blew an air kiss at my phone before I left the room and quietly crept through my house toward the kitchen where the reprieve of a cold water bottle awaited me. Once in the kitchen, I threw open the fridge and grabbed the first bottle I saw, eagerly gulping it down. When I finally released my hand from the refrigerator, I was frightened by a figure silently standing behind it. I jumped back, sloshing some of the water on my clothes.

"Shit! Grammy?! *Shit!*" I covered my mouth. "I'm sorry. I didn't mean to curse." I composed myself and searched through the dark kitchen for paper towels.

"Baby, it's fine." Her comforting, raspy voice soothed me immediately. She flipped on the lights to the kitchen as I placed my water bottle down and dropped to the floor with the towels to wipe up the spill.

My grandmother might've been an old woman, but she wasn't hunched over, she didn't have a hard time with motor skills, and she absolutely did not have a head full of gray hairs. She did have a few strands of silver lining her naturally black hair but not even much of that. She was fairly healthy for her age, and she was such a staple—a necessity in my family and in my life. She was the glue that held the lot of us together, and I couldn't imagine not spending at least one major holiday a year with her.

Before we'd moved, we shared most holidays with her, and anything different than that was an adjustment. She now had to split up her time since all her children and grandchildren were spread across different cities and states, but I still had the feeling she favored us.

"You're jumpy tonight, aren't you. Is there a reason why?" she asked, sitting down on a nearby stool.

"No reason, Grammy. You just snuck up on me." I stood and threw away the wet paper towels before grabbing my water bottle again.

"I did, didn't I?" She chuckled to herself, and I couldn't help but join her.

"I'm so glad you're here, Gram." I hugged her as she sat on the stool.

"I'm lucky to be here." She smiled and patted my butt. "Sit down,

Amelia, there's something I think we should talk about." She motioned to the seat next to her.

I was in no mood to have a deep conversation in the middle of the night. I was tired and tipsy as hell, but I wasn't *ever* going to turn down a request from Gram to talk. I sat down and stifled a yawn as I took another refreshing swig of water.

I could already guess the possible topic purely from the look in her eyes. It had by now become common knowledge within my family that I had named myself as a lesbian. I hadn't even once considered what my Grammy's position on this might be. It just hadn't seemed important enough to bring up in conversation with her—or maybe I was afraid of what rejection from her might feel like. Still, I loved my Grammy with all my heart; I anticipated seeing her every holiday season and checked in with her regularly throughout the year. I genuinely hoped that nothing would change between us after this conversation.

"My parents told you I'm gay. Didn't they?" She hadn't spoken yet, so I intervened in the silence. Her face looked concerned as she blinked a little before nodding. I sighed. "Gram, there's nothing wrong with me. There's never been anything wrong with me. I'm just different." I nervously gauged her reaction and was set to say more before she held up a hand to stop me.

"Baby." She shook her head then lifted her chin. "My beautiful and stunning grandchild. You're right. There's absolutely *nothing* wrong with you." Her brows were fiercely scrunched together as she spoke these affirming words. "I pity your parents, dear, for making you feel that way."

My mouth fell open, and I blinked several times. "You do?"

"Yes. I didn't instill that into your father at all. And your mother, as far as I know, wasn't taught to be so unaccepting either." Her soft, wrinkly hands took a firm hold of mine. "You are perfect. You are beautifully and wonderfully made. I think that's what the Bible said, and if so, it was certainly right. I'm not sure about everything else in it."

I released a chuckle, and a tear abruptly fell from my eyes.

"Oh, baby. Come here." She enveloped me into one of the warmest hugs I'd ever known. It was as if she could heal every rejection, every broken part within me with a single embrace.

She placed her hands on the counter after she pulled away and sat there looking forward but not at anything in particular. "Amelia, we are all delicate people." She turned back to me. "Now your parents... or anyone who is vehemently against something so important yet so personal as love. They're delicate people. Something that has absolutely nothing to do with them can incite them to become so unhinged you would think you were dealing with children.

But you," she pointed in my direction, "you're also a delicate person. And your love for another individual, whether a man or a woman, is a delicate thing. We all have the choice to make. Whatever that choice may be, just make sure it's the right one for you and you alone above everyone else—including that woman you love."

"What woman?" I questioned her as I wiped away more tears. I hadn't told my family about Alena yet. Since my arrival, I hadn't said much of anything concerning my sexuality. And it was clear that my parents were content to keep things that way and pretend they were doing the right thing by ignoring it.

"I know what it's like to look into the eyes of a young woman who's in love," she said with a smile. "Does she treat you well?" she asked warmly.

My voice cracked as I answered her. "She treats me *so* well, Gram. She cares about my heart—and even my health. She cooked for me when I missed you—I didn't even ask. She's the one who gave me this!" I picked up the necklace in my hands and her eyebrows rose as she examined it.

"How beautiful," she murmured, briefly holding the sun between her fingers. I couldn't find any more words to suitably describe Alena nor finish listing all the ways that she was the most amazing person I knew—aside from my grandmother of course. "She sounds like a keeper," she said tenderly.

I nodded, further clearing my face of tears.

"Your parents will come around. And if they don't it's their loss." She shrugged. "But don't worry, I already talked some sense into them when you fell asleep. I guarantee you that I will continue to do so until the day I am off this earth, Amelia. Your love deserves acceptance and support despite it not being the love your parents originally envisioned for you. That's the problem to begin with. You don't look like what they thought you might, but you're not supposed to. You are merely a physical extension of their love and nothing more. You are an original not a copy, and that's why I love you, my dear."

"I love you too, Gram," was all I could say as I sniffled pathetically.

"No matter what, remember this, Amelia." My grandmother looked at me seriously. "Always do what you must for love."

Chapter 25 Marigolds

My head was pounding as I stared into the darkness of my closed eyelids. *Not again.* My eyes fluttered open as I came further into consciousness, and I squinted from the blinding rays of the sun that poured in through a window. I could feel that I was laying on some cushy surface, but my legs were twisted up in a horrible position. I slowly situated them more comfortably as I rubbed my eyes and yawned.

I couldn't remember exactly where I was as my vision gradually became clearer—until I spotted a reclined lump snoring across from me. I then recognized the couch and the room I was in. I looked on the floor and saw Gabe wrapped up in some blankets with the same clothes he'd had on the previous night.

We'd gone out for dinner before attending a concert and pre-New Year's celebration in Destin, Florida. From the looks of it, all of us had drunk way too much. I could've sworn I had been pacing myself well through the night, but the sharp ache of my ever-increasing headache reminded me that I had not. I wanted to lay back down and finish sleeping it off, but I remembered I soon had a plane to catch.

Alena would be picking me up from the airport in Greenwood this afternoon. It was a compromise that I was able to make between me, my family, my best friends, and my girlfriend. My family had me through Christmas, Mya and Gabe had me right after Christmas and up until New Year's Eve, and Alena would have me with her to bring in the new year.

I bet they'll be happy I'm with her so they can kiss each other without my judgment, I thought as I lounged there watching my friends sleep. I didn't really care if they ended up together so long as they didn't break up. Mya and Gabe were a part of a short list of my favorite people. I got to see them evolve alongside me throughout our early years of adulthood. No one else had been through what the three of us had been through together, and that was too special to lose.

When I was finally ready to get up from the couch, I fumbled around for my phone before tiptoeing into the bathroom. My friends were still fast asleep, so I whispered with Alena on a FaceTime call.

"You look awful," she noted, chuckling quietly as she laid in bed.

"I know. I don't even remember coming back here. I'm pretty sure Mya's cousin drove us back, but I must've fallen asleep before we arrived."

"I'm just glad you're safe, and that you didn't drive all the way to Florida like you wanted to before. A flight makes it so much easier for you."

"Mm-hmm." I nodded. "Ugh, I have the worst headache," I complained. "Why do you look like you slept so peacefully?"

"Because I did. Are you jealous?"

"Of course I am," I snickered, sitting on the edge of the bathtub. "I'm jealous of that *and* of the pillow you're laying your head on. And the sheets around you too, but mostly of your shirt."

"What shirt?" she asked, panning down.

My mouth hung open, and I glanced around the empty room as if there were some chance my friends or Mya's family would accidentally catch a glimpse of Alena's breasts. "Are you wearing *anything*?" I whispered into the phone, my heart beating fiercely within my chest.

"What a silly question to ask." She brought the camera back up to her face where she wore a mischievous grin.

I groaned. "I should've got an earlier flight." I shook my head as if that would rid my mind of the fresh memory of her perfect breasts. She yawned then, and a moan escaped her mouth right afterward, which I knew wasn't purposeful. Or was it? Purposeful or not, it still caused an erotic stir inside me. "I hate to say it, but I have to get off this call. I'm having a difficult time not losing my mind over you right now."

She burst into laughter on the other end. "I barely even did anything."

"You flashed me," I whispered into the phone and suddenly I saw her breasts once again. "Ooh! Now you did it again!" I whispered too loudly then heard a movement in the next room. "Shit. I really gotta go now. I think I woke someone up."

"Aww, are you sure?" she sulked.

I bit my bottom lip hard. *No.* I blinked at her without answering.

"Can I at least tell you about my dream from last night?" she asked.

"Quickly."

"I umm, bought you a toy. And—"

"A toy? A *sex* toy? In your dream?"

She nodded, smirking. "It looks just like this one." She pulled out a bright toy from behind her.

Oh God. My face must've matched my internal reaction because she broke out in laughter again. A rustling sound then came from outside the room.

"Okay, I really have to go now." My voice was shaky. Why couldn't I just be there with her right now?

"Okay, baby. Call me when you get to the airport," she said.

"I will. I love you."

"I love you too." She blew me a kiss through the phone which I caught and returned to her before we hung up. I then left the room to see if my friends were awake.

"My stomach hurts," Mya complained as she stretched. She was on the longer couch.

"It's because of all the filth we put into our bodies last night," Gabe cheerfully explained. His makeshift bed on the floor didn't seem to dampen his morning mood one bit.

Mya rolled her eyes. "I know that Gabe, but guess what? It doesn't help my pain!"

Gabe chuckled as he stood. "It smells like breakfast up there."

"You are always hungry, I swear!" Mya criticized, adjusting her top. "I don't even want to think about eating right now."

"It does smell good," I said, walking further into the room and jumping back to my spot on the smaller couch. Gabe slipped into the bathroom.

"Were you on your morning booty call with the professor?" Mya asked frankly.

"Dammit, Mya, stop calling her that," I grumbled. "It's just, *Alena*. Alena, Alena, Alena!"

She snickered. "It *was* a booty call, wasn't it? With Alena."

My face suddenly went hot, and I wasn't sure if it was from anger or embarrassment. "Wrong," I said, folding the covers I'd slept underneath.

"Do either of you remember how we got here?" Gabe asked, emerging from the bathroom and wiping his wet hands on his hoodie.

"No," Mya and I answered simultaneously.

"Damn. We really were wasted," Mya said.

"Thank God for Vince," I said.

"Yes!" A brawny, dark-tan man came barreling down the basement stairs. "Thank the Almighty for me!" He laughed. "Breakfast is ready, you bunch of drunks!"

"What'd you do, Vince? Carry us all down here at once?" Mya asked.

"No," he answered seriously. "That one there could actually

walk." He pointed to Gabe who flexed one of his biceps at the revelation.

"But yes, you two were pretty light." He nodded and hustled back up the stairs.

"Amelia!" I heard a tiny voice call down from above. "Come look at my farewell picture for you!"

"Coming my sweet Lettie!" I shouted up. *Farewell picture? Who even taught her that word?* I thought sulkily. She was getting so big.

I cleaned up my space and tossed the sheets in the laundry room before dashing up the stairs to see my wonderful little friend.

The flight seemed to last a millennium, and every moment I wasn't in Alena's arms felt like wasted time. I nearly imploded as I stood by the luggage carousel at the baggage claim. Alena was already parked in the cell phone lot waiting for my call to come pick me up.

I impatiently stood in the crowded airport. I'd have thought most people would already be at their destination on New Year's Eve, but there were apparently plenty of people in the same boat as me. The carousel soon began moving and spitting out one suitcase after another, and I grew even more impatient. Within five minutes that felt like five hours, I located my hard-shell suitcase and hurriedly snatched it up as I dialed.

"I'm ready," I blurted out before Alena could even say hello.

"I'll be right there," she replied.

I rushed out into the frighteningly cold day, and a feeling of joy swept over me when I spotted her black Cadillac.

I could scarcely make out Alena in a pair of sunglasses through the darkly tinted windows. She slipped out of the car and made her way toward me, her curls freely bouncing with each strut. I cast my luggage aside and jumped into her arms. An unusual but pleasant scent penetrated my nostrils as she captured me.

"Oh my God, I missed you," she squealed out before kissing me roughly. I almost forgot we were in public as I slipped my tongue into her mouth and tugged her body closer. I could feel a smile on her lips as she pulled away. "We have to go, Amelia." She moved my suitcase upright and rolled it to the trunk of her car while I opened the passenger door and jumped in. She was soon next to me smiling and glowing. She grabbed my hand and squeezed before she looked ahead and drove away.

The two of us got caught up on our way back, and I gave her a hazy recount of my crazy drunken night with my friends. She had her own interesting stories, mostly to do with how she fared moving into Kevin's apartment with the help of both Jess and Nova. The two had been around each other before, but their personalities weren't very compatible. It had apparently been a funny interaction to watch, but everything worked out well in the end.

Alena had asked me the previous night if I wanted to return to my apartment before we went to her new place for the rest of our break. I was reluctant at first, but I did need a few changes of clothes.

When we pulled up to my apartment complex it was mostly empty. The complex was exclusively for college students, so it made sense that it was barren on New Year's Eve. Most occupants were likely still with their families and friends elsewhere. I turned to her. "Are you coming in?"

"Sure, as long as it's up to your standards for guests." She shrugged.

I never considered Alena visiting my place before, especially since it was the exact opposite of "safe" when I was still her student. It was probably still risky now, but there were barely any other cars around. I doubted anyone would be that concerned about a random tenant and her unknown lover going into her place in the middle of the day on New Year's Eve.

"Alright, let's go." I smiled.

She insisted on grabbing my suitcase again and rolling it to my door. I had no qualms about the cleanliness of my apartment; I was more concerned with what she might think of the design. The space was definitely cute, and I liked it, but it was simple—much simpler than what *I* might even expect from someone as artistically critical as me.

Alena rolled my luggage inside and evaluated the first room. I watched her observe the boring, white walls and cheap, wooden floors; the hanging icicle lights underneath the bar counter and the two bar stools with frumpy cushions. There were a few canvases on the wall—including the miniature painting from her—along with pictures of my friends and family. I did my best to add color to the room through the display of decorative pillows and throws on my couch. Many of my appliances also had an interesting flare to them.

"This is cute," she said. "It's chic."

I scoffed. "It definitely isn't that."

"Don't sell yourself short, Amelia." She dropped onto the couch. "It does the trick if you ask me."

"Thanks." I locked the door and slid down next to her. There was a twinkle in her eyes as she spoke to me, although I wasn't paying as much attention to her words as I was to the depth of her beauty. A strange feeling began to rise within me. She was as comfortable as she had looked in her own apartment the first night I visited—but her long, gorgeous body was now lounging on *my* brown sofa in *my* apartment.

I tuned back in enough to hear her complimenting my decorating skills again, but all I wanted to do right then was break in my couch with her. I felt hungry and thirsty for it. She didn't even need to be naked. I had no issues making her squirm beneath me with all of her clothes on if necessary.

"What're you so busy thinking about, Amelia?" she asked, stroking my arm over my coat.

I didn't mince my words. "How much I want to fuck you on my couch."

She smiled coyly but without looking surprised. "You're doing a lot of thinking when you could just make it happen," she said quietly.

There was my green light. I ripped off my coat while she shed hers, and then our lips came together, this time without any distracting factors to shorten the contact. It was much like our very first kiss; it felt electric, spine tingling, and almost wrong—but also *right*.

I wanted to make out with her for two hours straight, but I also wanted to be inside of her immediately. As I lost layer after layer of clothing, I didn't even think about how cold I probably was or would begin to feel by the time we were done. Either way it went, I could use her body to keep me warm.

The more layers she shed, the more I smelled her natural scent, along with the unusual but now highly recognizable perfume. I slid my hands down her body as we kissed, solely dressed in our bras and panties now.

"Are you wearing your Christmas gift, Alena?" I asked as I pulled away for a torturous moment and took another whiff. This was why I had been alerted to her smell back at the airport.

She nodded breathlessly, already clutching my body back into hers. After she successfully reeled me in, she whispered huskily into my ear, "C'est *Chanel Mademoiselle* mon amour. Maintenant tais toi."

Since when does she speak French?! I felt like coming before we even got into the real action. I didn't know exactly what she had said, but I knew French when I heard it. I decided for myself that she had said *let's fuck now,* and I refocused all my energy on that.

Once I was able to tug away her panties, she straddled my lap. She was remarkably warm and deliciously wet. It was too much for me to concentrate on anything else, so I did the only thing I was able to think about doing; I slammed two of my fingers inside of her.

Her radiating heat and the weight of her body rocking against me was enough to make me feel like I might not make it past the next few minutes without imploding. She moaned—too loud probably—but no one was here, so I worked my fingers harder until she grew even louder.

I could hardly breathe now from the pleasure beating in my chest but also because her body covered my face. Where else was she going to go? Her breasts were eye level, but she pressed so hard into me that I didn't have the opportunity to reach up and suck on her nipples.

The volume of her orgasm was lower than her preceding moans, which was probably a result of her face being tucked into the top of the sofa as she came. Before I had a chance to do anything further, she pulled herself off my fingers and pressed me flat on the couch. She didn't break eye contact with me as she removed her bra, her body still trembling from her release. I reveled in the view of my girlfriend's smooth beige skin which was lovely and bare.

"Damn, you're gorgeous." I wanted to shed tears at the sight of her. She pushed back her curls and leaned toward me, unhooking my bra and tossing it across the room. She smiled as she slid down my underwear.

"Was there a lot of turbulence?" she asked, tying her hair into a lazy ponytail.

"What?"

"On the plane." She pushed my legs up and moved her head between them. I bit down on my lip and drank in a harsh breath. The anticipation was killing me. It felt like it had been an eternity since her mouth was on me, and it still wasn't yet.

Wait. What did she say? Shit.

Alena kissed around my thighs, slowly. She wasn't looking at me now—just reviewing her meal apparently.

I remembered the question, and that yes, there had been turbulence. I had been anxious about it, in fact. My body had tensed every time the plane shook. At the time, the growing, gnawing ache between my compressed legs—from her call and suggestive messages—was easily overtaken by my fear of falling hundreds of thousands of feet from the sky.

"Yes," I shakily answered her embarrassingly late. "And if it wasn't so scary, I would've thought about you. I did think about you—holding my hand and comforting me but . . . I meant I would've thought about how I wanted you to—"

She blew her warm breath over my slit, then her tongue licked upright. "I'm sorry. What were you saying?" she asked sweetly.

I could barely even think at this point, aside from a short mental reminder to myself to breathe. Sex with her never got less difficult when it came to this. She always overwhelmed me with her tenacity and passion—and her beauty. Every time, it felt like I couldn't believe what was happening.

"It's okay, baby. We can talk about it later." She pushed her tongue inside me. Her hands clutched my thighs, and she held them open as she brought her head even closer, plunging her tongue even deeper.

I whimpered as she moved from inside me to lick and suck on my clit and even more when her fingers slid across my slick, delicate folds. There was a sharp pain on my thighs from her fingernails digging in, but I only slightly noticed. It was easy to ignore when there was a predominating surge of pleasure between my legs. Her right hand stayed attached to my thigh while the left outlined my waiting lips.

Go inside. "Please, Alena."

"Hmm?" she asked, her face still buried between my legs.

"I need your fingers," I gasped as her tongue sped up its movements. She didn't listen to me, and I knew it was purposeful.

I reached down, scrambling around for her hand—but even when I found it, she wouldn't budge. My short-lived groan of anguish turned into a whimper of satisfaction once she finally obliged. I remained unable to do anything but that as she drove her fingers into me. She then lifted her head from between my thighs and moved toward me, her face wet from my arousal. She kissed me while she kept up her thrusts below.

"I missed this, Amelia," she whispered, moving her kisses to my ear.

I couldn't have responded to her if I tried; nothing besides another moan at least.

"Are you going to come for me?" she asked, her mouth on my neck. She began sucking hard, and I knew it would leave a mark. She then traced her tongue from the bottom of my neck all the way up to my ear as she curved her fingers inside me—and I finally came.

We both received a taste of what we needed right there on my brown couch, and when we were done, we leaned tiredly against one another and slipped off to sleep.

Chapter 26 The Only One

"I just went grocery shopping this morning after we talked. I wanted to make you something special for our last and first dinners of the year," Alena explained to me as we ascended the elevator in Kevin's building.

"Really? I was hoping you would be that last and first dinner," I joked despite my actual hunger. "And I could be yours."

"Why are you even in school, Amelia? Being a comedian is obviously your calling," she said as the elevator opened.

The duffle bag I had switched out with my suitcase swung from her shoulder as we held hands and walked down the hall. It had gotten dark while Alena and I were busy in my apartment, so when we walked into her new unit the city lights made for a delightful view. The scene improved further when Alena clicked a remote that turned on the lights and music all at once.

The lights' settings made it look like candles were lit all over the room. It brought me back to the night when Alena and I were stuck in the darkness of her old apartment because of the storm. The memory prompted a fluttering, both in my chest and down below. She was so beautiful in the candlelight, every time, but that particular night she had been vulnerable with me. It was the first time we shared a sexual experience, and what a good one it was.

My lips parted as I took in the scene and wandered further into the apartment. I noticed a fresh bouquet of flowers on the glass coffee table by the TV. Rose petals were scattered across the floor leading to the bedroom. I stood in the kitchen admiring the room while she locked the door and set down my duffle. She then walked up behind me and brought her hands to my waist as she leaned into me.

"Merry Christmas, Happy Birthday, Happy New Year," she crooned. I turned around and stared into her brown eyes and she stared right back.

We said nothing, but we said everything. She technically looked the same as always, but I still couldn't get over her. Everything about her, inside and out, was absolutely wonderful.

"I love you," she professed, her eyes not moving from mine.

She'd beat me to it. "I love you too. I'm *in* love with you." I didn't think I was going to say that—but it was true, so I did. Her lips swiftly took over mine and suddenly the emptiness in my stomach was unimportant.

"Amelia, I'm so in love with you it drives me crazy. I'm honestly not even scared to be anymore," she confessed as she pulled away from me.

I sighed, relieved. "We're always on the same page." I closed my eyes and savored the moment. It felt like a dream, and I didn't want to wake up. Then her lips were on mine again, bringing me back to reality. She held me firmly until I opened my eyes.

"I've never felt like this before," she said. "I truly feel . . . *safe* with you. I didn't even know how much I was missing that." She bit her lip then picked up my duffle and took it to the bedroom. When she returned, she shrugged off her coat and stepped out of her shoes. "I'm about to start cooking."

"What are we having?" I asked, shedding my layers as well.

"Italian." She smiled and set our shoes on the rack by the door.

She washed her hands in the sink and grabbed some pots, filling one with water and turning the stove on high. Then she grabbed my hand and led me to the bedroom.

I watched over her shoulder as she ran me a bath. A soft R&B song was playing over the speakers now as I smiled at her. "Thank you, Alena." I already knew she would ask me *what for?* so I answered her upcoming question. "For my birthday gift and my Christmas gift and picking me up from the airport—and for cooking tonight, and this bath too."

She turned off the water and turned around, standing and consequently towering over me. She tugged on my necklace, sliding the sun between her fingers as she looked at me with a smile. "You're worth everything," she said and kissed my forehead. "Enjoy your bath." She winked at me and walked out, closing the door behind her.

I lay in the steaming tub with my head on the neck rest and my body relaxing from all the shenanigans I had put it through over the last few weeks. As I remained there, I thought of the future and what life could be like for Alena and me. I was now one semester away from graduating, and though I felt I should be more stressed, I was at peace. Even though the situation with Alena had been difficult, anytime we were alone and together I knew I could do anything—I knew *we* could do anything. I could tell my parents about her. I could make it through the next semester and proudly introduce her as my girlfriend. Her age didn't matter, her profession didn't matter, people's opinions didn't matter. It was Alena and I against the world as far as I was concerned, hopefully forever. She was my peace.

My hand went down to the silver necklace that I never took off, and my heart skipped a beat. I smiled to myself as I inhaled the mouthwatering aroma of basil and oregano that reached the bathroom. Alena was excited to cook tonight, and tomorrow we were getting brunch somewhere before enjoying another dinner here at the apartment.

Everything for the beginning of the new year was set, and I was here with my favorite person in the world; the woman whom I deeply loved. It was all finally perfect.

Alena looked smug as she watched me hungrily fork down the spaghetti bolognese she'd prepared. She sipped on her wine, bit into a roll, then slowly worked on her own pasta. I finished my food quickly, and I was standing to get seconds when she put a hand on mine. "How was it?" She was clearly holding in laughter.

"Damn good, so I'm getting more," I touted with a lifted chin.

"Eat as much as you want," she snickered, letting go of my hand.

I was soon at the stove scooping up my next helping. "Alena, my New Year's resolution is going to be cooking for you. I haven't done it once, and I don't want you to think it's because I'm incapable."

She chuckled from across the room. "Amelia, I actually enjoy cooking for you. I don't mind you taking over when you want to, but don't think you have to. There's nothing to prove with me."

"I still want to." I sat back down at the table and smirked. "My pussy can't be the only meal I prepare for you."

I should've known after dinner and drinks that Alena and I would end up naked in bed together. I meant what I had said about having her as my last meal of the year and me being hers. We'd accomplished just that, and it was now four minutes to midnight. We had been making love for over an hour.

The sound of my labored breathing filled the large room along with the music pouring in from the speakers. The sensuous love songs made perfect sense for this moment or for any moment with Alena. We had shared so much with one another since we met, and love was the most beautiful thing of all.

The taste of her arousal lingered in my mouth as she looked down at me with a smile. "You wanna know something, Amelia?" she asked, removing her fingers from inside me.

"What?" I questioned, my rapid breaths slowly but surely becoming more even. She was talking like she hadn't just brought me to the peak of another orgasm before stopping and denying me further. She chose a hell of a time to want to talk.

"I think we'll be together for a long time," she said with enthusiasm. "I really want to travel the world with you. I think that we could even get married one day . . . maybe start a family?"

"You'd want to get married again?" I asked curiously now, *almost* forgetting my denied release. Alena was speaking of a long life with me! *Marriage*, even if only vaguely, but we'd never broached the subject before. It was equally exciting and frightening.

"Of course!" she responded with a laugh. "I don't see myself floating in the unmarried abyss for too long a time when I love someone. I'm definitely marriage minded."

I eyed her steadily. "I am too . . . ." I didn't mean to sound hesitant, but I did, and she heard it.

"I don't mean tomorrow, Amelia." She sounded nervous now. "I need to get divorced first." She squeezed her eyes shut. "*Shit*, I didn't mean to bring that up. *God*."

"It's fine." I accidentally burst into laughter, but I was laughing more at myself than at her. My concerns about Teresa seemed so miniscule now, so it was comical to me. Besides, Alena's fingers were inside of *me* not Teresa—well, actually not anyone right now. I pushed my hips up at the remembrance of that.

She grinned sheepishly and pulled her hands further away from my body. "How about children? Would you ever want to start a family?" she continued.

We could make some kids right now if you stopped talking. We actually couldn't, but still. I briefly pondered the question, although I already knew the answer. "I definitely want children. I love kids. Even if we only adopt. I think it'd be cool to have a big family, but also kinda overwhelming."

Alena beamed. "I always wanted at least three."

"Yeah, they could be like a little group of friends," I concurred.

"Mm-hmm," she laughed into my neck.

"You wanna know something, Alena?" I copied her earlier sentiment.

"What?" she questioned, her lips moving away from my neck.

"I love you," I cooed, and I kissed her fervently.

"I love you too." She kissed me with far more depth than I had provided. It was a kiss that was sure to lead to more and a kiss I hoped might never end. I suddenly heard a commotion coming from the TV in the next room. A countdown.

Three! Alena finally resettled herself on top of me.

Two! She smiled. "Are you ready?" she asked me, and I could feel her hands return between my thighs. I was mesmerized by her. She was finally giving me what I wanted again, like she always did. That, and she was beautiful, and we were in love. I was happier than I had ever been.

One! Happy New Year!

A thousand memories floated across my mind as her lips danced with mine. I couldn't help but delight in the idea of starting a brand-new year with the love of my life. Despite any obstacles we might face, we would be a strong force together.

Our kiss grew so deep it felt like we might merge into one another. It must've been what she intended when she slipped her fingers inside me, causing me to gasp for air.

A feeling like this and a life with Alena is one I wished would last forever.

Acknowledgments

First of all, I am beyond grateful for every single supporter and reader! You are all so amazing! Many of you cheered me on as I worked to publish this book, and I am so thankful for that.

Thank you Uncle B. for always encouraging my creativity and being an open mind in our family. Thank you Rai for pushing me to publish this since 2019. You believed in this book before it was even close to being what it is now. Thank you Ingrida, Melody, and Jennifer. I love you all and your encouragement for my writing is never small to me; it means the world and I appreciate you.

Thank you to Carmen, my fantastic editor, as well as everyone else who had a hand in the publishing process of my debut novel.

I am the most thankful to God for my gift of writing. I love writing with everything in me, and I promise that I will keep doing this forever.

About The Author

Elia Johnson is a young writer of sapphic fiction and poetry. When she isn't writing, her time is spent reading, watching films, traveling, exploring nature, and loving on her friends and family. She has plenty more sapphic fiction and poetry books coming in the future, so buckle up and enjoy the ride.

Afterword

I first wrote *The Professor* on the couch of my college apartment the beginning of 2019, and it was probably the best thing I ever did in my life. It was a scary decision to make because I had only started writing down my stories a few months prior. When Alena and Amelia started materializing in my mind, I wrote the first scene which is still genuine to the first chapter. It just came to me one night; Mya was sitting there talking to Amelia, and I could see that *something* was going on between her and her professor.

I could never wait to figure out what was happening next. It didn't matter where I was or what time it was, I was writing. Before class, during class when possible, after class. I would listen to it on my computer and fall asleep to it at night. I was prouder of my writing than I was of myself the day I crossed the stage and got my four-year degree. I am simply not as fulfilled doing anything else.

This college love story is more than just your average pipe dream. It's a soft world to get lost in for a little while. It's experiencing love and joy and healing in its own ways. That's what it was for me at least and hopefully the same for many of you that read it. Whether it is a fictional world or not—a world I created or not—it's a real world. We can all do the same thing in a way. We can heal ourselves through ourselves and chase our goals and our dreams. Pick up something that we dropped. *Love always finds a way.*

I'm glad I had the audacity to write down this cute idea that I became obsessed with and to not stop. Although I didn't finish this story for years, I am here now.

This is a reminder to always finish what you started. Sometimes there are peaks and valleys that actually make things even better in the end. If there is anything that you left behind that you loved or got distracted from, I encourage you to return to it. It's inside you for a reason . . . that dream, that idea, that story, that song, that poem. Whatever it is, it's meant to be heard and to be shared and to be loved by others too.

Make it happen.

Made in the USA
Middletown, DE
01 November 2023